CONTRABAND

*

There was menace in the night sky over England: an international smuggling racket with far-reaching political implications.

Gregory Sallust knew nothing of this when, in the Casino at Deauville, he first saw the lovely Hungarian girl, Sabine Szenty. Nor did he know that, before the thing was finished, he, Gregory Sallust, to save Sabine from retribution she had surely earned, would once again become a 'Wanted' man . . .

BY DENNIS WHEATLEY

NOVELS

The Launching of Roger Brook
The Shadow of Tyburn Tree
The Rising Storm
The Man Who Killed the King
The Dark Secret of Josephine
The Rape of Venice
The Sultan's Daughter
The Wanton Princess
Evil in a Mask

The Scarlet Impostor
Faked Passports
The Black Baroness
V for Vengeance
Come into My Parlour
Traitors' Gate
They Used Dark Forces

The Prisoner in the Mask
The Second Seal
Vendetta in Spain
Three Inquisitive People
The Forbidden Territory
The Devil Rides Out
The Golden Spaniard
Strange Conflict
Codeword—Golden Fleece
Dangerous Inheritance
Gateway to Hell

The Quest of Julian Day
The Sword of Fate
Bill for the Use of a Body

Black August
Contraband
The Island Where Time Stands Still
The White Witch of the South Seas

To the Devil—a Daughter
The Satanist

The Eunuch of Stamboul
The Secret War
The Fabulous Valley
Sixty Days to Live
Such Power is Dangerous
Uncharted Seas
The Man Who Missed the War
The Haunting of Toby Jugg
Star of Ill-Omen
They Found Atlantis
The Ka of Gifford Hillary
Curtain of Fear
Mayhem in Greece
Unholy Crusade

SHORT STORIES

Mediterranean Nights
Gunmen, Gallants and Ghosts

HISTORICAL

A Private Life of Charles II (*Illustrated by Frank C. Papé*)
Red Eagle (*The Story of the Russian Revolution*)

AUTOBIOGRAPHICAL

Stranger than Fiction (*War Papers for the Joint Planning Staff*)
Saturdays with Bricks

IN PREPARATION

The Ravishing of Lady Mary Ware (*another Roger Brook story*)
The Devil and all his Works (*Illustrated in colour*)

Dennis Wheatley

Contraband

ARROW BOOKS

ARROW BOOKS LTD
3 Fitzroy Square, London W1

AN IMPRINT OF THE HUTCHINSON GROUP

London Melbourne Sydney Auckland
Wellington Johannesburg Cape Town
and agencies throughout the world

*

First published by
Hutchinson & Co (*Publishers*) Ltd 1936
Arrow edition 1960
Second impression 1966
Second edition 1971

Made and printed in Great Britain
by The Anchor Press Ltd.,
Tiptree, Essex

ISBN 0 09 005460 1

To

my old friend

FRANK VAN ZWANENBERG

In memory of many kindnesses

and because he likes

'straight' thrillers

Contents

I

Midnight at the Casino

When Gregory Sallust first saw the girl it was already nearly midnight on the last day of his holiday. He had made a leisurely tour of Normandy, stopping at some of the less pretentious inns where the cuisine was still unspoiled by the summer tourist traffic, and was ending up with three days of riotous living at Deauville.

It was a little early yet for that playground of the rich. Another ten days and *la grande semaine* would bring the wealthy and the fashionable, with their locust crowd of hangers-on, from every city in Europe; but the Casino was fairly full. English, French, and Americans jostled each other at the tables while here and there a less familiar type of face proclaimed a true Latin, Scandanavian, or Slav.

The women, for the most part, were middle-aged or elderly, except for a sprinkling of professional harpies. The majority of girls who filled the tennis-courts, the *bar du soleil,* and the bathing beach by day would be dancing, Gregory knew, and it was fairly easy for a practised eye like his to sort the few, who stood by their mothers or were gambling at the 'low' tables for a few francs, from their more adventurous sisters. The clothes of the latter, their jewels and general air of casual indifference to their surroundings, gave away no secrets; it was the way in which they watched the faces of their men rather than the piles of plaques, which represented so many thousand francs, that indicated to the shrewd observer where their real interests lay.

Gregory glanced again at the girl who had just come in;

then lowered his eyes to the man she was accompanying, a strange little figure, now seated at the table. He was not a dwarf yet he was curiously ill-proportioned. His body was frail and childlike, but his head massive and powerful. From it a shock of silver hair swept back, giving him a benign and priest-like appearance, but his rat-trap mouth and curiously pale-blue eyes belied any suggestion of mildness.

Catching sight of him had first drawn Gregory Sallust's attention to the girl, for Gregory knew him, which was not surprising since he knew most people of importance.

From his public school he had gone straight into the war but a nasty head wound had put an end to his trench service and he had been seconded to Intelligence. His superiors there thought him a cynical but brainy devil and came to value him as a reliable man who would stick at nothing to collect vital information. They had kept him on, specially employed in Paris after the armistice, during the whole period of the Peace Negotiations, and it was then that he had first come in contact with so many famous personalities.

At the time of the currency collapse in Central Europe he had left the Service to undertake certain confidential work for English banking interests in Vienna, and when that job had ended he had drifted into journalism in order to supplement his private income of a few hundreds a year.

That had led, a year or two later, to his being sent out to the Far East as war correspondent to one of the big London 'dailies'. On his return he had remained unemployed except for occasional literary work until an old friend of his had recommended him, as highly suitable to undertake a special investigation needing secrecy and brains, to a group of men who controlled one of Britain's greatest commercial corporations. Gregory had accepted the offer and as a preliminary had taken his fortnight's 'holiday' in Normandy. He was due back to make his first report the following day.

The girl remained standing behind her companion's chair, and Gregory watched her covertly. He was wondering if she was a *poule de luxe* or just some friend's girl in whom the old man was taking a fatherly interest; but Gregory knew that he was not the sort of old man to derive the least pleasure from the innocent conversation of respectable young women. He was almost a recluse, having cut himself off from all social life years before, and even when he travelled he rarely appeared in the public rooms of the hotels where he stayed owing to a super-sensitiveness about his physical shortcomings. On the other hand, he was by no means the type of old rip who travels with pseudo 'nieces' in his entourage. He was reputed to be colossally rich, but Gregory had never heard the word 'mistress' breathed in connection with his name.

She must be a *poule*, Gregory decided, but a devilish expensive one. Probably most of the heavy bracelets that loaded down her white arms were fake, but you cannot fake clothes as you can diamonds, and he knew that those simple lines of rich material which rose to cup her well-formed breasts had cost a pretty penny. Besides, she was very very beautiful.

A little frown of annoyance wrinkled Gregory's forehead, catching at the scar which lifted his left eyebrow until his face took on an almost satanic look. What a pity, he thought, that he was returning to England the following day. If only he had seen her soon after his arrival at Deauville it would have been fun to get to know her.

Gregory Sallust was no ascetic, yet it was quite a time since any woman had loomed on his horizon about whom he had felt that it was really worth while to exert himself. This girl was just the type to rouse him from his lethargy into sudden intense activity. He knew from past experience that he could sweep most women off their feet inside a week with the intense excitement of a hectic, furious, laughing, yet determined pursuit, and what magnificent elation could be derived from carrying a rich man's darling off from under his very nose despite her better sense and the rich man's opposition. Gregory had done it before and he would certainly have attempted it in this case if only he had had a few days left to work in.

The more he studied her, between making bets, the more the desire to do so strengthened in his mind. He could never bring himself to be anything but 'uncle-ish' to 'nice' girls, however attractive, and he barred respectable married women, except on rare occasions, on practical grounds. The aftermath of broken hearts and tear-stained faces with possible threats of being cited as co-respondent by an injured husband was, he considered, too heavy a price to pay. He preferred, when he took the plunge into an affair, a woman whom he could be reasonably certain was content to play his own game. Nothing too easy—in fact it was essential to his pleasure that she should move in luxurious surroundings and be distinguished of her kind, and so quite inaccessible except to men of personality even if they had the wealth which he had not. Then, when victory was achieved, they could laugh together over their ruses, delight in one another to the full and, when the time came as it surely must, part before satiation; a little sadly, perhaps, but as friends who had enriched life's experience by a few more perfect moments.

'*Rien ne va plus*' came the level voice of the croupier and Gregory realised, too late, that he had failed to place his stake.

Really, he thought, I'm behaving like an idiot and if I'm not careful I shall be thinking of that lovely face of hers for weeks. I've known this sort of thing happen to me before, so I'd better go home to bed before I get her too much on my mind.

He pushed the cards away from him and, collecting his chips, stood up. Then, just as he left the table, a simple action caught his eye while the players sat tense receiving their cards for a new deal.

The elderly man had pulled out his watch, but he was not looking at it. He held it in the palm of his hand and the girl was gazing at it over his shoulder. She nodded and, turning from the table without a word, walked quickly away.

Gregory knew that it was just on midnight and, as he watched the receding figure, so graceful in its sheath of heavy silk, he paused to wonder just what lay behind that little act. He was certain that neither of the two had spoken. Was the old man sending her somewhere or reminding her of an appointment? Anyway, she was just leaving the *salle*—and alone!

The temptation was too much for Gregory. True, he had only a dozen hours or so before he must pack and catch his boat but much could be done in a dozen hours. With a long loping stride he made his way to the *entre-salle*.

Before she appeared in her wraps he had already collected his light coat and dark soft hat and had a taxi waiting a few yards from the entrance of the casino.

Too old a bird to attempt to speak to her, he watched, a little surprised that no car was waiting to pick her up, as she walked down the steps and turned to the south along the gardens which fringed the *plage*. He gave her about five minutes' start, then boarded his taxi, giving the man precise instructions in fluent French.

The taxi slid along the asphalt road, easing down to a crawl when the lady once more came in sight. A moment later she turned round the far corner of the *Normandie*. The taxi speeded up until it came level with the corner. Gregory peered out. Opposite the Deauville branch of the famous jewellers, Van Cleffe et Appel, situated in the side of the Normandie Hotel, stood a large limousine. The girl was just getting in.

'Follow that car,' said Gregory softly to his driver, and then sat back again.

The limousine ran silently through the almost deserted streets, crossed the little *Place* with its now darkened bars, dress shops, and *confisserie*, then took the road to Trouville. The parent town, once fashionable in its own right but now, as Margate is to Cliftonville, the holiday resort of greater but less wealthy crowds, lay only a mile or so away, and their route ran through the suburbs which connect the two.

At Trouville Harbour the limousine halted. The taxi pulled up in the shadow of some buildings two hundred yards behind. Gregory turned up the collar of his coat to hide his white shirt-front and with his soft hat pulled well down to conceal his face leaned out of the window.

The girl had descended from her car and evidently dismissed it; for the limousine swung about and sped back towards the big villas and great hotels along the Deauville *plage*.

A man came forward from behind the deserted customs shed. Quiet greetings were exchanged. The girl called a solitary taxi that still lingered on the rank. She pushed the man in before her and bent forward to whisper an address to the driver then she too got in and the taxi moved off towards the centre of the town. Gregory sat back and his taxi followed.

For a few moments they wound in and out the old-fashioned twisting streets, then Gregory's taxi pulled up once more. The other stood some way along a narrow turning outside a lighted doorway. The man and the girl were getting out. Gregory could see now that the man was hatless and wore breeches topped by a leather airman's coat.

'Stay here,' he ordered as he stepped down into the street, softly closing the door of his cab behind him. The driver grinned. '*C'est une maison de passe, M'sieur. L'autre a de la chance ce soir.*'

'Thank you for nothing,' Gregory snapped. Then he smiled resignedly. '*C'est la fortune de guerre*' he translated the English idiom literally but incorrectly for the driver's benefit. It did not always suit him to draw attention to his proficiency in foreign languages; then, being a very thorough person, he took the trouble to walk quietly down the street to verify his taximan's statement.

The other taxi, now paid off, had driven on. The place seemed to be a cheap *café* open to the street. A few night birds were sitting silent, with drinks before them, at the little tables. The girl and the man were not among them but Gregory's quick eye had immediately noted a side door giving separate entrance from the street to the rooms above. He shrugged his slightly stooping shoulders impatiently. What an ass he had been to bother. The girl was a *cocotte* all right, and this was undoubtedly a 'house of accommodation'. It surprised him a little that so gloriously lovely a lady should consent to meet her lover in a sordid joint, but he knew well enough that women care nothing for such things if they happen to have got the great madness for a particular man. The old chap might be running her but obviously she was of the type who insist on having their freedom at certain times, and this was one of them.

He was just about to turn away when a sharp cry came from the room above the *café*. It was a little muffled by the thick window curtains, through which chinks of light filtered, but Gregory's ears were almost abnormally keen that night.

A sudden grin spread over his lean face. In three strides he had crossed the narrow street. His raised foot crashed against the flimsy lock and the private door to the rooms above swung open with a bang.

Crouched like a leopard, he raced up the narrow flight of stairs, dashed across the landing, and flung his weight against the only door beneath which there appeared a streak of light.

The room was not the *cabinet particulier* which he had expected but almost a replica of the *café* below. In one corner four men were writhing in a struggling heap. Three wore the blue cotton blouses of French dock labourers. The fourth, who lay beneath them, was the fellow in the airman's coat. The girl stood nearby with distended eyes, her hands gripping the sides of a little table over which she leaned, apparently too paralysed by fear to scream.

The situation would have been clear to a dullard's eye so Gregory wasted no time in thought. Seizing a bottle from a nearby table, he knocked it sharply against the wall, smashing off the punt. Then, waving the jagged end, the ugliest weapon in the world, he sailed into the fray.

2

The Coded Telegram

As Gregory leapt he saw a knife flash in the hand of one of the thugs. For a second it looked as if the vicious stroke would pin the young man to the floor, but Gregory struck with all his force. The jagged bottle bit through the flimsy covering of the dock rat's shoulder and into the grimy flesh beneath. With a sudden scream he dropped his knife and clutched at the torn and bleeding muscle.

The other two swung round, still crouching in the corner over the prostrate man, to face Gregory. With his free hand he seized a chair and flung it—just as the nearest was about to spring. It caught the man below the knees. He staggered wildly, grabbed at a frail table and went down with it on top of him. The other whipped out a knife and, with a quick twist which Gregory recognised in sudden fear as the manner of the expert, drew back his arm to throw it.

But they had all reckoned without the man in the airman's jacket. He was a hefty fellow, well over six feet tall, and broad in proportion. Despite his recent gruelling, it seemed that he had plenty of fight left in him for his muscular hand closed like a vice round the ankle of the knife thrower and, with a violent jerk, he brought him crashing to the floor.

Then he scrambled to his feet, pushed the girl roughly from his path, gasped out 'Thanks a lot' to Gregory, and dashed from the room.

The wounded thug was cursing vilely as he tried to staunch the flow of blood from his shoulder. The other two picked themselves up, and the knife thrower, a sinuous dark young fellow with crisp curly hair, cried wildly, '*Vite! Vite! Arrêtez-le!*'

Without so much as a glance in Gregory's direction all

three thrust themselves through the door and pounded down the stairs in pursuit of their late victim.

Gregory turned to the girl. She seemed to have recovered her self-possession completely and was watching him with a curious intensity beneath which, he just suspected, lay a faint amusement. He raised his eyebrows and smiled.

'I can excuse many things in the young,' he said softly, 'but not bad manners. Now, it would have been quite impossible for *me* to leave *Mademoiselle* so suddenly and without even one little word of farewell or a deep sigh of regret. . . . In fact,' he added seriously as if the thought had just come to him, 'I should find it difficult to leave *Mademoiselle* at all!'

'You follow me from the Casino. I recognise you,' she stated softly, ignoring his remarks.

'Lucky for you I did,' Gregory replied promptly.

She was French as he had supposed but obviously English came quite easily to her. It was the first time that he had had the leisure to study her at close quarters and the quick smile which twitched his thin lips showed that he was in no way disappointed.

A long coat of mink with a heavy double collar now hid her graceful figure, but above it rose her heart-shaped face with its broad low brow and little pointed chin. He admired again the dark pencilled eyebrows which curved back like the two ends of a cupid's bow, the points rising almost to her temples, and the sleek black hair, parted on the side and flattened on the crown but spreading into a mass of tight jet curls behind her small pink ears and on the nape of her neck. Then he noted the perfection of her skin. It was fresh and healthy as that of a child, and such light make-up as she wore was obviously only a concession to fashion.

As her large dark eyes held his with an unflickering gaze he was suddenly aware that she was no young girl but a very dangerous woman. The type which makes all other women bristle with jealousy and suspicion from the moment they enter a room, and for whom men have killed each other, and themselves, throughout the ages.

For the first time for years a real thrill ran through Gregory's body and even in that moment the thought came to him how wise he had been not to fritter away his emotions on lesser game while there were still women like this in the world.

'We must get out of here,' he said quietly but there was an imperiousness in his voice which had been lacking before, for the noise of the chase had hardly died away below when he caught the sound of hurrying feet from somewhere in the rear of the house. Next moment a door at the back of the room behind a small bar was thrust open and a thick-set bald-headed man in his shirt-sleeves burst in upon them.

As the new-comer's small dark eyes lit upon the overturned furniture he began shouting in voluble French.

'What is this! You make a scene in my respectable house! You break the furniture. I see blood! There is murder done! I will call the police!'

'Shut up!' snapped Gregory. 'You were in it yourself I expect. Any more from you and I'll give you a taste of this.' He waved the end of the broken bottle, which he still held, aggressively.

The man gnawed his walrus moustache in apparent indecision while he eyed Gregory stupidly for a moment, then he suddenly dived back behind the rampart of his bar and ran from the room as quickly as he had come.

Gregory wasted no time in argument. If the landlord of the place was not in with the thugs he was now making a bee-line for the telephone and the police would be arriving at any moment. Gregory knew just how inconvenient a French police inquiry could prove, even to innocent persons. They might hold him for days as a material witness against the thugs. To be mixed up in anything of that sort was the last thing he desired. But the lesson of Drake and the game of bowls on Plymouth Hoe was one which had always appealed to him. Time enough now to impress the lady first and run from the French police afterwards. So instead of hustling her out he dropped the bottle, held open the door and, removing his hat with a graceful bow, said courteously:

'*Mademoiselle*, the time has come for you and me to find pleasanter surroundings. I have a cab below.'

'I thank you, *Monsieur*,' she replied evenly, and the suggestion of a smile which played about her red lips as she walked from the room showed that she was not unappreciative of his poise and gallantry.

As Gregory made his bow, his eye had fallen on a flat, black notecase lying a few feet away from the corner where the tussle had taken place. He stooped swiftly, picked it up, and thrust it in his pocket. Then he strode after the girl and shepherded her swiftly down the stairs.

The street was still empty except for his waiting taxi a hundred yards away. The voices of the few night-birds now raised in excited argument within the *café* drowned the sound of their footsteps as he took the girl's arm in a confident grip and with long, but apparently unhurried strides, led her to the cab.

'The Metropole, Deauville,' he told the driver, and the man nodded with a quick grin as they climbed in.

The airman and the thugs had probably taken the other direction, Gregory assumed, since the taxi-man said nothing of the chase. Anyhow, the fellow could grin until he burst, for he, Gregory, had got the girl, and *what* a girl. She seemed to radiate warmth by merely sitting beside him as they bumped over the *pavé* of the old streets back to the harbour, and a faint delicious odour, not so much a definite perfume as the scent of daily coiffured hair, freshly washed silks and a scrupulously tended person—the hall-marks of a superbly *soignée* woman—filled the darkness of the taxi. The problem was—how to keep her?

'What would you like me to call you?' Gregory asked her suddenly.

'My name is Sabine.'

'Delightful—and the other half?'

'*Monsieur* is curious, but I do not consider it necessary that I tell. We part soon and it is not—er—*convenable* that we meet again.'

'*Parfaitement.*' Gregory bowed to her decision but with mental reservations. 'Sabine it is then but you seem to forget that the police are probably taking down our descriptions at the moment. Unless we can keep clear of them we shall both spend the rest of the night in the lock-up.'

'You think that—*pas de blague*?'

'I certainly do. That's why I told this chap to go to the Metropole—and here we are.'

He paid off the taxi with a lavish tip and followed her into the hotel.

'I leave you only for the moment,' she said as they reached the *entre-salle* and he watched her walk in the direction of the ladies' cloak-room.

But Gregory was not to be caught like that. She might give him the slip if he went into the lounge and sat down at a table so, instead, he took up a position where he could keep the door under observation and occupied himself by examining the notecase which he had collected from the floor of the upstairs *café*.

A quick survey of its contents caused him to smile with pleasure. Then he slipped the case back into his pocket and, lighting a cigarette, stood waiting for Sabine.

She appeared again a moment later and he noted with satisfaction that she had not left her mink coat in the cloak-room; thus enabling him to put a completely fresh plan into operation without delay. As they passed into the lounge he took her arm again and whispered:

'We won't stay here. There are so few people about at this hour we're certain to be noticed. We'll go out through the other entrance and along to the *Normandie*.'

'But why should there be people in quantity there more than here?' she questioned.

'There won't,' he answered tersely, 'but the taxi-man set us down here so it's as well to get out of this place as quickly as possible in case he's questioned.'

'As you will.' She allowed him to lead her out on to the

plage and they walked the few hundred yards to the other hotel. At the entrance he paused and faced her.

'Listen Sabine!' he spoke with unusual firmness. 'Any argument will draw attention to us. I am staying here, so there must be no fuss—you understand? Do as I say or else the police will get us and we shall both spend the night in some uncomfortable gaol.'

'But . . .' She was about to make a protest.

'Stop it,' he cut her short abruptly. 'I hate to remind you of the fact, but it was *you* who took the fellow who was attacked to the *maison de rendezvous*, so it is you whom the police will want to talk to. Remember, he may have been murdered by now for all we know.'

'All right,' she murmured and when he took her straight over to the lift and upstairs to his room she made no further protest.

'Now,' he said, having closed the double doors behind him and thrown his coat upon the bed, 'I think you had better tell me what you know.'

Again she regarded him with her large, calm, unfrightened eyes. 'How?' she asked.

'There's something going on, and I want to know about it.' Gregory's chin jutted out as he faced her in the quiet room, shut off from the corridor by the private bathroom, clothes closet and miniature hall, with its *toile de jouy* hangings and *rose du barri* colouring, warm in the pink lights of the shaded lamps.

He took the worn notecase from his pocket again and added quietly: 'Perhaps this will help us.'

The case contained 2,440 francs in notes of various denominations, the document which Gregory had already scanned at the Metropole, and a telegram. He spread out the latter and read it carefully.

'This is written out in pencil; by a woman I should judge. It's on a sending form so it has not yet been despatched; it says:

COROT CAFE DE LA CLOCHE CALAIS SIXTH 41 44 11 15 THENCE 46 SEVENTH 43 47 EIGHTH 43 AGAIN 47

Well, that doesn't help us much, since it's in code,' he added. 'But it's interesting all the same, and confirms my ideas about your charming self. Now, once again, what do you know?'

She stared at him with a lazy insolence in her hazel eyes.

'If I knew anything why should I tell? Also, I do not regard the chance of being questioned by the police as of sufficient importance to risk my reputation by remaining in your room.'

A sudden smile that could on occasion make Gregory's lean face so attractive flashed over it. 'Why?' he said softly with a new note in his voice. 'We are both bad hats anyway—aren't we?'

'Of course,' she murmured with an answering smile. 'And you are—how shall I say?—well, *emotionant* in your way—one does not often meet an Englishman with your personality—see how frank I have become. But I fear I have no time for gallantry at the moment.'

'Haven't you? I think you have.' Gregory took one of her hands and kissed it.

'No—no,' she shook her head. 'You are a nice person but at this time such follies are apart from me.'

'Are they?' He pressed nearer to her and his eyes said infinitely more than his words conveyed. But at that moment the telephone which stood on a little table near the bed shrilled loudly.

It was just behind her and she picked it up without the least hesitation. '*Ullo*,' she said, '*merci . . . ah bon! . . . Adieu.*' Then she replaced the receiver.

'As I thought,' she turned back to him. 'That call was for me. My friend whom you have seen with me in the Casino has many ways of knowing what I do. Someone in this hotel has told him of my presence here. He assures me that all is arranged so that there is no further likelihood of my being troubled by the police.'

She smiled—a little mocking smile of triumph at Gregory. 'You understand? I must return to my friend. This little adventure has been quite amusing and I thank you for your courtesy, but now, *Monsieur*—it is over.'

Gregory smiled too. 'I hate,' he said, 'to seem to press you; but I think you will see the wisdom of remaining here in hiding when I tell you I know from his papers that the man whom you lured to that dive tonight was an officer from Scotland Yard. If the French police knew that they would renew their desire to interview you despite anything that your very clever friend can do. So it seems to me that you are wrong, *Mademoiselle*, and that this adventure has only just begun.'

3

An Interrupted Idyll

'You mean to keep me here—against my will?' For the first time the self-confidence faded from Sabine's eyes. Almost instinctively she glanced behind her to see if there was another exit from the room.

Gregory faced her across the broad low bed. His back was to the only door which gave on to the miniature hallway of the suite. Tall, lean, the suggestion of a smile pulling at his thin lips, he noted with quiet satisfaction that he had at last broken through her armour of casual ease.

It was now well after one o'clock. Many of the wealthy crowd staying at the *Normandie* would, he knew, still be at the casino; while those who did not gamble or dance would already be in bed. The double doors, with the small hallway in between, separating the big room from the corridor, muffled the loudest sounds even in the day time; now, the unbroken hush of midnight hours pervaded the great hotel. In the soft light of the *rose du barri* shaded lamps against the background of the *toile de jouy* hangings Sabine's dark beauty glowed warm and alluring.

Not a flicker of an eyelid betrayed Gregory's determination to take with both hands this golden hour which it seemed that the Gods had decreed for him. The girl was no bread and butter miss but an adventuress, perhaps even a *poule de luxe*, one of those rare exotic women for the sake of whose caresses millionaires commit crazy follies and sometimes come to ruin, disgrace, and suicide. He had caught her fairly; he was even running some risk of trouble with the police for deliberately concealing her. She must pay toll but she should do so of her own free will in an hour or two. Gregory was by nature the joyful cynic and far too old a hand to rush his fences. He moved round the bed towards her.

'Listen!' he said. 'You lured that chap in the airman's coat down to that dive where he was set upon.'

'*Monsieur*, that is not true.'

Gregory dismissed her protest with a wave of his thin muscular hand. 'Owing to the break I gave him he may have got clean away. On the other hand, those thugs may have run him down and knifed him.'

'No—no. If so my friend would have told me of that when he telephoned just now.'

'*Touché!*' Gregory exclaimed, his smile broadening into a grin. 'A confession, my dear Sabine, that those cut-throats were in your friend's employ, *and* that you knew it.'

Her dark eyes flashed. '*Monsieur* is clever but it is sometimes dangerous to know too much.'

'A threat, eh? Come, that's ungenerous, since you'd be in Deauville police station at this moment if I hadn't got you out of that *café*. More, it's rank ingratitude when I propose to keep you here all night to save you from arrest.'

'My friend has said that I am in no danger of arrest.'

'You forget that your description will have been given to

the police by the *patron* of the *café*. They'll nab you for certain if you try and leave this hotel.'

'*Nab*—what is that?'

'Pinch—arrest. All the hotel porters and taxi men in Deauville will have been warned to keep a look out for you by this time. Remember, the man whom your friend's thugs tried to do in was an officer from Scotland Yard. When our special branch men operate on the continent they always keep in touch with the local police, so if he has escaped he will have made his report by now, and the authorities will be wanting you pretty badly.'

For a moment she was silent then, with a little sigh, she sat down on the arm of a low chair. 'I am so tired,' she murmured, passing her hand across her eyes. 'Perhaps you are right, *Monsieur*, but it is ungallant that you should take advantage of my situation.'

Gregory reassessed his chances. Her regal self-assurance of a few moments before had suddenly disappeared. It was as though a spring inside her had given away; she sat now hunched and dejected, a rather pitiful little figure, acute anxiety in her dark eyes as to the outcome of this difficult position in which her evening's adventure had landed her.

His experience of women made him certain that she was not shamming. She was an adventuress, of course, but not a *poule*, otherwise she would never have broken down like this. He was glad of that since it made the affair so much more interesting. Like a good diplomat he prepared himself to make concessions. The gods gave only in their own good time. They had been kind to place so rare a gift within his compass. Now he must wait upon their pleasure.

He smiled, one of those rare warm smiles which could at times make his grim face so attractive, and laid a hand on her shoulder.

'Don't worry please,' he said softly. 'I hope we are going to see quite a lot of each other in the future, so the last thing I want is to make you think me a bore. I only want to help you. I'm sure it's best for you to stay here the night. You can have my bed and I'll shake down with some cushions and the eider-down in the bathroom. We'll talk things over in the morning.'

She nodded slowly, not doubting for an instant that he meant exactly what he said.

'I think I might have guessed that I need have no fear of you. How wise you are, too, if you really wish to gain my fren'ship.'

'May our friendship ripen quickly,' he replied, and they smiled into each other's eyes like two expert swords-men about to enjoy a test of skill with buttoned foils.

'Pyjamas!' Gregory drew a clean pair, of peach-coloured silk, from a drawer and threw them on the bed. 'You'll have to use your fur coat as a dressing-gown I'm afraid—I'll need mine if I'm to sleep hard. They key's in the door, so you can lock it if you wish—but you needn't bother. Your virtue is as safe as the crown jewels for, shall we say, the next eight hours—or until you leave this suite—but after that, *gardez vous ma belle Sabine. Je deviendrai le loup dans le bois.*'

She arched her splendid eyebrows. 'Is that a challenge?'

'It is. I know nothing of your dealings with your elderly friend but I mean to take you from him even if I have to swing for it.'

As he spoke Gregory had been gathering up his things together with the cushions and the coverlet from the bed. He had no intention of losing the maximum effect of his withdrawal by prolonging the conversation. In the doorway he turned. 'Good night, little Red Ridinghood.'

Sabine inclined her head. '*Dormez bien,* my Big Bad Wolf.'

She was now a little uncertain if she was altogether glad to see him leave her so quickly.

Outside he locked the door on to the corridor, made up a couch for himself on the bathroom floor, undressed and, putting out the light, lay down to think.

His unusual resting-place did not trouble him at all. Gregory Sallust could sleep anywhere but his brain was busy with the events of the evening.

His tour through Normandy, spying out the land for the organisation which had engaged him in London, had proved completely abortive until this, the very last evening of his visit. Even now he had no certain knowledge that this strange adventure, into which he had been led by following Sabine, had any bearing upon the operations which he had been asked to investigate, yet he had a strong feeling that this might be so. The officer from Scotland Yard, who'd been attacked, might have been in Deauville for half a hundred different reasons, but it was Sabine's connection with that strange little man, with whom he had first seen her in the Casino, which intrigued him. That almost dwarf-like figure with the powerful head, pale stone-cold eyes, and shock of white hair above the broad forehead, was known to Gregory as one who had been engaged for years in great, and always sinister, undertakings. It might well be that he was at the bottom of the whole business. Even if that were not so, Gregory had found Sabine, a woman in a million; one of those rare beings who possessed all the attributes which appealed to his fastidious nature. Gregory Sallust felt that his evening had not been wasted. For a time he amused himself by conjuring up her face again in the darkness; then he turned over and slept peacefully.

Gregory made a practice of never being called and usually slept late in the morning, so he would probably not have woken until nine o'clock, but at half-past eight the bathroom door creaked and Sabine put her dark head round the corner.

As his eyes opened he stared at her in bewilderment; then the events of the few hours before flooded back to him and he sat up.

'I am so sorry if I disturb you,' she said, 'but I have been awake a long time and I am hungry; also, I would like a bath.'

'Right oh! Give me ten minutes, will you, and I'll see what we can do about some breakfast. Feeling better this morning?'

'A lot, t'ank you.' She smiled and shut the door.

He shaved his lean face with quick sure strokes, brushed his tumbled hair, slipped on his dressing-gown, and then joined her in the bedroom.

Her evening dress and stockings were still lying over a chair and she sat perched on the edge of the bed muffled up in her big fur coat.

'I've turned on the bath,' he told her, 'so in you go, and don't come out before I call you. In the meantime I'll order breakfast. What would you like? Just coffee and rolls, or something more sustaining?'

'May I have some canteloupe, also an omelette—*fines herbe*—I think.'

'You little glutton,' he laughed, 'of course you may, but we'll have to eat it off one set of plates, or else they'll tumble to it that I've got a visitor. Run along now and when you hear the waiter come in mind you stop splashing.'

As she left him, carrying away her clothes, he gave the order by telephone, and a quarter of an hour later the floor waiter appeared with the dishes and coffee upon a tray. He was accompanied by an under porter carrying a cabin trunk, which he set down carefully as he said: 'This has just arrived, *Monsieur*. I was ordered to bring it up to you at once.'

When the men had gone Gregory examined the trunk. It was addressed to him and he found it to be unlocked. On opening it, he saw a note inside; it read

Dear Mr. Sallust,

I trust that you have taken care of my little friend, Sabine. Some people in my position might find grounds for serious annoyance in her desertion of me, but at my age I can afford to be tolerant towards the escapades of young people. I only hope she was not disappointed in you.

Now that this little frolic is over, however, she will naturally wish to return to my care at the earliest possible moment. To facilitate that end I send under your name a complete outfit of her day clothes. Should she fail to rejoin me by midday I shall consider you lacking in appreciation of the courtesy I have extended to you and proceed to teach you a sharp lesson in good manners.

I do not sign this as Sabine will know from whom it comes.

P.S. My apologies to Sabine, please, that my servants are unable to find her Bassana powder. Also, although she is fond of it, I should be obliged if you will exercise your influence to restrain her from eating any fish for breakfast, since I am always a little doubtful of it in the summer months abroad.

Gregory grinned. He did not need to ask Sabine from whom the letter had come and, knowing something of the sender, he felt that the veiled threat was by no means an empty one; yet he had no intention of truckling to it. Sabine was far too beautiful a prisoner to be released because some risk might be incurred by a continuance of her company. Gregory was already planning in his mind the manner in which they might most pleasantly spend the day together. He slipped the note in his pocket and, knocking on the bathroom door, reported the arrival both of the trunk and breakfast.

Sabine joined him a few moments later clad in her evening dress and looking beautiful but slightly incongruous in the bright morning sunshine which was now streaming through the window.

Breakfast proved a gay and pleasant meal. They had to drink from the single cup and shared the melon and omelette with the happy laughter that springs from quick mutual attraction. All the distrust she had shown of him the previous night had disappeared.

When the meal was over he waved a hand towards the trunk. 'You had better change now, I think, into day clothes, while I have a bath and get dressed myself. But what shall we do afterwards? How would you like to spend the day?'

She became grave at once. 'I must get back and rejoin my friend. Otherwise he will be angry and when he is angry it is not good.'

Gregory raised one eyebrow, the left, until it met the white scar running down from his forehead, which gave him at times such a Mephistophelean appearance. 'You're not out of the wood with the police yet, you know,' he said, 'and if you go off on your own they may pinch you for that affair last night.'

'If that is so, they may do so if I am with you, *n'est ce pas?*'

He shook his head. 'I don't think you need worry as long as you remain with me because, you know, that Scotland Yard man owes me something. By turning up when I did I probably saved his life. He's bound to take that into account so the chances are that if you're caught with me they'll prove much more reasonable about you than if they catch you on your own. Besides, the wolf knows the forest and you're much more likely to escape altogether if you let him be your guide.'

'That may be so—but my friend? He will make trouble if I do not return.'

'Listen.' Gregory leaned forward eagerly and took her hands. 'I'll put it to you another way. If you wish to do so you are perfectly free to walk out of this room now. From the beginning I've never had the least intention of turning you over to the police, I'm sure you know that, but if you go now I may never see you again. All I'm asking is for another hour or two with you. This is the last day of my holiday. I'm returning to England this evening by the five o'clock boat. You said last night you might give me your friendship for sheltering you here and asking nothing of you in return. Now is the time then. Won't you be very sweet and kind, risk a spot of trouble with the old man, and spare me a few hours today? Just long enough to drive somewhere and lunch together in the sunshine. I'll have you back in Deauville and safe at home by four o'clock. I promise.'

'You have been kind—and generous.' She hesitated a second. 'But this may be most dangerous for you.'

'Danger has never stopped me doing anything I wanted to yet, nor you my dear. We're two of a kind and thrive on it—be honest now—aren't we?'

'*C'est vrai*,' she said softly. 'All right then, I will do as you wish, but the consequences—they must be upon your own head.'

'Splendid!' With a quick gesture Gregory pulled her to her feet and kissed her on the cheek. 'Quick now and change—while I get my clothes on.' With a happy laugh he swung away from her and two minutes later he was singing lustily in his bath.

When he returned he found her dressed in an airy primrose summer frock and large picture hat, which suited her dark beauty to perfection. She had repacked the cabin trunk with her evening clothes and, but for the tumbled bed, the room now showed no traces of her occupation.

'Now to make our get-away,' he exclaimed and, picking up the telephone, he gave swift orders in French that his car should be driven round from the garage and left outside Van Cleffe et Appel, the jewellers, at the side of the hotel.

'We'll give them ten minutes,' he said, turning back to her, 'then slip down the service staircase, just in case there's a large blue policeman waiting to wish you good morning in the lounge, although they can hardly know you went to earth here last night.'

Only a good-natured chambermaid hid a smile of understanding as she passed them hand in hand on the service stairs. They slipped through a side door into the restaurant then, under cover of the cider-apple trees, out through the court-yard. The car was waiting at the spot to which Gregory had ordered it. His plan had worked without a hitch yet those few minutes of suspense made a bond between them; for both felt a little like naughty children who were slipping away to play some forbidden game in spite of the prohibition of stern elders.

Gregory turned the car to the left, along the front, then left again on to the fine main road, and so out of the town between the rows of big Edwardian villas. He had already settled it in his mind that they should lunch at the famous Guillaume Conquérant Restaurant at Dives, but it was still only ten o'clock, so he drove straight through to Cabourg and then turned inland along the road to Caen.

When he discovered that Sabine had never visited the old Norman capital, except to dine at that resort of gourmets, the Champs d'Hiver, he parked the car in the square and they got out.

They spent an hour laughing and talking as they walked round the market and inspected the Cathedral then, after an early cocktail, they picked up the car again and drove back to Dives, that little village at the mouth of the river, from which William the Conqueror set out so many centuries ago with his Norman knights to invade England.

Neither Gregory nor Sabine were strangers to the celebrated hostelry, which is the principal centre of interest at Dives today, and they were soon seated at one of the small tables in its ancient flower-decked courtyard, receiving the ministrations of the *maître d'hôtel*.

The August day was one of torrid heat so they decided on a cold luncheon: *Consomme en gelé, Canard Montmorency,* and *Fraises de bois*.

Sabine had lost all trace of the anxiety which she had previously shown in playing truant to that powerful and sinister figure whom she termed her friend. She was protesting gaily that she could not possibly manage a third helping of the excellent cold duck, dressed with foie gras and cherries, when Gregory saw her face go suddenly blank.

'What is it?' he inquired anxiously.

She leaned across the table, laying her hand swiftly on his; her smooth forehead creased into a frown. 'That man,' she whispered. 'Quick, he is just going through the gate. Oh, but you must be careful.'

Gregory glanced over his shoulder and was in time to catch one glimpse of a tall broad-shouldered well-dressed fellow, who dragged one leg slightly as he walked.

'Who is it?' he asked.

'The Limper; that is the name by which they call him,' she murmured. 'Is it by chance, I wonder, that he is here, or has my friend sent him? Be careful of yourself, please. It would make me miserable now if any misfortune were to happen to you.'

'Is he so dangerous then?'

'Very, I t'ink. At least, many people are afraid of him.'

'Well, I'm not,' Gregory laughed, 'but thanks for the warning, and thank you far more for your concern for me. But tell me this: why do you mix with such people? Have you got to or is it from choice?'

She shrugged. 'It is my life.'

'I wish you'd tell me more of yourself, and more of your, er—friend.' As he spoke he was speculating again as to whether Sabine could possibly be the old man's mistress. The thought that it might be so filled him momentarily with one of those gusts of cold fierce rage which made him capable, at times, of sacrificing his egoism to become a killer; not from jealousy, but because some queer streak in him leapt to the defence of the beautiful, the precious, and the rare, utterly regardless of all man-made laws, conventions, shibboleths. He had been born five hundred years after his time, knew it and, even in his more sober moments, was inclined to glory in the fact.

She shrugged again. 'I prefer that you should not question me. In a little time now we must part and it is better that you should know nothing of me.'

'Yet I mean to. Believe me Sabine, we shall meet again—and soon.'

'I do not say I would be averse to that—but no! At this time I am apart from men. It is too dangerous—dangerous for you. Please, after today forget that we have ever met. It would be better so.'

'Tell me one thing,' he urged. 'When you speak of your friend, do you really mean your lover?'

'How absurd you are,' she laughed. 'But no, perhaps, not altogether absurd, for he is a most fascinating and interesting person. He has no time for women though, I t'ink, and uses me only as a cog in his machine.'

'To lure unsuspecting young policemen to their death, eh?'

He smiled, his flaming anger having evaporated as quickly as it had come.

'No, no, not that. Those thugs, as you call them, would not have killed him. Their orders were only to get back the telegram that he had stolen.'

She spoke hastily in her anxiety to deny the suggestion that she might have led the officer to his death and, in so doing, had said more than she had intended. Gregory was quick to note the flush that mounted to her cheeks. The telegram was now reposing in his breast pocket and as soon as he had the chance he meant to get a cipher expert on to decoding it, if possible, since he had felt from the beginning that it might hold the key to the mystery in which he was so interested.

'Do you know the code in which that telegram was drafted?' he asked casually.

She helped herself to a few more wood strawberries from the little wicker basket which reposed between them then said slowly: 'If I did I would not tell you and, since you speak of it, much trouble could be saved if you would give that telegram to me. If I could hand it to my friend on my return I should escape his anger. Also, he would be grateful to you and perhaps allow that we meet again.'

Gregory shook his head. 'I'm sorry, but I'm afraid that's impossible. I'm sure you'll be able to make your peace with him when you get home in an hour or so now, and I mean to keep the telegram at least, as a small souvenir of our adventure.'

She shrugged and lifted up her coffee cup. 'As you will—but you would be far wiser to do as I suggest.'

'No. I have to return to England in any case tonight, so even with your friend's permission I should not be able to see you again for a day or two, although I mean to, whether he likes it or not, as soon as I can. Here's to our next merry meeting.' He tossed off his liqueur of vintage Calvados and beckoned the waiter to bring the bill.

As he was paying it she stood up, saying that she must

leave him for a moment, but would rejoin him at the car. He watched her go, a gracious sylvan figure, then he stood up himself and walked slowly through the creeper-covered gateway round to the garage.

His car was not where he had left it in the car park, but a blue-overalled mechanic met him and told him that, having noticed the car had a flat tyre, he had run it into the garage. Then the man hurried off on some errand saying that he would be back again in one moment.

The car park was deserted and, all-unsuspecting, Gregory turned from its strong sunlight into the deep shadow of the ancient stables. As he rounded the corner a tall figure with raised arms leapt forward casting a cloud of black dust straight into his face.

It was pepper. Too late, he shut his eyes and thrust up his hands. Searing red-hot pains seemed to stab through his eyeballs. The infernal stuff was in his mouth and nostrils making him choke and gasp. Then, as he staggered back, blind and helpless, a powerful fist caught him a terrific blow in the stomach and he doubled up, writhing in agony upon the ground.

4

Enter an Eminent Edwardian

'And that,' said Gregory two nights later, 'was the last I saw of the delectable Sabine.'

Sir Pellinore Gwaine-Cust sat back and roared with laughter.

'Well, I'll be devilled!' he exclaimed when he had somewhat recovered. 'The minx fooled you properly, and no wonder your eyes are in such a state. Still, there are as good fish you know . . . Have some more brandy, my boy, have some more brandy.'

'Thanks.' Gregory picked up the decanter and poured a further ration into the big Ballon glass that stood on a little table at his elbow. His host's brandy was as rich, as full-flavoured, and of as fine a vintage as the man himself.

Sir Pellinore was one of those remarkable products which seem peculiar to England. Born in 1870, the heir to a pleasant property on the Welsh border, which had been in his family since the Wars of the Roses, he came into his inheritance in the naughty 'nineties, while still a subaltern in a crack cavalry regiment. He had an eye for a horse and a pretty woman, and an infinite capacity for vintage port, but no one had ever accused him of having any brains. He was distantly connected with royalty, and numbered three dukes among his first cousins, so from his youth upward he had known everyone who mattered by their Christian names, yet not one in a hundred thousand of the general public had ever heard of him. He had shot everything that is shootable, including men, and received a brief notoriety from a particularly well-deserved V.C. in the South African war, but as he had never courted publicity he soon slipped from public notice again.

Early in King Edward VII's reign a crisis had occurred in Sir Pellinore's financial affairs which had made him consider it desirable to resign his commission rather than sacrifice his ancient patrimony. Some people in the city had offered him a directorship, entirely, of course, on account of his social standing, but curiously enough they found him a surprisingly regular attendant at their board meetings, where he displayed a blunt persistence in acquainting himself with the minutest details of the company's affairs. After a little, the people in the city discovered that if they had a particularly tricky transaction to negotiate with an Armenian or a Greek the best thing to do was to leave it to Sir Pellinore; true he had no brains, but he possessed a strange direct way of putting matters to such people. He was so transparently honest that they never quite knew what had come over them, until they were back in the Levant. Other directorships had been accepted by Sir Pellinore, although he always modestly declined the chairmanship of any company with which he was connected.

For services in the Great War he had been offered a peerage, but declined it on the score that there had been a Gwaine-Cust for so many centuries at Gwaine Meads that the tenants would think he had sold the place if he became Lord something-or-other.

He had always dealt with his co-directors with that same disarming frankness which he displayed to Americans and Greeks; his formula being, 'Well now, you fellows, just pay me what you think the job was worth—say half what I've saved the company, eh? That's fair. No cheating there. Mustn't rob the shareholders, must we?' He was now exceedingly rich.

He inhabited a vast mansion in Carlton House Terrace to which admirals, generals, diplomats and cabinet ministers came to unburden themselves when their affairs proved particularly difficult. Not for advice, oh no! because everybody knew that Sir Pellinore had no brains, but he was as safe as the grave and a decent sort—one of the old school with a curiously direct way of thinking, an eye for a horse or a pretty woman, and an infinite capacity for vintage port.

His only son had died of wounds during the Great War, and it was Gregory who, as a very young subaltern, had carried him back out of the hell of Thiepval Wood on the Somme, in 1916, at imminent risk to his own life. That was how he had come to meet Sir Pellinore who, times without number, had offered him lucrative permanent posts in his companies, but Gregory had a loathing of routine and just enough money of his own to be independent.

He had a direct way of thinking too, however. That was why they liked each other and why, when one of the great corporations which Sir Pellinore virtually controlled, found their interests threatened, he had said to the board, 'I think I can get you a man. Very able feller. Much more likely to get to the bottom of this business for us than one of those beastly agencies. If you care to leave the matter in my hands . . .'

Now, Gregory warmed the precious liqueur in the bowl-shaped glass with his palms, before sniffing its ethers appreciatively. Then he glanced round the big quiet library where they were sitting after dinner. '*She* didn't fool me, you know,' he said.

Sir Pellinore closed one bright blue eye under a bushy white eyebrow. 'Tell that to the marines, my boy. Been fooled often enough myself by women. Not afraid to admit it either. She tipped off that Limper feller and he did the rest. Gad, I'd have given a packet to see you afterwards. How mad you must have been.' He gave his long thigh a ringing slap, and roared with laughter again.

'Not a bit of it,' Gregory protested. 'If Sabine had put the Limper on to me he would have searched me afterwards for a certainty, and taken the telegram when he had the chance, but he didn't. He obviously couldn't have known I had it. All he was interested in was getting Sabine out of my hands under instructions from his boss. Here's the telegram to prove it.'

'Well, maybe you're right.' The baronet took the flimsy sheet and read it out:

COROT CAFE DE LA CLOCHE CALAIS SIXTH 41 44 11 15 THENCE 46 SEVENTH 43 47 EIGHTH 43 AGAIN 47

'What d'you make of it?' Gregory asked.

'Nothing. Never was any good at figures, much less codes. Never had much of a brain for anything at all.'

'No.' Gregory grinned. 'Yet the father of all the Rothschilds would have buttoned up his pockets and knocked off work for the day if he had heard you were going to pay him a visit in his office.'

'What's that!' Sir Pellinore looked up sharply.

'Well, you know what I mean.' Gregory continued to grin unashamedly. He knew his man and treated Sir Pellinore in private as few of the baronet's co-directors would have dared to do.

'Insolent young devil.' Sir Pellinore returned the grin. 'Good thing there aren't many more of your kidney knocking about. World wouldn't be fit to live in. Honestly, though, I can't make head or tail of this thing. However, I've got a pal in the Admiralty decoding department and I'll get him on to it tomorrow. Never do anything yourself that you can get other people to do for you. Remember that my boy. Better than any tip for the Derby. Lots of fools have paid me good money to get other people to do their work for them.'

'I can well believe you,' said Gregory succinctly. 'Have you still got any of that pre-War Kummel?'

'What, the original Mentzendorff?'

'Yes.'

'Why?'

'Only that I've always found it an excellent aid to thought and I can get fine brandy in other people's houses but you seem to have cornered all the pre-War Kummel in London.'

Sir Pellinore brushed a hand over his fine white moustache and got up. He stood six feet four in his socks and could still have flung most men over thirty down his stairs if he had wanted to.

'Drat the boy,' he muttered as he pressed the bell. 'Another bottle gone and even Justerini's can't find me any more. But I'd sooner you drank it than most people I know. At least you appear to appreciate the stuff and I wouldn't mind a spot myself. Now you shall tell me what you really did with that attractive young woman.'

'There's nothing more to tell.'

'Come on, you young rascal. You had her in your room all night.'

'Even so, I promise you . . .'

'Expect me to believe that! Is it likely! Still, I'll let you off. It's nice to find a youngster who refuses to tell tales out of school. Crawshay, bring me a bottle of Kummel. Out of the bin mind. Not that muck we have for parties.'

'Very good, sir.' The under butler bowed in the doorway and disappeared as quietly as he had come.

'Now! Let's have this thing clear.' The baronet sat back in his deep arm-chair. 'Do you really think you've tumbled on to something or just got yourself mixed up in some shady deal which doesn't matter two hoots to us.'

Gregory shrugged. 'I can't say for certain. It may not concern us at all. On the other hand it may be what we're after. Anyhow, I intend to follow it up.'

'Follow up that young woman is what you mean, my lad.'

'Certainly, but I have a hunch that I won't be wasting my time as far as the other thing is concerned. Remember, it was a Scotland Yard man whom those thugs attacked.'

'That's true. All the same, policemen must have their nights off, like other people, and it's quite probable this wench told you a whole pack of lies to cover up her affair with the fellow. Women are marvellous liars—marvellous. Ha! here comes the Kummel.'

The under butler had arrived with the cob-webbed bottle still uncorked upon a salver, and Sir Pellinore took it from him. When the door closed behind the man he said to Gregory, as he gently tapped the wax off the top of the bottle, 'Never allow my people to uncork old liquor. Servants don't understand that sort of thing these days. Cork's gone to powder, like as not. If so, they push it in and ruin the stuff. One thing I always do myself.' With a skilful sideways twist of the wide spiral corkscrew he drew the cork, smelt it, and then poured out two generous rations. For a moment they both sniffed at the old liqueur, then sipped it.

'By Jove! How right I was to ask you for this,' Gregory murmured. 'Smooth as cream, isn't it, but what a kick.'

Sir Pellinore nodded. 'Pity you didn't have some of this to give the girl at Deauville, eh? But I'll bet you managed without it. Where were we now? You were saying you had a hunch that you'd got on to something really big. What makes you think that? On the face of it, you know, it's only a brawl in a *café* in which it happened that a Scotland Yard man was mixed up.'

'Yes, on the face of it,' Gregory said slowly. 'But I wonder if you remember a conspiracy which took place a few years ago when, by means of arson, sabotage and paid gunmen, a combine endeavoured to gain control of the entire film industry?'*

'Yes, they murdered poor John Bamborough and a number of other people, didn't they? And Hinckman, the Trans-Continental Electric chief, who engineered the whole business, died while evading arrest.'

'He was supposed to have been drowned in a marsh, somewhere down in Surrey, but that's never been proved. However, Hinckman was only the figurehead. There was a far more sinister figure behind the scheme really. A man who controls almost limitless capital and who is believed to have been mixed up with all sorts of financial rackets during the past few years—Lord Gavin Fortescue.'

'What, Denver's brother?' Sir Pellinore's white eyebrows shot up into his forehead.

'Yes. He's the Duke of Denver's twin, but whereas Denver is a fine upstanding figure, Gavin is a sort of freak. Not a dwarf exactly but very short, with an enormous head and a tiny little body, like a child's in its early teens. They say that his abnormality together with the fact that he was born second, and so failed to inherit the dukedom, embittered him to such an extent that it turned his brain. The story goes that he even attempted Denver's murder when they were boys together.'

'That's so! I knew 'em both. Know Denver well today but I haven't seen Gavin for years. He travels a lot I believe but wherever he goes he lives as a recluse. He's immensely rich and made every penny out of crooked deals. He hates his fellow men like poison and has sold his soul fifty times over to make his millions. Armaments, dope, white slaving on the grand scale, he's been in them all; but he's so powerful in a

* For particulars of this conspiracy see *Such Power is Dangerous*, Arrow Books.

subterranean sort of way that nobody's ever been able to get enough watertight evidence to pin anything on him yet. He's not a man, but a warped inhuman devil. I'd put him at the top of the list as the cleverest and most ruthless criminal brain in Europe at the present day.'

Gregory nodded. 'Well, that was the man who gave Sabine her instructions before she left the Casino.'

5

Superintendent Marrowfat Takes Certain Steps

'Good God, man! Why didn't you tell me this before?' Sir Pellinore sat forward quickly.

'Because I'm a born story-teller and always save the tit-bit till the last. I could make a fortune writing thrillers if I weren't so darned lazy; but I think you'll agree now that I'm on to something big.'

Sir Pellinore drank again of the old Kummel. 'I agree entirely. This is worth opening a bottle for. I wouldn't be surprised if Gavin Fortescue isn't the king-pin in the whole of this devilish business we're up against. You're right, my boy, right every time in your intention to follow this up. What's your next move?'

'I want a plane. It must be fast, fool-proof and whatever make has the least noisy engine.'

'You can have a dozen if you want them.'

'One's enough, thanks.'

'Want a pilot too?'

'No, I'll pilot myself but that's why I want it fool-proof. I'm a good bit better than most amateur pilots but all the same I never take a single risk that isn't necessary. Most of my work will be night flying and I'll have to observe as well as fly the plane, so I want the sort of thing that flies itself almost, if you can get it for me.'

'Most planes do these days. Anyhow, the best machine that money can buy shall be at your disposal at Heston tomorrow. What then?'

'We'll see what your pal at the Admiralty can do to decode the telegram although I'm doubtful if he'll make much of it. You see, it's not a cipher where the numbers can be changed down on a sliding scale until one finds their equivalent. The numbers probably apply to things or places so only the people who have the key can read the thing. Still, where it says sixth, seventh and eighth, I think it's a fair bet that dates are implied as today is the fifth of August. If they are dates the inference is that something's going to happen tomorrow, the sixth, so I shall have a cut at getting in on it. Anyhow, I propose to be snooping round the *Café de la Cloche* in Calais tomorrow night.'

'Good, but as the police are already mixed up in this I think you ought to co-operate with them if possible.'

'The police hate civilians butting in on their affairs.'

'That's true, but since one of their men was attacked it's up to us to give them any information in our possession, whether they're after the same thing or not. The Commissioner is in Scotland at the moment but I'll get on to the Assistant Commissioner and arrange an appointment for you to meet somebody at the Yard in the morning.'

Gregory shrugged: 'Just as you wish, although I doubt if much good will come of it.'

Sir Pellinore Gwaine-Cust was an extremely efficient person. When he took an affair in hand it rarely suffered from the delays which are a bane in the life of ordinary business people. All he ever asked was a plain answer to a plain question and if anybody suggested to him that a certain routine must be followed he was apt to be devastatingly terse in his remarks to the routinist. He retained in his employ a well-paid squad of private messengers and always used them in preference to the post as the standing order was instant dismissal for any one of them who failed to return with an answer—even if they had to stay up all night to get it.

In consequence he was able to inform Gregory by telephone at eleven o'clock the following morning that the Admiralty decoding department had vetted the telegram and agreed that the numbers in it applied to things or places and, therefore, were quite undecipherable without a key. Also, that a plane, which would meet his specification, was now awaiting him at Heston, and that he had arranged an appointment for him at twelve o'clock with Superintendent Marrowfat at Scotland Yard.

At five minutes past twelve Gregory was ushered into the Superintendent's room. It was a cold, inhospitable-looking office; the only cheerful thing in it being its occupant.

He was a large man, very large, weighing a good eighteen stone, and Gregory was reminded for a moment of that stout inspector who spends his life perambulating the courtyard of Buckingham Palace watching the great men of the world come and go.

In spite of Superintendent Marrowfat's bulk he showed no sign of physical deterioration. He could move as quickly as most of his colleagues and Gregory judged that he must, literally, possess a punch which could fell an ox. He had a round red cherubic countenance, friendly blue eyes, and a shock of tight carrot-coloured curls upon his head.

'Sit down, sir.' The Superintendent waved a hand towards a chair on the far side of his desk; then pushed over a box of cigarettes. 'Will you smoke?'

'Thanks.' Gregory took a cigarette and lighted it.

'The A.C. tells me that Sir Pellinore Gwaine-Cust rang up to say you had some information which might be useful to us and, if that's so, we should be very pleased to have it.'

'May anything I say be used in evidence against me afterwards?' Gregory asked with a cautious smile.

The big man laughed: 'We're not wanting you on any charge as far as I know so I don't think you need worry about that. This is just a private interview.'

'Right oh,' said Gregory. 'I'm not worried as far as you're concerned, but I'm particularly anxious not to have my copy-book blotted with the French police, so I'd like you to give me your undertaking that you won't pass anything I'm going to tell you on to them; that is, about myself.'

The Superintendent scratched his ear. 'Well, providing you haven't committed a felony in France. Anyhow, I think you can leave it to me to use my discretion.'

'Good, then I'll give you just the bald facts. On the third instant I had just completed a little motoring tour in Normandy ending up at Deauville. That night at the Casino I saw a very striking-looking girl in the company of an elderly man who was known to me by sight. Just before midnight he pulled out his watch and, without saying a word to the girl, showed it to her.

'She left him at once and, as I was interested in the pair, I followed her. She picked up a private car outside the Normandie Hotel and drove in it down to Trouville Harbour. There she dismissed it and a few moments later met a man, evidently by appointment, who came out from behind one of the customs sheds. He was wearing an airman's jacket. The pair took a taxi through the old part of the town, dismissed it outside a little *café* in a narrow street, and went upstairs to a room on the first floor together.

'I was just about to give up the chase, having made up my mind that I was butting in on some love affair, when the sound of fighting came from the room above the *café*. I dashed upstairs and found three dock labourers had set upon the man in the airman's kit. I went to his assistance and he managed to get away. The thugs went after him, leaving me alone with the girl.

'By that time the people in the *café* downstairs were raising Cain and the proprietor yelling for the police. I didn't wish to be mixed up in the affair and be delayed for an investigation, so I determined to get out as quickly as I could, taking the girl with me. But, before I went, I noticed a pocket-book lying in the corner which had evidently been dropped during the struggle.

'Later, when I went through it, I found that the owner's name was Wells, and that he was one of your people attached to the special branch. I got the girl away and as I wished to find out more about the business I gave her shelter for the night in my hotel to save her from being arrested. That's the part I want you to keep under your own hat and not give away to the French police.'

Superintendent Marrowfat nodded, and Gregory went on:

'She refused to give me any information, but I managed to hang on to her during a good bit of the following day and took her over to lunch at the Guillaume Conquérant Restaurant at Dives. Afterwards, when I was going to get my car to motor her back to Deauville, I was set upon, probably by a man whom she had pointed out during lunch and whom she referred to as the "Limper". In any case someone chucked a handful of pepper in my face and gave me a biff in the stomach.

'By the time I was fit to stagger round again my car had disappeared and the girl with it. When I got back to Deauville I found that my car had been returned to the hotel garage but I was only just in time to catch the boat for England that night. That's the story for what it's worth—and here's your man's pocket-book.'

'Much obliged. Now, can you give me a description of this young woman?'

Gregory hesitated a second. He had no desire to put the police on Sabine's track, whatever she might have been up to, but Sir Pellinore had been insistent that he must give the authorities all the information he had so he could hardly avoid complying with the Superintendent's request.

'I can give you a sort of description,' he said, 'but I doubt if it will be very much use to you because, while one woman may be extremely beautiful, and another as plain as the back of a cab, their bald description about height, colouring, and so on, might tally almost completely. This one is of medium height, with what I suppose you would call a heart-shaped face. She has black hair parted at the side and curled at the back of the head. I couldn't tell you the colour of her eyes exactly; pencilled eyebrows, like ninety per cent of women these days, and that's about all there is to it.'

'Nationality?' prompted the Superintendent.

'French I should think: she speaks excellent English though.'

'Age?'

'About twenty-six.'

'Body?'

'Good figure, fairly well-developed bust.'

'Legs?'

'She'd get in the front row of the chorus on her legs all right.'

'Nose?'

'Straight.'

'Complexion?'

'Roses on pale bronze, but she was touched up, of course, like any other smart woman.'

'Cheeks?'

'Full.'

'Ears?'

'I didn't notice.'

'Mouth?'

'Full curved lips.'

'Teeth?'

'Small, white, even.'

'Forehead?'

'Broad.'

'Hands?'

'Plump, pointed, with the usual crimson nails.'

'Carriage?'

'Very upright.'

'Jewellery?'

'She was wearing a big sapphire on the third finger of her right hand, when I saw her, and four—no five, diamond bracelets; the heavy expensive sort, you know, and she had a pair of big pearls in her ears.'

The Superintendent stopped making notes on the pad in front of him and remarked: 'Well, I've had worse descriptions than that to go on.'

Gregory smiled ruefully. The description was far more full than he had intended to make it.

'I think we may assume too,' the Superintendent went on, 'that, in your view at least, she was not as plain as the back of a cab, but extremely beautiful, since you risked getting yourself knifed on her account after only having seen her for a few moments.'

'I followed her because it was part of my job,' said Gregory tonelessly.

'Just as you wish. Now, what about the man she pointed out to you and referred to as the "Limper"?'

'I only caught sight of him for a second and his back was turned towards me. He was a tall fellow, over six feet I should say, dressed in a smart, light-grey, lounge suit and a Homburg. He dragged his left foot a little. That's all I can tell you.'

'Thanks. It's a pity though that you can't tell us more about him, because he might be an old friend of ours whom we've lost sight of for some time. The lady, of course, we knew all about before.'

'The devil you did!' exclaimed Gregory.

'Yes. Wells got away all right and naturally he gave us details of the occurrence in his report. He'll be glad to have his pocket-book back. The woman's not French, but Hungarian, and you're right about her being a goodlooker. He laid stress on that in his description of her.'

'If you had it already why on earth did you bother me for it then?'

'Just a matter of routine, sir. We have rather a habit here of checking up as often as possible.'

'Checking up whether I was lying to you, eh?'

The big man's eyes twinkled. 'I wouldn't exactly say that, but I always like to establish the mental orientation of my visitors as far as possible; if you understand what I mean. Now, what can you tell me about the elderly man who was with the girl at the Casino?'

'I don't think you'll need any description of him. It was Lord Gavin Fortescue.'

For a second the Superintendent's blue eyes went curiously blank, but not a muscle of his face betrayed his sudden interest, and a less acute observer than Gregory would have missed his carefully concealed reaction.

'Lord Gavin Fortescue,' he repeated casually. 'Yes, we can get particulars of him easily enough, as we can of most well-known people. Are you quite sure though that it was Lord Gavin?'

'Certain. I could hardly be mistaken—could I?'

'No. Once seen never forgotten, as the saying goes,' the Superintendent replied, admitting that he was quite well acquainted with Lord Gavin's strikingly unusual appearance. 'Strange, though, to find a gentleman like him mixed up in an affair like this—isn't it?'

'Is it?' Gregory countered. 'He's such a queer bird I should have thought it quite possible you had him on your records already.'

'Really now.' Marrowfat's eyebrows shot up in bland surprise. 'I can't imagine why you should think that. We know nothing of him officially.' He lowered his voice and leaned forward confidentially. 'Now, just what's your view of this business, sir?'

Gregory shrugged. 'I'm afraid I haven't got one—at the moment. It's clear, of course, that the girl lured your man down to that *café* where the thugs set on him.'

'Very interesting,' nodded the Superintendent. 'In your view, then, Lord Gavin Fortescue sent those thugs to lay out our man?'

'That's about the size of it.'

'What d'you think he was after?'

'I haven't the faintest idea, but I hope to find out in the course of the next few days.'

Superintendent Marrowfat raised his carroty eyebrows again. 'But what's your interest in the matter, outside the lady, may I ask? It's hardly your business to ferret out Lord Gavin Fortescue's affairs.'

'No, but I'm engaged on a private investigation for Sir Pellinore Gwaine-Cust at the moment and the two things may link up together.'

'What sort of thing are you investigating?'

'That is Sir Pellinore's affair, and if he hasn't told you it's hardly my place to do so. He was hoping though, I think, that you might agree to my working with your people.'

Superintendent Marrowfat shook his large round head. 'I'm sorry sir: I'm afraid we can't agree to that. You see it would be quite contrary to regulations and I don't think the matter Inspector Wells was sent over to look into can have any bearing on a private issue which appears to rest between Sir Pellinore Gwaine-Cust and Lord Gavin Fortescue. We're very much obliged for the information you've brought us all the same.'

The Superintendent was glancing through the papers in the wallet. 'You didn't happen to find a telegram in this by any chance—did you?' he asked after a moment.

'I'm afraid not.' Gregory lied glibly. He had never been particularly keen on police co-operation and since his offer of assistance had been rejected he had no intention of letting them have a sight of what he considered to be his best card.

'Pity,' said the big man, searching Gregory's face with innocent blue eyes. 'Wells had no time to make a copy of it and the thugs must have got it back after all.'

'That's what they were after then. Well, if you'd prefer that I should continue to act on my own I'm afraid there's no more to be said—is there?'

'That's so, sir. Of course, if you tumble across any criminal activities during your investigations you're entitled to call upon the assistance of the police. In fact, it's your duty to do so, but it wouldn't do for us to mix ourselves up with Sir Pellinore's private concerns. If we once started doing that sort of thing we should never hear the end of it.'

'Right oh! Superintendent. Maybe you'll be hearing from me again later on.'

The Superintendent extended a large plump hand. 'That's it, sir. Much obliged to you I'm sure. I don't think there's any necessity to inform the French police that you concealed the lady for the night and I'm very grateful to you for having come to Wells's help so promptly when they were giving him a rough house. Good morning to you; and thank you.'

As the door closed behind Gregory the big Superintendent suddenly became amazingly active. He grabbed his desk telephone and, after a moment, bellowed down it.

'That you Wells? I've just had that bird here who helped you out at Trouville. Gregory Sallust's his name—a clever devil if ever there was one—he wanted to work in with us but, of course, I couldn't have that. Listen though, you're the lucky one. Lord Gavin Fortescue's in this. It'll be the biggest thing that's happened in years and it means promotion for you if you handle it right. Come up to me at once, but put some good men on to trail Sallust as he leaves the building. He's not to be lost sight of day or night. He's pinched that telegram, but he's going to lead us to something or my name's not Marrowfat.'

6

The Secret of *Mont Couple*

From Scotland Yard Gregory walked round the corner to Westminster Bridge and took the underground down to Gloucester Road, where he had rooms comprising the first floor of No. 272.

He could well have afforded better quarters but the building was the property of one, George Rudd, who had been his batman in the war and had ever since remained his devoted henchman.

Mr. Rudd eked out a precarious living by letting the upper floors of his house, generally to students at the London University, and doing odd jobs for the retail grocer who had the old-fashioned little shop on the ground floor.*

When Gregory returned he found Rudd in his sitting-room polishing some eighteenth century silver-hilted rapiers. Rudd was a great polisher and always seemed to find some difficulty in disposing of his hands unless he had something to occupy them. He was a medium-sized man with yellowish hair, close cropped and bristling at the top of his head, but allowed to grow into a lock in front, which he carefully trained in a well-greased curve across his forehead. A small fair moustache graced his upper lip but, as he always kept it neatly trimmed, it failed to hide the fact that his teeth badly needed the attention of the dentist. His eyes were blue quick, humorous and friendly.

'Like to come on a trip with me to France?' Gregory asked him.

'Not 'arf sir.' The ex-soldier removed the butt of a Gold-flake that dangled from his lower lip. 'Is it gay Paree, or one of them places on the coast, where the girls from the Folley Berjares disports themselves in pocket handkerchiefs during the summer months?'

'No, this is business. I've got a private war on.'

'S'treuth! Who are we going to cosh this time?'

'That's the devil of it: I don't quite know.'

'Well it's all the same to me sir but I pity the poor devils if you've got it in for 'em. Shall we be taking the armaments?'

* Further particulars of Gregory Sallust, Mr. Rudd, and his curious caravanserai in Gloucester Road are to be found in *Black August*.

'May as well. We'll probably need them before we're through.'

Rudd replaced the rapiers above the mantelpiece and took two big automatics from a drawer in the writing-table. They were greased and polished to a superb degree of oily efficiency and he fondled them with loving pride.

'A bag apiece is all we'll need,' Gregory went on. 'Just in case we have to stay the night anywhere. By the bye, we shall be flying.'

'Must we go risking our necks that way as well, sir?' asked Rudd ruefully. 'No nasturtions on you as a pilot sir, but I always feel it's more homely like in a nice comfortable train meself.'

Gregory grinned. 'No, we've got to be birdmen this trip and it's probable we shall be flying backwards and forwards across the Channel until we're sick of the sight of the damn thing.'

'Very good, Mr. Gregory, just as you say,' agreed Rudd philosophically. 'But I hopes we has long enough on the other side between trips to knock off a bottle or two of that vin rooge in one of them estaminaies.'

'Do you ever remember me going hungry or thirsty in all the years you've known me?'

'No sir, and pray God I never will. You've always been a rare one for your victuals; though a bit queer in your tastes, if I may say so.'

Gregory refilled his case with cigarettes then picked up his hat. 'I'm going to lunch now. Have everything packed by three o'clock and the car here ready to run us down to Heston.'

'Right you are sir, and if there's any time over I'll be rubbin' up me French.'

Rudd's French was mainly English, shouted very loudly and clearly with the addition of 'Kompronevous' at the end of every other sentence, so it was not greatly improved by the time Gregory returned and found him seated outside the grocer's in the car, with the bags strapped on behind.

The afternoon was the sort one always hopes for in early

August, but rarely gets; sunshine so brilliant that the passing people were walking perceptibly slower than usual; the women were in their lightest frocks and nearly all the men had abandoned their waistcoats. The ice-cream vendors, beside their tricycles, were doing a roaring business, and that lazy hush filled the air which made London seem temporarily a city of the tropics.

At Heston many people were taking advantage of the fine spell. Quite a crowd was gathered on the flying ground watching the planes come and go. Gregory presented his credentials at the office, while Rudd garaged the car, and a few moments later an official led them over to a hangar in which reposed a very up-to-date looking monoplane.

It was an enclosed two-seater Miles Hawk, cruising speed 180 m.p.h., but as it was fitted with a retractable undercarriage Gregory knew that would give it an extra 15, and by the use of the supercharger he could rev her up to a good bit over 200.

For twenty minutes he discussed its engine, speed, and capacity with one of the mechanics then he took it up for a trial flight. When he landed again Rudd knew from his expression that he was satisfied. Sir Pellinore had functioned with his usual reliability and provided a machine which met entirely with Gregory's requirements. At a quarter to five, with Rudd in the observer's seat, Gregory called 'contact' and took the air.

He headed straight for Calais, but did not descend at the landing ground; instead, he turned eastwards and followed the coastline as far as Dunkirk, carefully scrutinising the ground beneath him. There, he turned on his track and flew south-westward until he reached Cape Gris Nez, then he turned once more and finally came down at the Calais airport a little before seven o'clock.

Having parked the plane, and refuelled it to capacity, he left instructions that he might be returning in it to England that night. Then, in a taxi, he drove to the *Mairie* and inquired the whereabouts of the *Café de la Cloche*.

At first no one seemed to know it but, having penetrated at last to a musty little bureau, where an old woman sat writing a spidery hand in a well-thumbed ledger, he learned that the place was a poor sort of *estaminet* a kilometre outside the town on the road to Boulogne.

As they came out again from the *Mairie* in the evening sunlight he remarked to Rudd: 'Our birds won't operate until after dark in any case so there's no sense in making ourselves conspicuous. We'll go to the Hotel Terminus. So few people stop in Calais that I cannot think why it should be worth the proprietor's while, but it's a fact that it has a first-class cellar, and the fresh-caught local soles cooked a special way are a thing to dream over.'

'That's O.K. by me, sir,' agreed Rudd, 'although I'd rather have a good steak and chips. I never was one for these frenchified foods, in a manner of speaking.'

'You shall have a *Château Briand*, which is French for an outsize steak, to your own cheek, and a bottle of *vin rouge* to wash it down.'

The queerly assorted couple obtained an excellent meal, entirely satisfactory to both their divergent tastes and, by the time they had finished, darkness had fallen.

During dinner Gregory had been carefully considering the problem of how he could best install himself at the *Café de la Cloche* without arousing suspicion. To visit it was simple enough, but he might have to remain there for several hours, and from the description which the old woman at the *Mairie* had given him of the place, it hardly seemed one at which a well-dressed traveller would choose to linger. True, he had brought a disreputable looking old raincoat for just such a possibility—the pockets of which bulged with his gun, night glasses, and a big torch—but that hardly seemed enough.

The fact that Rudd was so obviously an Englishman, and could hardly speak a word of French was also certain to raise comment in such an out-of-the-way spot. He could leave Rudd outside, of course, but he preferred to have him with him so that he could send him off at once to shadow anybody whom he wished to have followed. Moreover, if this *estaminet* were the headquarters of a gang there was a possibility that one of the thugs who he had come up against in Trouville might be there and, if he were recognised, a rough house was certain to ensue. Gregory was perfectly capable of taking care of himself but all the same it would be a comfortable thought to know that Rudd was with him. From past experience he knew well that the excellent Mr. Rudd could prove a magnificent ally and an extremely ugly sort of customer in any fracas.

After dinner, by an offer of lavish payment, he managed to hire a car to drive himself from a garage. It was a Citroën and had seen better days but that suited his purpose admirably.

At ten o'clock they packed themselves into its worn seats and Gregory drove slowly out of the town; explaining to Rudd his plan of campaign as he did so.

'I want to snoop around at this place a bit,' he said, 'and unless I can get what I'm after I don't want to leave until they chuck us out. We're on a motoring holiday—you and I—and another bloke named Brown. We intended to move on to Boulogne tonight, but this wretched old bus let us down a few hundred yards from the *estaminet*. We've sent poor old Brown to footslog it back into Calais and come out with a mechanic to do the necessary repairs.

'In the meantime we've dined damn well, and that's the truth God knows, but we'll give them the impression we've dined a damn' sight better; not tight you know, but just about half a one over the odds, so what's more natural than we should knock off a few more drinks at this place while we're waiting for old Brown and the motor merchant.

'If he fails to turn up in an hour or so we may think it a bit strange, in fact even funny that the poor blighter's lost his way, but by that time we'll be fairly well ginned up and not caring two hoots in hell for anybody. We'll start talking of making a night of it as we refresh ourselves with further potions of the local poison. Round about midnight we'll agree that old Brown's lost himself and obviously returned to the hotel in Calais, where we spent last night. Then we'll say, for the benefit of anyone who's listening, that we'll do the same ourselves and foot it back when we feel like bed. It's not likely they'll turn us out as long as we look like buying another drink off them since there are none of these fool early closing laws in France. If they do, we'll know that there's something fishy going on, then we'll have to continue our watch outside. Get the idea?'

'Yes, sir. Sounds like a first-class pub crawl, without the crawl in it, ter me. I've often wished there weren't no early closing hours in England.'

While Gregory was speaking they had driven clear of the last houses of the town and were now out in the open country with the rolling downland all about them. A few minutes later a solitary building came into view at the roadside on the brow of a low hill.

'That'll be it, unless I'm much mistaken,' said Gregory, 'so I think it's about here we'll ditch the car.'

He slowed down and ran it off the road into a shallow gully, then climbed out, remarking: 'I don't want to leave her on the road in case some fool breaks his neck by crashing into her. We'll say we had to run into the bank to avoid a speed maniac and that the jolt snapped something. We don't know what as we're not mechanics, only holiday-makers who've bought a cheap car for our trip.'

Side by side they trudged up the slope to the solitary building. It proved to be no more than a couple of ancient flint-walled cottages knocked into one, but a creaking sign above the doorway established the fact that it was the *Café de la Cloche*. Before it, on the stony ground, stood a few rusty iron tables and battered chairs. The place was shuttered but lights came through the cracks of two windows and from beneath the heavy door. No other sign of life showed about the place and it was wrapped in a deep silence.

It was so old and tumbledown that Gregory allowed his vivid imagination to play upon it. He felt that it had probably already been an inn in Napoleon's day, frequented by gay

Hussars and Chasseurs of the Guard from that mighty 'Army of the Ocean' that the Emperor had assembled on the nearby downs for his projected invasion of England in 1802. It was just the sort of place too, where spies might have met by night in those far-off times, to exchange secret intelligence about activities in the Channel ports after having run the gauntlet of the British fleet in some lightless lugger, while ten years earlier, aristocrats escaping from the Red Terror might have made rendezvous there before their final dash into exile and safety.

Dismissing his romantic speculations, Gregory kicked open the door and walked in with Rudd behind him. Inside, the place was like a hundred small *estaminets* which they had visited behind the lines, years before in the Great War. A bar ran down one side of the room; behind it on the shelves was a meagre collection of bottles, mostly fruit syrups, many of which, from their tattered labels, looked as though they had stood there for generations. A dark, blowzy, sullen-eyed French girl sat behind the bar knitting. A handful of men occupied three out of the five cheap wooden tables covered with red-and-white checked clothes. One group was playing dominoes; the rest were talking in subdued voices. All of them had the appearance of French peasants or fishermen. The air was heavy with stale tobacco smoke, the fumes of cheap spirits, and the odour of unwashed humanity.

'*Monsieur?*' said the girl, standing up and abandoning her knitting.

Gregory asked for whisky, but she had none, so he changed his order to cognac and she poured two portions from an unlabelled bottle into thick glasses.

He had become suddenly garrulous and friendly. Leaning across the bar he told her about their 'accident', and laughed somewhat hilariously at the thought of poor old Brown now trudging back to Calais. Then he went on to speak of their holiday; purposely refraining from using his best French and helping out his apparently scanty knowledge of the language with frequent vivid gestures.

The girl proved a poor audience. She was a dull creature and her share in the conversation was limited to polite meaningless expressions and a series of nods.

When the topic of their holiday was exhausted Gregory asked permission to remove the bottle to a table in the far corner and, with Rudd, parked himself at it.

So far he had purposely refrained from even glancing at the other visitors; giving them ample time to accept this invasion of their haunt by strangers. They had settled down again now after having listened with one ear to the story he had told the girl behind the bar.

When he had seated himself in the corner with his back to the wall, so that he could survey the whole of the low raftered room, he scrutinised each figure in turn while keeping up a desultory conversation with Rudd. He carefully hid his satisfaction as he noticed that one of the three men who were talking at a table near the doorway was the dark, curly-haired young thug who had thrown a knife at him a few nights before in Trouville. Mr. Corot of the telegram, Gregory decided to assume for the moment.

Pulling his raincoat up round his ears, and his hat down over his eyes, he shifted his chair a little so that Rudd should come between him and the Frenchman in case the fellow happened to glance round. He had no desire at all to be recognised at the moment.

At a little before eleven the domino party broke up and the players left the *estaminet*. Only five others, including the curly-headed knife thrower, now remained, and they were all seated together. Gregory and Rudd were halfway through the litre bottle of brandy. It was cheap, fiery stuff, but both of them possessed heads like rocks and if they had ceased drinking Gregory knew they would soon be informed that they had outstayed their welcome.

They talked together in English but avoided all mention of the real reason for their presence at the *café* in case 'Corot' or one of his friends should understand the language.

It was a dreary business waiting there for they did not know quite what, but something to happen, and Gregory was thankful when, at about a quarter past eleven 'Corot' stood up, obviously summoned by a few musical notes upon a motor horn, twice repeated, from a spot not far distant on the road outside.

As he left the inn the notes on the motor horn were sounded again with evident impatience which gave Gregory the opportunity to say casually to the girl behind the bar, 'I wonder if that's our friend, poor old Brown, who's found our ditched car at last and is wondering what's happened to us. As he wouldn't know we're here I think we'd better go and see.'

He pulled out a note and paid the bill in a leisurely way, treating the girl to some cheerful half-tipsy badinage before he left, in order to avoid the appearance of deliberately following the other man.

It was Rudd who, fearing that they would miss the fellow in the darkness unless they left without further delay, muttered something about 'not keeping old Brown waiting any longer', and pulling Gregory by the arm led him outside.

'Good lad,' muttered Gregory directly they were clear of the *café*. 'We managed that exit splendidly. Now, where's our curly-haired assassin got to?'

They could not see the man but fifty yards down the road stood a car. Keeping in the shadows they made their way along the side of the *estaminet* and then by a wide detour through an adjoining field until they came opposite the place where it stood in the roadway.

Like the majority of French roads, there was no hedge separating it from the field, behind which they could shelter, but only a ditch, so they had to get down on their hands and knees and crawl the last twenty yards to avoid being seen against the skyline.

The car was a powerful limousine and 'Corot' was standing by its doorway on the side nearest the ditch. A faint light lit the interior of the car and Gregory smiled in the darkness as he recognised the small hunched figure on the back seat. Then he caught his breath for beyond Lord Gavin sat Sabine; looking even more beautiful than his memory of her. He grasped Rudd's arm and pressed it.

'Take a good look at the old boy,' he whispered. 'That's the fellow we're after; Lord Gavin Fortescue's his name. Looks like an archbishop, doesn't he, but he probably deserves to die kicking at the end of a rope more than any man in Europe. Think you'd know him again?'

'Sure thing, sir,' Rudd whispered back. 'Looks like a monkey on a stick ter me, but 'e's got a distinguished sort of dial I will say. And ain't his girl friend a bit of orlright.'

Lord Gavin was talking in a quick low voice to 'Corot'. The watchers could not catch his words but they saw him pass over a sheaf of papers.

The handsome knife thrower touched his checked cap; then closed the car door and it was driven away at a high speed towards Boulogne.

For a second Gregory considered attacking the thug for the purpose of seizing the papers he had just received from Lord Gavin, but the chances were that, if they set on him, his shouts would bring his four friends tumbling out of the *café* before they could master him and get away. In any case, Gregory decided, more valuable information would probably be obtained by remaining under cover for the time being and following the man to see where he went.

'Corot' only waited long enough for the dust, thrown up by the car, to disperse, then he returned to the *estaminet*; but only to poke his head inside the door.

A moment later, the four others joined him outside and, as the whole party set off together up the road, Gregory saw that all five of them were now carrying things that looked like fat cylinders or oil-drums, slung across their backs.

He gave them a few minutes' start; then followed. It was easy to keep the group in view as the road switched-backed towards the rising ground and on each low crest they stood out plainly silhouetted against the starlit sky. After a mile they left the main road and took a track leading in the direction of the coast. Along this Gregory and Rudd had more difficulty in keeping sight of them as it wound in and out among the dips and hillocks of the deserted downland.

No lights were to be seen in any direction and Gregory knew that they were now well inside that desolate wind-swept triangle, entirely lacking in roads and villages, which lies between the three points; Boulogne, Calais and Cape Gris Nez.

A good two miles were covered, then the Frenchmen turned in the direction of Boulogne again, leaving the track to trudge over the short coarse grass. There was little cover in this open country which made the shadowing of them more difficult. Gregory had to drop much further behind, allowing them time to mount each gentle slope and disappear into the next shallow valley before he and Rudd dared to move on again, in case one of them should turn suddenly and realise that they were being followed.

Twice Gregory lost his quarry for a moment but on each occasion he managed to pick them up again because, all unsuspicious, they were laughing and talking as they walked, and their voices carried clearly on the light airs of the still warm night.

They had long since left behind the last twinkling lights of Calais Town. It was over an hour since they had left the inn and in all that time they had not passed a single farmstead or seen a human being. As the slopes began to rise more steeply Gregory realised that they were moving towards the high ground which dominates that uninhabited area and is known as *Mont Couple*.

The group in front suddenly fell silent and must have turned off in a new direction for Gregory lost the shadowy blurr of their moving figures in the semi-darkness for the third time, and now, although he chanced discovery by trotting forward a hundred yards he failed to regain touch with them.

Cursing his ill luck he stumbled up a low mound and, pulling his night glasses from his raincoat pocket, began to scan the surrounding country. For ten minutes or more, with Rudd beside him, he swept the darkened downlands, first in one direction then in another, without success, until he suddenly caught sight of a faint glow which had just appeared a quarter of a mile away, throwing the line of the next ridge up into sharp relief.

For a moment he thought it might be caused by the lighthouse at Boulogne, but that had a sweeping beam, whereas this remained steady. With a word to Rudd he thrust his night glasses back in his pocket and they set off towards it.

As they advanced the silvery glow grew perceptibly brighter, throwing all the surrounding country into a heavier darkness. Halfway up the ridge Gregory suddenly slipped to his knees pulling Rudd down beside him. From that point they wriggled up the last hundred yards on their stomachs. At the crest Gregory caught Rudd's arm to stop him proceeding further and gave a low chuckle.

Below them stretched a broad shallow dip in the very centre of the high ground they had been traversing. The men they had followed had already set up two of their cylinders, from which there now hissed bright acetylene burners, and were busy with a third at the far end of the valley bottom. Soon they had completed their work and had all five flares going, spaced at irregular intervals, but marking out a fiery T at one end of a fine stretch of level grassy land hidden from any casual observer beyond its ring of encircling hills.

Suddenly Gregory pricked up his ears. He had caught the hum of an aeroplane. A moment later the noise ceased and a big bomber passed low overhead outlined in black silhouette against the starry sky then, sinking rapidly, came to land over the flares, taking its wind direction from their formation.

Its pilot taxied it towards the further slope and there the five men met it; but Gregory's attention was taken from it momentarily by the sound of another plane coming up from a different quarter which circled slowly overhead, came down into the wind, and taxied up alongside the first arrival.

For the next quarter of an hour plane after plane arrived at little more than minute intervals; but Gregory's eyes were now riveted upon the activities of the men on the ground. Their number had increased to half a hundred and these had not landed from any of the planes. They were emerging from a shadowy patch at the far side of the valley and all carried cases or bales upon their shoulders which they were busily loading into the first few aeroplanes to arrive at this secret depot.

At first Gregory was puzzled as to where the men with supplies were coming from. There were no roads or tracks within a couple of miles of this lonely spot so they could not have been brought by motor or lorry and no dumps were to be seen; although the men kept disappearing into the shadows in an irregular chain to return each time carrying a fresh load of cargo for the waiting fleet.

Touching Rudd on the arm he began to crawl stealthily along the crest of the ridge, keeping just within the belt of shadow, until he could get a better view of the place from which this chain of supplies continued to make its mysterious appearance.

After covering two hundred yards he was able to view the proceedings from a fresh angle and noticed what looked like a black slit in the seaward slope of the natural basin below them. It must be, he guessed, the entrance to an underground passage leading down through the old chalk caves to one of the little fishing villages, Sandgatt or Wissant, on the coast a mile or so away.

Rudd had been drilled to silence in the old days when, as Gregory's batman, they had gone out together time and again into 'no-man's-land' on the western front; but now he could restrain his curiosity no longer.

'What's the game, sir?' he asked in a hoarse whisper.

'Smugglers, my boy,' said Gregory grimly. 'For the last two years this outfit has been costing Britain half a million pounds a month in revenue but there's more to it than that. These birds are out to wreck the old firm of J. Bull, Home, Dominions and Colonial unless we can stop 'em. D'you feel like running a marathon?'

'Orders is orders and got to be obeyed,' said Mr. Rudd

'Come on then.' Gregory drew back into the deeper shadows and stood up. 'We're going to run now—run as we've never run in our lives. We've got to be in the air again before Gavin Fortescue's fleet starts on its way to England.'

7

In the Silent Hours

Ordinarily Gregory was a lazy devil, in fact he prided himself upon being a master of the gentle art of idling gracefully. He never ran when he could walk, stood when he could lean, leaned when he could sit, or sat when he could more comfortably lie down. He loathed every form of exercise and had been regarded as a crank at his public school because of his open hatred of all ball games. He would, perhaps, have proved highly unpopular on that account if nature had not endowed him with other assets; a lean sinewy body, which made him a dangerous opponent in a scrap, and a bitter caustic wit to which the games enthusiasts found it difficult to reply. Moreover, he was quixotically generous and the ringleader in any devilry which could alleviate the monotony of the dull scholastic round. In consequence, he had been forgiven his idiosyncrasy and let off the penalties which would have been meted out during their first terms to most youngsters who had such heretical tendencies and, later, he established a definite reputation as a 'bad man' which earned him much admiration among the younger boys.

Perhaps it was the very fact that he had made it a life rule never to exert himself unnecessarily which accounted for his continued fitness. It so often happens that footballers and rowing blues run to seed and put on fat when they are compelled to abandon their regular hours of sport through the ties of business or professional life, whereas Gregory, never having put himself to any strain, had retained his supple figure and his wind unimpaired.

He could not, of course, compete with a trained athlete but he had a wonderful reserve of strength and when he felt it necessary to use it he could put up a far better performance than the average man of his age.

As soon as they were clear of the slope he broke into a long loping trot which Rudd, who was half a head shorter, but of far more muscular build, found it difficult to keep up with.

The going for the first mile over the coarse grass was tiring and tricky, as they felt it too risky to show a light, but when they reached the track Gregory produced his big army torch and lit the way as they ran on side by side.

Luck was with them when, panting and breathless, they reached the road, for they had hardly gone two hundred yards along it in the direction of Calais when a lorry loaded with fresh vegetables came rattling up behind them. Gregory hailed the driver in French and offered fifty francs for a lift into the town. The man blessed his luck and, gasping from their exertions, they scrambled on to the back of the vehicle.

'So it's smugglers we're after,' said Rudd when he had regained his wind. 'I thought smugglers was a back number since we beat old Boney at Waterloo.'

'Not a bit of it,' Gregory assured him. 'Free trade put them practically out of business for several generations but since protection came in with the National Government the whole racket has started up again. You see, there's a packet of money to be made now for anyone who can get silks and cameras and a score of other things into England duty free; and for the last year or two smuggling has assumed enormous proportions. The big concerns won't handle the stuff, but any amount of contraband is jobbed off cheap through some organisation in the East End to scores of little shops all over the country, which enables them to undercut the big corporations. That's why Sir Pellinore's people are getting so het up. Their turnover's been going down thousands a week in the last eighteen months and this new smuggling racket is the reason. But there's a more sinister side to it than that. I've been put on to try and run this dangerous organisation to earth; so that we can hand particulars over to the authorities and have it mopped up.'

'Seems like you've succeeded pretty quick, sir.'

'Good Lord no! What we've seen tonight is only one thread in the tangled skein. These people must be operating on a huge scale. They've probably got half a dozen bases on this side, because if they sent every cargo from that dip in the downs the French police would get wind of it before long. We've got to find out where they land their stuff in England and how they distribute it afterwards too.'

'Seems a chancy game ter me, anyhow, with all the planes there are flying about these days. Some bloke might fly over casual like any old night 'nd spot those flares.'

Gregory shook his head. 'Didn't you notice the flares were placed irregularly—so that the valley would not have the appearance of a proper landing ground from the air? Besides, Gavin Fortescue is as wily as the traditional serpent: we've got to give him that. If anybody visited that base in the day time there wouldn't be a thing to show what's going on, not even a cart-track, because the goods are all consigned to one of the little fishing villages on the coast and brought up underground through the caves.'

'Maybe, Mr. Gregory sir, but what abart all them planes? They've got ter have 'angars, ain't they? Though I didn't see none.'

'Of course you didn't—because the planes are not kept there. Each one is probably registered as a privately owned machine and housed separately somewhere between here and Paris. Then, when these night birds get their orders, they go up, only land here long enough to take on their cargo and are away again over the sea. I doubt if the whole operation takes more than half an hour so, if they don't use any one base too frequently, the chances are all against their being rumbled in an almost uninhabited stretch of country like this.'

'Half an hour, eh! Blimey, we'll have to make it snappy then if we're to be in the air before they hops it.'

'Ever known me run without reason?' Gregory replied tersely. As he spoke the lorry was rumbling into the outskirts of Calais. Leaving Rudd, he crawled forward and spoke to the driver, asking him to take them direct to the airport for an extra ten francs.

The man complied and five minutes after their arrival they were in their plane, Gregory having already thrust a note into the oily palm of the mechanic and asked him to telephone the garage with particulars of the spot where they had abandoned the hired car. Next moment they were in the air.

Gregory did not make straight for the secret base on the downs behind Cape Gris Nez. The place was so near by the measure of air travel that he would have been compelled to fly low over it and, perhaps, give away to the smugglers the fact that they were being watched. Instead, he spiralled round and round to gain altitude then, when he had reached three thousand feet, turned the plane's nose towards the west.

It was the dark period, between moons, and he guessed that the smugglers had purposely chosen this, and the succeeding dates mentioned in the telegram, to run through their cargoes; but there was little cloud, and many stars lit the August night. By their faint glow it was quite possible to make out the coastline and his position was easily ascertainable from the harbour lights of Calais and Boulogne.

As they passed over *Mont Couple* he felt a stab of disappointment. The flares in the hidden valley were no longer burning so he assumed that the secret fleet had already sailed but he turned his plane seaward in the hope that he might yet pick them up.

They had been cruising for about five minutes and were well out over the water when Rudd tapped him on the shoulder and jerked a grimy thumb towards their tail.

Gregory looked back towards the coast and saw what it was

that had caught Rudd's attention. Dead in their rear certain stars in a long oval patch of sky seemed to be blacked out for a moment and then show up again. It was the smuggler fleet behind them and Gregory cursed himself as a fool for not having realised that the flares were only necessary to guide the planes in to their unofficial landing ground. Directly all the machines had arrived the flares would be put out in order further to shorten the time in which discovery of the secret base was possible by a casual plane passing over.

He began to climb again. His intention being both to gain further altitude and, by the resulting loss of speed, allow the smuggler feet to pass under him. Ten minutes later he was up at five thousand feet and dimly silhouetted below him against the sea stretched the long line of heavy bombers; but now they were climbing too and he judged that they meant to pass over the English coast at as great an altitude as possible, in order to escape drawing attention to themselves by the roar of their engines.

He climbed still higher as they passed beneath him, and altered his course a little when he noted that the fleet was now veering to the north.

Soon he picked up the lights of the English coast lying thousands of feet below to his left and, having acquainted himself with the varying flashes of the Kent lighthouses that morning for just this purpose he was able to check his course as almost dead northward, with Dover and the South Foreland light on his beam.

The smuggler fleet was a good way ahead, below him now and still climbing, but he hoped that if he could maintain his present distance they would lead him in to their English landing ground without suspecting that they were being followed. Unfortunately, visibility ahead was by no means so good as it had been over the French coast, and a moment later they passed through a cold wisp of cloud.

Gregory grabbed the throttle lever in his left hand and pushed it through the gate of the quadrant, bringing his supercharger into play and decreasing his distance a little, as he feared to lose the squadron; but they flew on, still gaining height, and apparently taking advantage of the cloud patches rather than avoiding them. A few moments more and he could see only two machines on the extreme right wing of the flight.

Cursing the clouds, he mounted again, hoping to get above them but the upper layers proved thicker than any he had yet encountered and now the smugglers had disappeared. The sound of their engines was of no assistance since the roar of his own blacked out any other vibration; and as they were flying without lights he could only hope to spot them again in a clear patch then they momentarily obscured a star here and there.

For another ten minutes he flew on; still towards the north. He could no longer see the coastline below him but judged that they must have left Deal behind on their left and were coming up to Ramsgate. In the dense cloudy masses through which they were now flying it seemed that all hope of sighting his quarry had vanished, so he decided that his best course was to get down below the cloud banks, pick up the coast, and cruise along it on the off chance that he might spot the smugglers when they came down towards their secret landing place. He had little hope that luck would favour him as it was probable that each machine would make for a separate destination, perhaps far inland, but it was worth trying.

Five minutes later he was free of the clouds and picked up Ramsgate with the North Foreland light beyond it. Then he suddenly banked steeply to the left for he had just spotted a single plane tearing through the night sky over Thanet.

It might only be some amateur pilot practising night flying but, on the other hand, it just might be a single unit now detached from the smuggler squadron. Setting the controls, he pulled out his night glasses and focused them upon the solitary night flyer, then grunted with disappointment. It was not a big plane such as he had hoped to see, but a passenger machine, probably a four-seater.

They were well inland now and heading west-north-westward. The solitary plane was a thousand feet below them and, as Gregory came down, he picked up a long irregular broken chain of lights upon his right which, although the town was dark and the holiday-makers long since sleeping, indicated the deserted front at Margate.

A few moments more and he could see the sea again; the north Kentish coast where it runs towards the Thames estuary. Westgate, Birchington and Herne Bay lay somewhere ahead of him.

The other plane was dropping now towards a great belt of trees a little inland from Birchington. Their massed foliage stood out darkly in the faint starlight against the flat arable land which surrounded them on every side. The ring of trees was at least two miles in circumference and several broad open spaces in its centre suggested that the place was a private park.

From his greater altitude Gregory watched the solitary plane through his night glasses as it descended. Another moment and, circling into the wind, it floated down towards one of the bare patches in the very heart of the great belt of trees.

Instantly Gregory swung away to the south again; knowing that immediately the other plane landed its engine would be switched off and the roar of his own machine would attract attention.

Diving now to gain speed he headed away from the big tree-girt enclosure, then flattened out and returned ten minutes later at a height sufficient only to ensure escaping that aerial death trap, the grid system, with its thousands of pylons now forming a network over England.

As he sighted the tall tree-tops again, standing out stark and black against the naked Thanet landscape, he decided to chance any pylons and risk a landing. A broad field lay below him. He could not guess if it was corn already harvested or stubble, but switching on his landing light he turned his plane towards the prevailing wind, and came down gently.

His luck was in. The plane bounded lightly for fifty yards and he was able to bring it to a standstill without turning over.

'Stay here,' he shot at Rudd. 'If the village constable happens to be on the prowl after poachers say we had to make a forced landing—and that I've gone for petrol. Better get out the corkscrews and picket the plane in case the wind gets up. The machine we followed may have nothing to do with the outfit I'm after, but anyhow I'm going into this place to find out a bit more about it. I may be away some time.'

'I get you, sir,' Rudd muttered, and Gregory tumbled out on to the ground.

The field was ridged with coarse stubble; but he was soon out of it and across the low ditch into a winding lane which followed the curve of a thick, six-foot hedge, overhung by the leafy branches of massed trees on its far side.

The place *was* evidently a private park and a splendid site for secret landings, Gregory thought, remembering the several fine open meadows, separated by patches of woodland, but all enclosed within this outer belt of trees which surrounded it entirely.

He ran lightly along the lane, hoping to find a break in the hedge or a place where he could scramble over easily, but it was in good repair and he covered two hundred yards before he found a suitable spot.

A grassy bank below the hedge sloped up a little for a foot or more and from it protruded the stump of an old tree. By mounting on the stump he was able to fling himself bodily on the top of the hedge and slip down on the far side.

It was pitch dark there and he did not dare to use his torch; not knowing how deep the ring of trees might prove at this point and fearing that a light might be spotted by the people who had landed in the plane.

He ran into a tree trunk, barked his knee, and swore angrily then, more cautiously, with hands extended in the darkness, he crept forward. The eerie silence of the night-shrouded glade was broken only by the snapping of twigs beneath his feet.

As his eyes became accustomed to the gloom he could just make out the boles of the big trees in time to avoid them, but the belt was much deeper than he had supposed, almost a strip of woodland, and he had to tiptoe a hundred yards before he emerged into the open.

He found himself then in a meadow, but there was no house or out-building in sight, such as he had expected. Turning right he warily continued his advance, sticking closely to the line of trees in order to be able to take cover behind them, if necessary, at a moment's notice, until he came up against an iron fence which bordered a gravel drive.

Remaining in the field he broke cover and proceeded, parallel with the drive, towards the centre of the park. After what seemed an interminable time the big field ended and he came to another wood. Clearing the fence he plunged again into heavy darkness down the driveway between the overhanging trees.

A moment later he caught a glimmer of light through the tree trunks and tiptoed forward until he reached the edge of the wood. Upon his left there was another great open space, a lawn with meadows beyond, perhaps, and on his right the drive broadened into a wide sweep before a long three-storied house, up to which trees and bushes grew at both its wings.

The light came from an uncurtained downstairs window, and by it Gregory could see clearly now a big closed car drawn up in front of the porch. As he watched, the light in the window was switched off, then four people came out of the darkened doorway and got into the car.

The engine of the motor purred. Next moment the beam of powerful headlights threw a golden glow on the gravel drive. Quick as a cat Gregory leapt back into the shadows and crouched there, dazzled for the moment by the blinding glare, and almost certain that his presence must have been discovered; but the car turned on the sweep and roared away in the opposite direction from which he had come, down the west drive which led to the Birchington Gate of the park and the road to London.

His glimpse of the car's occupants was brief but the man at the wheel and another seated beside him, like chauffeur and footman, had been wearing leather jackets so Gregory guessed them to be the pilots of the plane, while Lord Gavin Fortescue was hunched in the back seat and, next to him, wrapped in heavy furs above which her delicate profile rose as beautiful as a cameo, Sabine had been sitting.

Gregory released his breath with a little sigh of satisfaction at the success of his hunch to follow the solitary plane. It had led him to Lord Gavin's headquarters in England, which was, perhaps, more valuable even than finding one of the places where the contraband was landed.

As soon as the car had disappeared he stepped out from the trees and examined the front of the house. It was now in total darkness and the whole place seemed to be unoccupied. He scanned the lawns before it for the plane, but that was nowhere to be seen, so he assumed it had been run into a hangar, and tiptoed towards the far end of the house to see if he could find any building in which it might be garaged.

Passing through the shrubberies there he came upon some greenhouses and then two high windowless buildings which he thought might have been built for squash or as covered tennis courts.

He beat a gentle tattoo with his finger-tips upon the locked door of one of these while he considered the situation. He felt that his luck was very definitely in tonight and that the house might hold all sorts of interesting secrets. This was far too good an opportunity to try and unearth some of them for him to even think of rejoining Rudd and flying back to London yet awhile. The problem was how to force an entry into the house?

Behind the big brick buildings he could just make out, in the faint starlight, a row of outhouses, stables and garages. Proceeding between them with a cautious, almost cat-like step, he passed a fifteen-foot brick wall with espaliered fruit trees on it; the eastern extremity of a fine walled garden. Turning right, he found himself at the back of the house itself. This too was wrapped in heavy silence and no light came from any of the windows.

Tiptoeing forward across the gravel, so that it barely crunched under his feet, his shoulders hunched, his eyes alert, like some prowling cat, he stalked along the rear side of the house, examining each window with the aid of his torch, which he now no longer feared to show as the place seemed to be quite deserted.

At last he found a spot suitable for his purpose; a small uncurtained window through which he could see a sink. The place appeared to be a scullery and a corner of the window frame was broken. Getting his fingers into the aperture he wrenched with all his might. There was a sharp crack of splintering wood as the catch was torn from its socket and one half of the window swung out towards him. Reaching inside he undid the bolt which held the other half and drew the casement wide open.

Gripping the sill with both hands, he put his head inside, and was just about to lever himself up when he caught the sound of a stealthy footfall on the gravel close behind him.

8

A Night of Surprises

Gregory jerked his head out of the window and spun round to confront a tall man who had just emerged from the shadows of the shrubbery half a dozen yards away.

The man was alone and did not appear to be armed. A caretaker or keeper perhaps, thought Gregory. He swung his torch meditatively in his right hand. It was long and thicker than a policeman's baton. The big automatic was in his pocket but he had no intention of using it in England, or anywhere else for that matter, unless he found himself trapped and his life in actual danger.

'Come here,' said the man, 'and no monkey tricks or you'll regret it.'

Gregory came three slow steps forward. He meant to hit the man, and hit him very hard indeed, so that there should be no necessity to hit him a second time. The side of the neck was the place; just in line with the jaw bone. A good crack there, over the jugular vein, with the torch would out the fellow before he had time to shout for help and bring any friends he might have about the place on to the scene of action.

Gregory's empty left fist lifted in a feint, but dropped again almost as quickly, when the man took a swift step backwards and snapped: 'Stop that. I've got a gun here.'

It was only then Gregory realised a thing that he had failed to notice before owing to the difficult light. The man's right hand was thrust into his jacket pocket, which bulged ominously.

For a moment Gregory hesitated; wondering whether to risk an attack. To have to surrender tamely to one of Lord Gavin's men would not only be infuriating but definitely dangerous. He would probably be thrown into some cellar and guarded closely until Lord Gavin visited the place again and, knowing how utterly unscrupulous the crooked financier was, he did not fancy that prospect at all. He knew that if Lord Gavin made up his mind that he had been spying upon his secret operations he was capable of having him murdered. The interests he had to conceal were so vital and far-reaching that he certainly would not hesitate at taking human life in order to protect them.

On the other hand, this tall fellow who had caught him just as he was about to break into the house seemed a cool customer; not at all the sort to be trifled with. Here, in the silent depths of this great park, a mile or more from the main road or any other habitation no one would hear the shot if the fellow used his gun; and it was highly probable that Lord Gavin had given instructions that if a spy were found about the place this fellow was to take no chances, but shoot rather than risk an unauthorised visitor getting away with any information he might have secured.

Discretion seemed the better part of valour. Gregory had just made up his mind to accept the situation, in the hope that an opportunity would occur for him to turn the tables later, when he caught the sound of gravel crunching underfoot again.

The other man heard it too and half-turned his head. Next second a voice yelled: 'Jump, sir!' and a dark figure leapt from the shrubbery on to the man's back.

As Gregory sprang sideways, to avoid the bullet if the man's gun went off, the other two crashed to the ground together.

They rolled over once, then Gregory stepped in, bringing his heavy leather-covered torch down with a dull thud upon his late captor's head. The man went limp and Rudd, wriggling free of him, staggered to his feet.

'Gawd! You bashed him proper an' no mistake. Ain't killed him 'ave you?'

'I don't think so,' Gregory muttered. 'I was careful to avoid his temple and caught him on the top of the skull. Show a light, will you. The bulb in my torch has bust.'

Rudd pulled a torch from his pocket and shone it on the prostrate man's face. He was a nice-looking, freckle-faced, sandy-haired fellow of about thirty, with a trim little upturned moustache, and not the type at all that Gregory would have expected to find among Lord Gavin's gunmen.

'He's all right,' said Gregory, after rolling back one of the man's eyelids. 'He'll be coming round in a few minutes I don't doubt, so we'd better truss him up. How did you happen to come on to the scene so opportunely?'

'Well, it was this way sir. You'd 'ardly 'opped it into the lane before another plane comes sailing down and makes a landing in the next field to ours. Hello! I ses to myself, what's all this abart? So I goes over to investigate. I was just in time to see this bloke here beating it across the field at the double towards the park so I follows cautious like. When I reach the lane he was shining a torch about, looking for footmarks in the long grass I reckon, where you had trampled it down as you went along. He comes to a tree stump and hikes himself over the hedge into the park, so naturally I gives him a minute and then 'ops over too. I lorst him for a bit among the trees—dark as 'ell it was, and I barked me knuckles on one of the tree trunks something cruel—but I picked up our Albert again as he was crossing a field be'ind 'ere, and tagged him round the 'ouse. Then when I crep up close enough I found 'e'd got the goods on you—in a manner of speaking.'

'Darned lucky for me you did,' said Gregory. 'It was a good thing his gun didn't go off though when you jumped him.'

'That were the only thing I was scared of, but I 'ad to take a chance, and I know you're pretty nippy on your tootsies.'

'He probably had the safety catch still down, but in any case with your weight on his neck the bullet would have gone into the gravel.' As Gregory spoke he was lashing the man's feet securely together with the belt of his raincoat. Their prisoner was now groaning a little and breathing stertorously.

Rudd pulled off his belt for Gregory to tie the man's hands and then shone his torch again. As the light streamed on to the limp unconscious head Gregory suddenly let out a sharp low whistle.

'Hang on a minute! I thought I'd seen this chap's face somewhere before when we looked at him just now, and by jove I have, although it was only for a minute.'

'Is he one of the bunch you made hay of a few days ago in Trouville, sir?'

'No,' sighed Gregory. 'I wish to God he were. This is the young policeman whom I rescued.'

'Blimey! Here's a fine how-de-do. We've been and coshed a copper.'

'Never mind. As it's the chap I helped out before perhaps he won't run us in this time. Undo his feet again and I'll try and bring him round.'

They were both kneeling beside the policeman's body when a door creaked in their rear and a light suddenly illuminated the bushes. They swung round to see a woman silhouetted against a brightly lit doorway a few yards from the scullery window. She was a broad-bosomed middle-aged female. Her tousled grey hair, thick dressing-gown, and bare feet thrust into old slippers, showed that she had been roused from her bed by the recent scuffle. In her hand she held a large Mark V service revolver. She held it very steadily and it was pointing at them.

'Stand up you two,' she said, 'and put your hands above your heads. Then you'd better tell me what you're up to.'

Taken completely off their guard, the two men obeyed.

'What's your friend doing on the ground?' asked the woman sharply.

'He's met with a slight accident.' Gregory's voice was low and amiable as he strolled casually towards her.

'Keep your distance,' barked the woman. 'I've got a revolver here and I 'ave orders to use it.'

Gregory halted a few paces from her. He possessed more courage than most men but one thing that really scared him was to see firearms in the hands of a woman. They were so much more likely to go off unexpectedly.

'All right,' he said soothingly. 'I'm not a burglar and I wouldn't dream of harming you. As a matter of fact the chap on the path there happens to be a friend of mine and a police officer.'

The woman's face showed a stony disbelief at this surprising statement.

'Is he?' she said sarcastically, 'then he'll be pleased to see his friends from the station at Birchington as soon as I've had a chance to get on the telephone to them.'

As she spoke she stepped out of the doorway and sideways along the wall of the house keeping it at her back and the three men covered by her revolver. 'Pick him up both of you,' she said, 'and carry him inside. Then I can get a better look at you. Come on, be quick now. I don't want to catch my death of cold standing about in this heavy dew all night.'

Rudd took the policeman's shoulders and Gregory his feet. Then, followed by the woman, who never lowered her weapon for a single instant, they carried him into the house.

'Straight down the passage,' she ordered and then, addressing Gregory who brought up the rear: 'If you try and trick me I'll put a bullet in your back. Straight on now and the third door on your right.'

'Thank you, mother,' said Gregory amiably, 'but I'd rather have a nice cup of warm tea in my tummy. When you're tired of holding that thing I'll hold it for you and you shall make me one.'

They proceeded along a stone-flagged passage, evidently the servants' quarters, but when Rudd thrust his way backwards through the third door on the right Gregory saw that it was a heavy baize-covered affair which led to the main part of the house. For a moment they were in semi-darkness and he contemplated dropping the policeman's feet to swing round and tackle the woman, but she closed up on him as he passed through the swing door and, jamming the muzzle of her pistol firmly in the small of his back, switched on the lights.

He saw that they were in the main hallway of the house; a fine apartment from which a broad staircase led to the floors above. There was a long settee in one corner and, on a small table some way from it, stood a telephone.

'Put him on the couch,' said the woman, making straight for the instrument.

They dumped the policeman; who was now groaning loudly and showing signs of coming round. Then Gregory held out a quick restraining hand to the woman.

'Please, one moment,' he begged. 'The police won't thank you for lugging them out at this hour in the morning to arrest one of their own people Hang on until this chap comes round. I swear to you on my honour that he *is* a policeman. He'll be able to tell you so himself in a minute.'

The woman had her hand on the receiver; but she did not lift it.

'What was he doing unconscious behind the house then?'

'He was unconscious because I knocked him out. Mistook him for somebody else in the darkness.'

'And who may you be, I'd like to know.'

'A friend of Lord Gavin Fortescue's.' Gregory lied unblushingly. 'Honestly, Lord Gavin will be furious if you bring the local police into this. The chap we knocked out is from Scotland Yard and that's quite a different matter, but the last thing which Lord Gavin would want is to have a lot of flat-footed country constables mixed up in his affairs.'

The policeman's eyes flickered open and Rudd pulled him up into a sitting position on the settee. He groaned again and for a moment put his head between his hands; then he lifted it painfully and stared about him.

'Better now?' asked Gregory. 'I'm terribly sorry I knocked you out. I was under the impression that you were someone else, but you remember me, don't you? We met a few nights ago at Trouville.'

'Yes—yes, of course. I remember now: you got me out of a nasty mess didn't you? I didn't know it was you either when I caught you trying to break into this place—but I'm afraid I'll have to ask you for an explanation.'

'Plenty of time for that,' said Gregory easily. 'I think we're working on the same thing; but from different angles. We've landed ourselves in a new mess since you passed out though. This lady here with the heavy armaments, I don't yet know her name . . . '

'Mrs. Bird,' the woman supplied non-committally.

'Well, Mrs. Bird seems to think that all three of us are up to no good here and she's just about to phone for the local coppers. I think it would be a good thing for all of us if you can persuade her not to.'

The policeman stood up a little groggily. 'Mrs. Bird,' he said, 'my name's Inspector Wells, and I'm down here on special work for Scotland Yard. Here is my card of authority. Just look it over will you, and you'll see that it's all in order. Then I think you can leave this business safely in my hands.' As he spoke he extended the card he had taken from his pocket-book.

'Stay where you are. Don't you dare come a step nearer,'

rapped out Mrs. Bird. 'What's the good of showing me that thing. Specially printed for the purpose, I haven't a doubt. Some people sneer at reading detective fiction but I don't. It gives respectable folk a lot of tips about your sort of gentry.'

Gregory grinned. 'One up to you Mrs. Bird. I'll bet you're thinking of that Raffles story, where he came in and got Bunny out of a tight corner by turning up dressed as a policeman and arresting him in the South African millionaire's house.'

A gleam of appreciation showed for a moment in Mrs. Bird's sharp eyes. 'That's it,' she said. 'Good stories those. We don't get many like them now; more's the pity.'

'If you'll excuse me madam you're making a serious mistake.' Inspector Wells drew himself up. 'If you like to phone the local police you are, of course, quite within your rights to do so; but it's going to cause a lot of unnecessary inconvenience to everyone concerned.' The Inspector was thinking at the moment what a fool he would look among his colleagues if the woman did hand him over to the local police as one of a gang of housebreakers.

She shook her head stubbornly. 'I may be right and I may be wrong, but what were you doing in our grounds I'd like to know? As for inconveniencing the local police what do we pay rates for. You stay where you are young man and don't you move a muscle while I telephone.'

A stair creaked above them and they all glanced up. Unheard by any of them a young girl had appeared on the landing and was now descending the broad straight stairway. She was barefooted and clad only in her nightdress. Two long plaits of golden hair coiled about her head made a halo gleaming in the light. Her blue eyes were wide open and staring. Instantly they all realised that she was walking in her sleep.

9

The Real Menace to Britain

'Don't wake her!' whispered Mrs. Bird. 'Not a sound please—or the poor lamb may get the shock of her life.'

In two silent strides Gregory was beside the older woman. His left hand closed over her right and in a single sharp twist he forced the revolver from between her fingers.

It had happened before any of them had had time to even think and a cynical little smile twitched the corners of his lips as he whispered: 'Now, *I'll* hold the gun, Mrs. Bird, while you make me that nice cup of tea.'

If looks could have killed Gregory would have fallen dead upon the spot. Mrs. Bird's homely, but normally pleasant, features became, for a second, distorted into a mask of almost comical indignation and dismay but she brushed past him without a word and hurried on tiptoe to the foot of the wide staircase.

The girl was now halfway down the flight. She was quite young, eighteen or nineteen perhaps, slim as a boy, with only faintly rounded breasts and hips. The lines of her beautifully moulded figure showed clearly through the thin flowered chiffon nightdress. Her face was small and delicately chiselled; her creamy cheeks were slightly flushed in sleep. Above her short straight nose and white forehead the great oriel of plaited hair formed a shimmering golden crown. There was something ethereal and fairy-like about her as she moved slowly down towards them which made it seem hardly possible that she was warm flesh and blood. The young Inspector's mouth hung a little open as he gazed up at her, completely fascinated; he thought that in all his days he had never seen anything quite so lovely, either human or in a work of art.

Mrs. Bird mounted a few stairs and took the girl very gently by the arm. With hardly a pause she turned in her tracks and began to walk up the stairs again; led now by the elder woman.

'Wells,' said Gregory in a sharp whisper.

'Eh?' The Inspector started as though he had been woken from a trance.

'Go up with them. There may be another telephone upstairs.'

Wells nodded and with one hand on the banister rail began to tiptoe upstairs after the two women.

As the little procession disappeared from sight Gregory let out a sharp sigh of relief, released the catch of Mrs. Bird's revolver, broke it open, and emptied out the bullets.

'Weren't she a pretty kid?' murmured Rudd. 'Almost like a fairy orf a Christmas tree; only wanted a wand and a couple of wings.'

Gregory shrugged. 'Pretty enough, but quite brainless I should think. Anyhow, it was a bit of luck for us that she turned up when she did or we would have had to waste more time arguing with the old woman.'

When Mrs. Bird and the Inspector came down the stairs again Gregory asked her sharply:

'What's the name of this place?'

'Quex Park, Birchington.'

'Good, now before we go on any further I want you to satisfy yourself that our friend here really is a police inspector. The quickest way is for you to get on the telephone to Scotland Yard. You can describe him to them then and they'll soon tell you if he's one of their people, or not. D'you agree?'

'That sounds sense,' she said, a little subdued, now that she no longer had the whip hand over them.

Wells gave her the number, but Gregory insisted upon turning it up in the London Directory, so that she could have no grounds to think that they were trying to trick her; then he made her put through the call herself.

The result proving satisfactory her attitude changed at once from acute suspicion to apologetic interest.

'Not another word, please,' Gregory protested. 'You were

perfectly right to hold us up and you did it darned well into the bargain but now, joking apart, would it be troubling you too much if we asked you to make us a cup of tea? We've been up all night and I'm sure the others could do with one too.'

'Certainly, sir, of course I will. Maybe you could do with a bite to eat as well. What about some nice scrambled eggs for an early breakfast?'

'That'd be splendid and really kind of you. Rudd, you go along with Mrs. Bird and give her a hand. I want a word with the Inspector.'

'Certainly, sir,' said Rudd cheerily. 'I'm a dab at scrambling eggs I am, as you know well enough from past experience.'

Mrs. Bird bridled. 'You'll do no cooking in my kitchen young man, but you can help with the plates and things.'

As they left the hall Gregory moved over to Wells, who had sat down on the settee again.

'Now let's try and get things straightened out a bit,' he said. 'I'm awfully sorry about having banged you over the head but it would never have happened if it hadn't been for the stupidity of your own people in refusing to allow us to work together.'

'Don't worry about the knock you gave me.' Well's freckled face lit up with a boyish grin. 'You were at the Yard this morning, weren't you? I was talking to the Superintendent about your visit only a few minutes after you'd gone. Of course the position is a bit unusual and it's against our principles to work in with civilians. That's why the Super had to turn down your offer. But it's quite clear now it would be wiser for us to come to some working arrangement.'

'I'm glad you feel that way. You know most of my end of the story; what about yours?'

'I know what you told them at the Yard this morning and that you're acting on behalf of Sir Pellinore Gwaine-Cust but you didn't give away what you're investigating for him.'

'Need we fence? I'm trying to get to the bottom of the international smuggling racket. It's costing some of his companies a packet owing to unfair competition by the ring who're dealing in illicit goods upon which no duty has been paid.'

'Right. Well, I'm after the same thing. In the ordinary way the prevention of smuggling doesn't come under the police. It's the business of the Customs and Excise people to check up on suspected goods which have already been imported and the Inspector of Water Guard deals with prevention along the coasts. We're only called in to make arrests, and so on, but the loss in revenue during the last year has mounted to such a fantastic figure that it's got to be stopped. The Yard were asked to undertake a special inquiry and they've given me a chance at it as my first independent investigation. It looks to me like a biggish job too.'

'A biggish job!' Gregory echoed, a satirical edge to his tone. 'I'll say it is. The biggest that any policeman's been called on to handle in the whale of a while. I'm not being rude. I mean that. If you handle this thing right you'll be made for life, but, if you don't, it'll break you and lots of other people who're higher up the ladder than you are, as well. But go on. I must know all you've done to date if I'm to give you any help.'

Wells did not like Gregory's faintly contemptuous manner but he was shrewd enough to recognise that he was in contact with a far more dynamic personality than his own, and somehow, he could not help feeling attracted to Sir Pellinore's rakish-looking representative. His professional admiration had been aroused too, by the swift efficient way in which Gregory had relieved Mrs. Bird of her revolver instantly the opportunity occurred, so he went on quietly:

'I was put on to this special work about six weeks ago and, so far, I've spent most of my time trying to get a lead from the British end of it; working back from the retailers, who are cutting the prices of their goods, to the wholesaler and so, eventually, to the actual importers of contraband. It's been an uphill job, because silk stockings and things like that are such universal commodities, and there's no law which compels a retailer to keep an official record of his purchases or sales.

'Take spirits now, they're different, because there's been a heavy duty on them for generations. Years ago a law was passed which compelled every dealer in spirits to keep an excise ledger. Say a man has five hundred gallons of whisky down from Scotland, or foreign spirits for that matter either, he gets a permit with it directly it's checked out of bond, then he has to give a permit in his turn to every customer who buys the stuff, and enter the transaction in his book. Every few months an excise officer visits each dealer and examines his figures, which gives a pretty satisfactory check up, you see. It's illegal for a dealer to sell spirits without passing on a permit to his customer and, if the amount permitted out exceeds that permitted in, the excise man would start asking awkward questions at once.'

'How about odd bottles?' Gregory inquired.

'Oh, they're allowed a certain margin to cover that. The system's not altogether watertight as far as the pubs are concerned, where most of the stuff goes out in tots over the counter. There's a certain amount of smuggling in spirits still done but they can't operate on the grand scale; as they can with silks and other goods where there's no check up at all.'

'You didn't have much luck then?'

'Not much to begin with, but the police net's a wide one once it starts to operate, and this dealing in contraband has grown to such huge proportions recently that I knew I'd get what I was after in due time. We traced some goods from a dress shop in Birmingham to a wholesale house in Regent Street and I put the chap who runs it through his paces about a week ago. Of course he swore he had no knowledge there was anything fishy about the parcel he'd handled and said that it'd been sold him through a French house, by a woman representative, as bankrupt stock. That's why the price had been unusually low and he'd been glad to get the goods as a bargain.

'He hedged a lot about the French people he'd bought it from and then gave me the address of a firm in Lyons which had actually gone out of business a week or two before. I managed to rattle him pretty badly though by telling him that if he couldn't put me on to the woman who'd sold him the goods I'd have to run him as a dealer in contraband himself. Then I gave him twenty-four hours to think it over.

'Next day he gave me a description of the lady you met in Deauville. But I said that wasn't enough and I couldn't let him out unless he put me on to her. He didn't like the idea one little bit; seemed to think something unpleasant might happen to him if he blabbed. Well, as I pointed out, no one would know where I got my information so there was no reason to suppose they'd ever know who'd split. Then he told me the deal had been done in the lounge of the Carlton, where he went to meet the lady: evidently, of course, because she didn't want to be seen in his offices, and he believed that when she was in London she stayed at the hotel.

'My next move was to the Carlton and the management there gave me every assistance they could. The lady proved to be a Miss Sabine Szenty. We circulated her description through the usual channels and asked for the co-operation of the French police as well. They found her for us in Paris where she has some connection with a genuine silk stocking factory.'

Gregory frowned on learning that Sabine was so much more deeply involved than he had supposed; but Wells continued without a pause:

'That made the job fairly easy. Headquarters have allotted me a plane for this special work, and I had no trouble in getting faked credentials from a respectable firm here, so I flew to Paris as their buyer.

'I presented myself at the firm's offices, said I was interested in their goods, and my people might be willing to do business with them. When it came to prices they were remarkably low and they told me the goods could be delivered from their warehouse in London. They haven't got one actually: I checked up on that, but they intended to supply me with contraband through one of their agents here, of course, so I decided to place an order anyhow, and get a fresh line on their methods of delivery, but I made a lot of fuss and bother as I didn't want to clinch the deal until I'd got in touch with the lady herself.

'At my third call I was lucky. They'd evidently come to the conclusion I was a troublesome sort of bird and called her in to vamp me into signing up. She's the goods all right—I'll give her that—but not quite the type that appeals to me and, anyhow, when I'm on a case I'm about as cold as Mount Everest. I asked her if she'd take lunch with me just to celebrate this new business tie-up we were making between her firm and mine. She didn't want to, I could see, although butter wouldn't have melted in her mouth to all outward appearances. I don't flatter myself I'm the sort of chap a woman like that would waste her time on out of office hours either, but this was business and the order I was proposing to give made it worth her while to treat me nicely, so she came along. Seeing the sort of woman she was I took her to the *Meurice*.'

'The devil you did.' Gregory grinned. 'Lunched her at the *Meurice*, eh. By Jove! If that's the way the police treat suspected persons I shall consider turning crook myself.'

Wells laughed a little ruefully. 'Lord knows I'll never get that back on my expenses account. The prices just made me shudder; but she's a sport all right. As far as talk and apparent interest in me were concerned she really did me proud. If I hadn't known what was behind the scenes, and been a genuine buyer of ladies' underwear, I might almost have thought she'd fallen for me; but being a policeman puts you wise to the way women can act pleasant when they want to and not think another thing about it the second you've gone out of the door.

'After that lunch I hadn't got much for'arder, but she was paged—wanted on the telephone outside and she left her bag behind. That was my big opportunity. You bet I took it. You'd be surprised how quick trained fingers can go through a lady's bag in an open restaurant with everybody looking on but no one noticing; and inside was the telegram addressed to Corot.

She'd evidently written it out ready to send off just before leaving her office.

'I had no time to make a copy so I pinched it. Only thing to do. Then when she got back, although I'd paid the bill and we were just about to make a move, she asked for a liqueur and more coffee, so we sat on until the restaurant was nearly empty. She had warmed up quite a lot by then and really started in to vamp me properly.'

Gregory kept a perfectly straight face but his humour was intensely tickled by the vision of the delectable Sabine stooping to conquer this nice but unsophisticated young policeman in complete ignorance that he already had her taped.

'She asked me if I'd ever been to Deauville.' Wells smiled. 'I hadn't as a matter of fact. Then she told me she was off there that afternoon and began to chip me about being a staid unadventurous English businessman: "Why not come too?" she said. "Take a few days' holiday. I shall be there and the bathing is delicious on that long sunny beach. I have many engagements but I like you and would put some of them off in order to be with you. Tonight now, I have to dine with a friend but I have no engagement for supper. You tell me that you are not married? All right then; forget your business for a few hours and meet me at midnight tonight in Deauville to give me supper. That is romance."

'Well, it might have been romance, if she'd really meant it that way, though of course I knew she didn't. I was wondering what the game was and couldn't guess what she was after but the opportunity to follow her up seemed far too good to miss. As I had a plane at my disposal I put it to her that I'd fly her down to Deauville if she liked.

'She said, "yes" to that and we had another ration of Cointreau on it. I met her again at Le Bourget at half-past five, by arrangement, and flew her to the sea. We took a taxi from the airport to the town and she pointed out the place where she would meet me that night. I'd asked her already where she'd like to have supper but she said she knew a little place that would just suit us. In the meantime, there were all sorts of reasons why we should not be seen together; which of course, if I'd been the business-man she thought I was, would have added to the romantic mystery of the game. I turned up at the Customs sheds that night just as she had told me and she picked me up a few moments later. You know the rest.'

Gregory nodded: 'So that's why the telegram was on a sending form and had never been despatched. Obviously she missed it from her bag almost immediately after you'd pinched it and made up her mind that she must get it back. It would have been easy enough for her to send a duplicate but she didn't want you to retain possession of the original and, I suppose, she had to have a bit of time to make her plans before she could arrange to have you laid out.'

'That's about it,' Wells agreed. 'If I hadn't been a fool I should have made a copy of it and mailed it off to the Yard that evening; but she was so charming after lunch that I don't mind confessing she really made me half-believe she'd developed one of these sudden passions for me as I've heard some foreign women do. It never occurred to me she was after the telegram, but you got that in the end, didn't you? Although you never told the Superintendent so.'

'No, since he wouldn't co-operate,' Gregory smiled, 'I kept it dark, but I acted on it and went over to the *Café de la Cloche* last night.'

'The Super guessed you'd got it so he had you shadowed all yesterday. I left Heston only about ten minutes after you and I sat around the Grand Hotel doing my best to comfort myself with sandwiches while you had a damned good dinner; because I was afraid that you'd recognise me if I went into the restaurant. When you left I went after you in a taxi but, as a little time elapsed before I could get one, the fool driver failed to pick you up and took the wrong road, so the only thing I could do was return to the airport and keep your plane under observation. That was a cold and miserable job enough but I stuck it until you turned up hours later and I was in the air within two minutes of your leaving the ground. I hadn't the ghost of an idea what you were up to, but

I thought there was a real chance you were on to something, so I sat on your tail until you landed here outside the park.'

Gregory grinned. 'D'you mean to tell me that you never even saw the smugglers' fleet?'

'Not a sign of it. I didn't even know there was one although, of course, I assumed they were running the stuff in by air.'

'No. I suppose you had your eyes glued on my plane all the time and that's how you missed spotting the others.'

'Why in the world didn't you follow them?' Wells expostulated. 'It was a chance in a thousand to find the place where they actually land the stuff.'

'Naturally I meant to but it wasn't quite as easy as all that. I lost them in the clouds somewhere south of Ramsgate and I only picked up a single plane that landed here when I came down low over Thanet later on.'

'This *is* one of their receiving bases then?'

'I don't think so.' Gregory shook his head. 'The plane I followed in wasn't a cargo carrier. I had to land outside the park, as you know, but I managed to get into the grounds in time to see Lord Gavin Fortescue, Mademoiselle Sabine, and a couple of men, who were probably pilots, leave by car.'

'By jove, your night's work wasn't wasted after all.'

'Far from it as I've managed to locate one of their bases on the other side as well.'

'Good man. Where was it?'

Gregory's eyes narrowed a fraction. 'Before I let you in on that I want you to promise me something.'

'What?'

'That if we succeed in rounding up this mob you'll take no action against Mademoiselle Sabine Szenty.'

'Sorry, I can't. It would be more than my job's worth. I don't bear the lady any ill will for the way she led me up the garden path at Deauville; but she's in this thing up to the neck. She's operating a stocking factory in Paris as cover for supplying contraband, she's actively assisting in running the goods, and even travelling them this end as well.'

'Know anything about Lord Gavin Fortescue?' Gregory asked casually.

'Not much. Of course we have it on the records that he's been mixed in with all sorts of shady deals but we've never been able to get enough evidence to bring a case against him.'

'Well, believe me, he's a devil incarnate and while I'll give it you that the girl's probably acting the way she does largely from sheer love of adventure, she was probably forced into it originally through some hold that the old man's got over her. Now, I'm not boasting when I say that I can give you some real help in clearing this thing up. You'll admit yourself that I've done more in twenty-four hours than you have in six weeks; discovered one of their bases on the other side, and run this place to earth, which is obviously Lord Gavin's forward operation headquarters. As the price of my further help I want you to give Sabine a break when you pull these people in.'

'You've been lucky tonight,' Wells said thoughtfully, 'though it wasn't all luck I'll admit. But what further help can you give me?'

'The location of one of their French bases to start with and for future operations my association with Mademoiselle Sabine. If you arrest her prematurely, on some minor charge, you'll ruin the whole shooting-match, and you can't work her yourself now because she's already aware that you're a Scotland Yard man. On the other hand I can. I got her out of a nasty hole in Deauville and we parted on a very friendly footing, so if your people can locate her in London tomorrow morning, assuming that she's on her way there now, I can get in touch with her again and follow up the whole business without her suspecting what I'm after. See the line of country?'

'I do and it's a good one. All the same I can't promise to let her off. The best I can do is to say that we won't press the case against her more than we have to and we'll see to it that she gets the maximum benefit of any extenuating circumstances which she may be able to plead before the court.'

Gregory stood up, pulled out a cigarette, lighted it, and

began to walk up and down impatiently. 'But you can't understand!' he burst out. 'This girl's only a pawn in the game.'

'She's engaged in smuggling and I can prove it,' Wells said doggedly. 'She is running a permanent business in order to evade the customs and facilitate the importation of contraband silk.'

'Silk!' Gregory swung upon him angrily. 'Haven't your people told you the truth about what's at the bottom of all this?'

The Inspector's eyes opened wider. 'What on earth d'you mean?' he asked in a puzzled voice.

'Know anything about the present situation in China?'

'No. What's that got to do with it anyway?'

'Only that the Japs have organised smuggling gangs to break down the customs barriers of Northern China that are costing the Chinese Government a hundred million dollars a year in revenue, wrecking their home industries, and making it utterly impossible for the duty paid goods of other nations to compete in the same market. It's the same sort of thing we're up against here. Britain's been a free market too long for our business rivals to submit tamely to our protective laws. Our enemies are engaged in a desperate attempt to smash up the whole of our new commercial system. If, consciously or unconsciously, Sabine can enable us to defeat their ends what the devil does it matter if she has been cajoled or trapped into placing her stocking factory at Gavin Fortescue's disposal as a blind.'

Wells hesitated. 'How d'you know that is so?'

'I don't, but do you never use deduction?'

'I prefer to stick to facts and I know she's smuggling silk into this country.'

Gregory stared at the younger man stonily. 'Is that all you're after? Good God, you're in the Special Branch. You know where the Bolsheviks last concentrated all their energies don't you—Spain, and Spain went Red in consequence. Having done their work there they're concentrating now on France. Any fool could see that who reads his daily paper. Next it will be our turn and you sit there talking about *silk*!'

'I'm afraid I'm rather dense,' confessed the Inspector. 'You've just said yourself that the smugglers are out to wreck our protective barriers. Surely silk now constitutes one of the most important items in our tariffs?'

'Of course. But don't you see that if silk can be smuggled in other things can as well. To bankrupt our business houses and cut our customs revenue in half is only their first objective. Unless we can checkmate them they'll start dumping anarchists and agitators here by the hundred—all the scum whose full-time job it is to spread discontent and ruin. Then they'll send cargoes of illicit arms to their secret depots, and bombs, and poison gas and every sort of foulness to desecrate England's green and pleasant land. For God's sake man! Forget petty larceny for a bit and give me a free hand to stop that arch-traitor Gavin Fortescue staging a Red Revolution.'

10

The Strange Tenant of Quex Park

Five minutes later Mrs. Bird put her head round the door and announced: 'Baked beans and very good butter, all good people come to supper.'

Gregory smiled at the old tag as they followed her out of the hall and down the stone-flagged passage. He had managed to convince the Inspector of the real menace to Britain which lay behind the modern smuggling racket, and given him particulars of the secret depot on the Calais downs, after an agreement had been reached that they should pool their intelligence for the future.

Those were the best terms he could get, as he had never intended for one moment to withhold such vital information and he had demanded immunity for Sabine only in the hope that he might be able to trap the Inspector into making some promise which might prove useful later, while knowing quite well that the officer had no power to release her once she had been arrested.

In Mrs. Bird's cosy sitting-room they found Rudd busily dishing up generous portions of scrambled eggs on to large squares of thick hot toast.

All four of them set to with gusto having acquired a remarkable appetite from their night's adventures. When they had done the Inspector turned to their hostess.

'Now you're satisfied that I'm a police officer, Mrs. Bird, I'm sure you won't object to my asking you a few questions.'

'Ask away young man,' she said cheerfully. 'Being a law-abiding woman it's my duty to answer.'

'Good; perhaps you'd tell us then, in your own words, how long you've been here and what you know about the owners of this house.'

'I don't know a thing about them except what I've heard from the gardeners who keeps the place in order. He's a Major Powell-Cotton; a fine gentleman and a great hunter, so they say. There's a museum next to the house where he keeps his trophies, lions and tigers and all sorts of fearsome-looking beasts, though stuffed of course. He and his wife shot every one themselves, and they're away now in some un-Christian place looking for white leopards, if you ever heard of such a thing—have been for months and may be for another year—so meantime the Park's been let through an agent.'

'I see. Then you're not employed by the owner, but by the tenant.'

'That's right. Lord Gavin Fortescue's his name. He took the place from the March quarter and engaged me himself a few weeks later. Bit of luck for me he did too.'

'Why—particularly?'

Mrs. Bird's thick eyebrows shot up into her lined forehead. 'Why?—you're asking. Well, I'd had a worrying time before. You see, I was housekeeper to a Doctor Chalfont who lived at Dulwich. That was his daughter, Milly, you saw walking in her sleep, poor lamb. Her mother died when she was a baby and I was her nurse. We lived very happy at Dulwich, the Doctor and Milly and me, but last November the Doctor died and when we went into things we found he'd left next to nothing. He was such a generous soul, always a'giving and a'giving and refusing payment from poor patients who couldn't afford it. If we'd ever thought we might have known he never had much chance to save. He was only fifty-two so he probably expected to live a lot longer and put something by, or maybe he thought that Milly would be married before he died.

'Anyhow, we found the house didn't belong to him and the few bits of furniture didn't bring in much after the lawyer was paid, and Milly having no relatives at all it was for me to do the best for her I could. Fortunately I've been a careful woman so I had a bit tucked away in the bank for me old age, as you might say, but not enough for the interest on it to keep the two of us, even living very quiet, and my money would have gone in a year or so if I hadn't been able to get a job.'

Wells nodded sympathetically and the broad-bosomed Mrs. Bird went on: 'One day I saw an advertisement in the paper —"Caretaker wanted for country house, occasionally visited by tenants, must be able to cook, no other staff kept." Well, that might not have suited everybody as it looked a lonesome sort of post and most caretakers aren't much good in the kitchen, but it suited me all right so I put on my bonnet and went up to apply, as the advertisement said, to the office of the Carlton Hotel.

'I was shown up to a private sitting-room where there was a funny little deformed creature who told me he was Lord Gavin Fortescue and that the advertisement was his. He asked me no end of questions about the doctor and the life I'd led, but in the end he seemed satisfied and agreed that Milly might live in the house with me too. He made a point of it that I was to have no other visitors though, even for a cup of tea, because there's all sorts of valuables in the house. He was afraid that if people came to the place they might speak about them to other folk outside and that might lead to a visit from the burglars. Very scared of having burglars in his absence, he was, and he asked me if I was afraid of handling firearms.

'I said I wasn't afraid of burglars *or* firearms and that seemed to please him quite a lot because he told me he would have put a man in; except that it was so difficult to find a man who could cook. As he flew backwards and forwards from France quite a lot on business he'd be landing in the grounds, sometimes late at night, and want a meal. He put me through it proper about the cooking too, as to what I could do and what not. A very particular gentleman he seemed but it wasn't for me to argue about that so Milly and I moved in last February.'

'That's all nice and clear Mrs. Bird,' the Inspector nodded. 'Now, will you tell us what's been happening since.'

'He didn't come near the place for a month, except to settle us in. It was then he gave me the revolver with instructions that if I saw anybody in the grounds at night I was to shoot first and ask questions afterwards. He said the police wouldn't make any trouble about it, me being a lone woman in a house like this, and that my first duty was to protect the property. He said too, he'd prefer me not to go into Birchington or any of the other places round about, or make friends with the local people and that I'd have no cause to bother with the tradesmen calling because all our food would be sent down from London, except fresh vegetables and fruit, as it is—in big cases marked "Fortnum"—and very good food too. Towards the end of April. . . .'

'You hardly see a soul apart from the gardeners then?' Gregory interrupted.

'No, and not much of them either. All but one old deaf chap and a couple of lads who look after the glass houses and keep the place tidy have been lent to a charity institution by the owner of the estate while he's away. It's for a big new building they're putting up near Canterbury and a lovely place they're making of it too I'm told. They have to live near their work, of course, so the head gardener's cottage has been empty since we've been here and he only comes over once in a while for an hour or so to see that the others is not neglecting their job.'

'How about the lodge keeper? I suppose there is one in a place like this.'

'Well, he had an accident poor man, soon after we got here.'

'What sort of accident?' Gregory asked quickly.

'Knocked down by a motor car, he was, just outside the park gates, but his Lordship behaved very decent about that. Sent him away to have treatment at Bournemouth, and his wife and children with him—all expenses paid.'

Gregory exchanged a significant glance with Wells. 'Then apart from your foster daughter and yourself there is not a single person sleeps on the estate now.'

'That's so, sir.'

'You were going to tell us what happened at the end of April.'

'Well, his little Lordship came down and stayed the night. Then next day a gang of workmen arrived to build a big shed at the edge of the trees on the far side of the house. A few days later he turned up again in an aeroplane which was garaged in the shed. Since then he's been backwards and forwards quite a lot, mostly at night time, and he never stays more than a few hours. Sometimes there's a tall gentleman with him, who's got a game leg and sometimes a dark lady. Very lovely she is; but some sort of foreigner. She was with him tonight and he always has two men too who fly his plane. He gives very little trouble and pays my wages regular as clockwork. Always very civil, too, though silent, and it never entered my head that there could be anything tricky about him until to-night. You wouldn't think it yourself, would you, him being a lord and a rich one into the bargain?'

The Inspector smiled noncommittally. 'And is that all you can tell us Mrs. Bird?'

'It is. And now it's my turn. It's funny somehow that it never struck me as queer before, this landing in aeroplanes at night and him not wanting me to make friends with the people round about. Isn't he a lord at all?'

'Oh, his name *is* Lord Gavin Fortescue,' Gregory assured her, 'but the fact of a man having a title doesn't necessarily prevent him being a criminal.'

'The sooner we get out the better then. It's hard to lose an easy job but I've got Milly to think of.'

'I hope you won't decide to do that, Mrs. Bird,' Wells said quickly. 'There's not the least likelihood of these people doing you or Miss Chalfont any harm and if you say nothing about our visit they won't have any reason to suspect you of knowing that the police are interested in their activities. If you can see your way to stay on here just as though nothing had happened it'd be a very great help to us. You see, I'd send a man down to keep in touch with you outside the Park and through him you could let us know each time Lord Gavin or his people come and go from here.'

'That's all very well, young man, but if they're criminals, as you say, they might murder us both in our beds one night.'

'No, no! Their business is smuggling silks and other dutiable goods over from France and I feel certain that they won't do you the least harm. There's another point too, if you leave at once you'll be out of a job again, whereas if you're prepared to stay on and give us your help I think I can promise we'll be able to find a comfortable billet in a decent family for you, when it's all over, through the police organisation.'

Mrs. Bird considered for a moment. 'It'd be a big load off my mind if you could. All right, I'll stay then.'

'Splendid.' The Inspector stood up. 'Well now, I haven't got a search warrant but since you're going to give us your help you won't mind if I have an unofficial look round the house, will you? I just might spot something which would be useful to us later on.'

Mrs. Bird nodded agreement, but Gregory shrugged. 'As they only use this place for secret landings, and never stay here more than an hour or two, I doubt if you'll find anything of interest. Anyhow, I'm going to leave you to it and get back to London. Poor old Rudd looks as though he could do with an hour or two's sleep.'

Rudd yawned. 'You've said it, sir, but you're looking fresh as a daisy yourself. How you manage to keep going at times like this has always bin a poser ter me.'

Wells came out to see them on their way and accompanied them through the shrubbery at the side of the house round to its front. It was past four o'clock and in the faint light of the early summer dawn the coppices and broad meadows of the park now showed up clearly. To their left, from a group of trees a few hundred yards away, a turret rose, crowned by an openwork steel spire which looked like a small replica of the Eiffel Tower or a wireless mast, adding an extra fifty feet to its height. On the fringe of another group of trees, a little nearer, to their right, they could now see a big wooden shed.

Gregory jerked his head towards it. 'That's the hangar where they house the plane. Having all those trees behind it explains why I failed to spot it last night.'

'They've certainly got the very place for their job here,' Wells commented. 'That steel mast above the tower must be visible for miles. It's perfect for a signal light to bring in other planes that don't know the lie of the land.'

'Well, what does A. do now?' asked Gregory, preparing to move off.

The young Inspector laughed. He was in high good humour as a result of his night's work. 'A., being you, calls at the Carlton tomorrow and endeavours to make contact with B., the lady in the case. It looks like more than even chances she's staying there again and I daren't go near the place. She'd flit at the bare sight of me, knowing now that I'm a policeman, while C., being myself, returns to dull routine, sending a junior here to keep in touch with Mrs. Bird and the Park under observation.'

'Right, then. So long, Inspector.' Gregory turned away with Rudd beside him and set off down the east drive towards the field where he had left his plane.

Wells went back into the house and his inspection of it

soon assured him that Gregory's view had been correct. It was only used as a port of call from which Lord Gavin and his associates came and went without arousing the suspicions of the residents in Birchington. No papers which might throw further light upon the conspiracy seemed to be kept there. The drawers of all the desks and bureaux were unlocked and empty and there was no safe in the house.

The two tall windowless buildings behind the conservatories to the west, which Gregory had thought might be squash or tennis courts, proved to be the Museum holding the magnificent collection of Major Powell-Cotton, the absent owner of the estate. Vast cases, occupying in some instances the full length of the walls and twenty feet or more in height, contained jungle scenes where the great stuffed beasts, elephant, rhino, sable antelope, baboon, kudu, giraffe, and countless other varieties of wild beasts were mounted in life-like postures, plunging through tall grass or wallowing in muddy streams, so that they could be seen in all the splendour of their natural habitation.

On other walls of the buildings were ranged smaller cases containing native costumes and weapons, the grotesque masks of African witch doctors, collections of fearsome-looking beetles and a thousand other items of interest, brought from every corner of Africa, India and Tibet by the great hunter.

As Wells could make no further move of importance in his investigation until he learned whether Gregory had managed to get in touch with Sabine, he saw no necessity to hurry back to London, so he spent over an hour admiring the great beasts and studying the curiosities in the smaller cases. It was half past six before he got back to Mrs. Bird's kitchen again and with her he found Milly.

The girl had been woken early by the crunch of his feet on the gravel under her window an hour before. Looking out and seeing a strange man in the grounds she had rushed to tell her foster-mother who told her of the surprising events which had happened during the night.

Milly was dressed now in a light-blue summer frock that

enhanced the blue of her eyes and set off to perfection her delicate colouring and golden hair. When Wells was introduced she was agog with excitement at meeting a real detective from Scotland Yard.

Mrs. Bird, who was cooking breakfast for the girl, suggested that the Inspector could do with another cup of tea before he left and that, while she was getting it ready, the pair of them should go out and pick some fresh raspberries in the garden.

Nothing loath, the Inspector left the house again with Milly and she took him along a path behind the Museum buildings to a big walled garden.

She seemed a shy young creature and he found himself unaccountably tongue-tied, although he had an inward desire to start a conversation which might prolong the pleasure of being with her alone in the great garden, now made more lovely by the hush of the early summer morning.

'Your work must be awfully interesting,' she said at last.

'Rather,' said Gerry Wells. 'I've been lucky, too. I'm the youngest Inspector that's ever been seconded to the Special Branch.'

'You must be very clever then,' she said shyly.

He found himself blushing as he met the candid gaze of her large admiring eyes. 'Oh, no,' he hastened to protest, 'lucky that's all. I did quite well at school though, managed to get a scholarship and, as a matter of fact, I owe a great deal to my dad. He was a mechanic in the R.A.F. in the Great War. Now, *he's* a clever fellow if you like; so good at his job they kept him on afterwards in the technical department where the new planes are designed. He taught me all I know about engines and how to fly when I was quite a boy. That's one of the things that's led to my promotion because, you see, we haven't got a great many pilots in the force, but nowadays we have to move with the times and flying comes in useful.'

'It must be wonderful to fly,' she murmured.

'Take you up sometime,' said Gerry, 'that's if you'd care to go.'

'I've always thought I'd be frightened to fly but I wouldn't be frightened with you. If you'd like to take me.'

A happy grin spread over his freckled boyish face. 'That's a date then, although I may not be able to take you up for a bit yet, not till this business is over.'

'Is it a very dangerous business?'

'Well, perhaps you might say so in a way, but I've seen a good few rough houses in the last ten years and I can look after myself fairly well. Three crooks set on me a few nights ago over in Trouville but I managed to get away.' The Inspector felt a twinge of conscience as he failed to mention Gregory's assistance; but he refrained from doing so from the very human desire to impress the girl.

Milly's eyes grew larger and rounder than ever. 'You must be very brave and very strong,' she said.

He drew himself up instinctively among the raspberry canes and tensed the muscles of his fine shoulders. 'All in the day's work,' he said casually, 'and of course police training helps a lot. We're taught ju-jutsu you know, and various wrestling holds, which gives us a bit of an advantage. I rather like a rough and tumble now and again. It keeps me fit. Are you—are you interested in cricket?'

'I love it,' said Milly, who had once in her life been taken to the Oval. 'I think it's a splendid game, don't you?'

'Yes. I'm pretty keen myself. As a matter of fact I play for the first eleven of the Flying Squad.'

'Fancy your being in the Flying Squad; that must be awfully thrilling. You have to chase car bandits, don't you?'

'Yes. I've done quite a lot of that, but it's not so interesting as this special job I've just been given. It's a real big thing, this is, and if I pull it off it might mean promotion again.'

'Oh, I do hope you do. Wouldn't it be wonderful if they made you a Commissioner?'

Gerry smiled. 'That's a bit too much to hope for yet I'm afraid, but you never know if I might not end up as an A.C., in another twenty years or so.'

If the truth be told they ate more of the raspberries than

they picked, yet the little basket that Milly carried was full now and there was not room in it for another one. They would both have liked to linger longer but there did not seem to be any excuse to do so and for the moment neither could think of another line of conversation so, in an embarrassed silence, they returned to the big house.

Mrs. Bird met them with the news that Milly's breakfast was ready and pressed the Inspector to join her for a second meal. He accepted for the pleasure of remaining a little longer, managed two cups of tea and a further ration of raspberries, then when there no longer seemed any reasonable excuse for delaying his departure another moment he reluctantly said good-bye, but Milly volunteered to walk with him as far as the gate of the Park and see him off.

In a silence that was almost painful they walked down the east drive side by side and leaving the park crossed the field to the Inspector's plane. He unscrewed the pickets and stowed them in the cockpit then turned to say good-bye.

Milly held out a frail little hand and laid it in his big brown one. 'Shall we—shall we be seeing you again soon?' she asked

He smiled. 'I hope so; just as soon as I can manage it. With crooks in this place it's part of my job now to keep my eye on it.'

'Well, knowing that, we shan't be the least bit frightened,' she said simply. 'But do take care of yourself, won't you?'

'Rather,' he grinned, 'as you've been nice enough to ask me to.'

11

The Beautiful Hungarian

Sir Pellinore Gwaine-Cust stretched out his long legs and regarded Gregory with an approving stare. 'And what's the next move my boy—what's the next move?' he asked with sudden briskness.

'Lunch,' said Gregory. 'I'm a complete fool to introduce you to the girl, of course, because it's almost certain you'll cut me out. But someone's got to give us both lunch at the Carlton and I thought it might as well be you.'

'Cut you out, eh! Well, if she's all you say she is, dammit, I might have a shot at it, specially if you don't do your stuff better than you did at Deauville. Are you certain she's at the Carlton, though?'

'Yes. I rang up to find out immediately I got home.'

'D'you speak to her?'

'Good Lord no. I just ascertained from the office that they had an angel called Szenty beneath their roof. She hasn't the least idea that Wells got on to her in the first place through the fellow she sold the stockings to in Regent Street when she was staying there before. You see, she'd never heard of Wells's existence until he presented himself as a business man at her office in Paris. She can't know we've rumbled Quex Park either and that Mrs. Bird told us Lord Gavin engaged her while he was staying at the Carlton in February—which gave us a second line on it being their port of call in London.'

'Then she's not expecting you. She may be out.'

'I doubt it. She couldn't have got in till about three o'clock this morning so the chances are all against her being up and doing before mid-day. Anyhow, I thought the risk small enough to snatch a few hours' sleep. Not that I needed them particularly but it's my old campaigner's habit of taking a nap while the going's good. Quite sound really, as I may be up again all night tonight.'

Smart and fresh in a double-breasted light-grey summer suit Gregory certainly did not look as though he had spent a good portion of his night crawling over Calais downland and scrambling through the coppices of a Kentish park.

'I don't quite see, though,' Sir Pellinore said after a moment, 'where I come in about this luncheon business. What the deuce d'you want to drag me into it for?'

Gregory grinned. 'For one thing, it might amuse you; but, for another, I can't just go and hang around the Carlton on my own. Sabine's a clever woman and she'd smell a rat at once; guess the police had run her to earth there, and that I was acting with them. That's the one thing we've got to keep out of her lovely little head at all costs. My plan of campaign is to walk round the corner now and park myself in the lounge; tip a bell-hop to keep his eyes open for her then, when she turns up, I shall be just as surprised and delighted as though I had really run into her casually. I shall immediately inform her I am waiting there for *you* and that we're lunching together. Then you come on the scene proving that I'm not a liar and my meeting with her a pure coincidence.'

Sir Pellinore grunted. 'And what do *I* do if you please? Stand about in the street looking like a loony until you come and whistle for me?'

'Certainly not. You'll be in Justerini's office, next door. You always get your drink there so they'll be delighted to see you and refresh you with another ration of this excellent sherry. Immediately the bell-hop lets me know that Sabine's come down in the lift he'll slip out of the Pall Mall entrance and fish you out of Justerini's. Then you will stroll in to find me doing my stuff with her in the lounge.'

'Say she's already got a luncheon appointment?'

'In that case, you'll have to content yourself with my company I'm afraid. We've got to chance that but unless it's a very important appointment indeed you can put your money on my persuading her to break it.'

'Conceited young devil,' laughed Sir Pellinore. 'All right, you win. But what's the procedure saying we manage to get this wench as far as the luncheon table?'

'You order the best lunch that you can think of, which should be pretty good, and later on you pay for it. Then you go off to your club, or the house here, for a nice afternoon nap, suitable to a man of your years, leaving me in sole possession of the lady.'

'What happens then?'

'Allah, who knows all things, will give me inspiration, but my main policy is to stick to her as long as I possibly can on one excuse or another. Tonight's the seventh and in our now-famous telegram the numbers 43 and 47 follow that date, so presumably they'll be operating again, but from different bases. If I can hang on to Sabine long enough maybe she'll telephone while I'm with her or let slip some little bit of information which will give me a chance to follow her up when I can't keep her with me any longer.'

Sir Pellinore stroked his fine white moustache and stood up. 'What a lucky young dog you are. If I had my way the company wouldn't pay you a cent for this investigation; you're going to get far too much fun out of it.'

'On the contrary they'll have to pay extra as compensation for the damage I'm doing to my conscience.' Gregory laughed cynically but there was no laughter in his heart. To conceal his troubled thoughts he pursued the jest. 'Here I am having to force myself into following up some rotten game by taking advantage of the confidences of the girl I'm in love with.'

'You! In love! Never been in love in your life.'

'Well, I'm not too old to learn,' countered Gregory modestly, 'and I certainly don't want to see Sabine sent to prison.'

'Yes; awkward that—very awkward—but I won't have you going romantic. It's bad for the health, bad for business, and it doesn't suit you.'

'On the contrary, the very thought that I may be lunching with Sabine in about half an hour puts me right on the top of the world. Come along now or you won't have time for that glass of sherry at Justerini's.'

A few moments later the two men left the house and sauntered down Pall Mall together in the bright August sunshine. Gregory was a tallish man but his queer cultivated stoop made him seem almost short beside Sir Pellinore's magnificent height and upright figure. At the Pall Mall entrance of the Carlton they parted; Gregory disappearing into the hotel and Sir Pellinore into the door of his wine merchants which was less than a dozen yards away.

It was a little after half past twelve and an inquiry at the hotel office assured Gregory that he had been justified in not hurrying; Sabine was still in her room. He secured a page boy and, tipping the lad lavishly, gave him his instructions, posting him near the florists and within sight of the lift. Next, he spoke to the porters, both at the Pall Mall and Haymarket entrances of the hotel, describing Sabine to them as an additional precaution in case she slipped by the page unrecognised, and told them that if she went out they were to fetch him at once from the lounge. Then he parked himself at a small table and ordered a double gin fizz which he felt to be a particularly suitable drink in such sultry weather.

Nearly three quarters of an hour went by and he was beginning to fear that Sabine might be lunching quietly in her suite when the page came hurrying along to inform him that she had just come down and was leaving her key. Without losing an instant Gregory strode from the lounge and into the street by the Pall Mall exit, raced round the corner into the Haymarket, and came sauntering gaily into the hotel's other entrance, just as Sabine was about to sally forth.

'Hello!' he cried, throwing wide his arms to bar her passage. 'What heavenly luck. Is it really you—or am I dreaming things?'

She smiled as he seized her hand and kissed it. 'But yes, it is most surprising that we should meet so soon again.'

'Not really,' he assured her, 'since you chance to be in London. It's such a tiny world for people like ourselves who always move around the same old haunts. You were going out—but you mustn't. I can't possibly let you.'

Her face grew serious.

'You have no reason to detain me, as you had in Deauville.' Under her statement lay the suggestion of a suspicion.

'Only the reason that was at the bottom of everything before—my frantic desire to be with you, unless, of course, you've blotted your copy book again and want me now to save you from the London police. Come in and have a cocktail.'

She shook her head. 'That would be nice but, really, I must not. I have to lunch at Claridges and I am already late.'

'Ring up and put them off—please do. It seems a thousand years since I've seen you but I've been dreaming of you ever since. Now I've found you again I absolutely refuse to let you go.'

'But this is business,' she protested.

He laughed. 'What in the world can so lovely a person as yourself have to do with such a dreary thing as business; or do you mean that you have some job to do for that old devil I saw you with in Deauville?'

'*Mais non*, when I say business I mean commerce. You see, I am a business woman. Representative, you say, of a house in Paris, but that you could not know.'

'Really? How extraordinary!' Gregory's face expressed blank astonishment at this gratuitous information but he added blandly: 'Somehow it seems so out of keeping that anyone like you should have to face the daily grind, but then everybody's in business these days, aren't they?'

She shrugged. 'It has become necessary that most people should work since old families lost their money in the war years, and after, but I should be miserable if I had to lead always an idle life.'

'Well, you're going to take an hour or two off today anyhow,' he declared. 'Surely you can put off your appointment until tomorrow. Nobody could possibly want to do business on a lovely sunny day like this.'

He saw her hesitate and pressed home his advantage. 'Come on now. I'm lunching here with a friend of mine, but you'll find him charming—a delightful person—Sir Pellinore Gwaine-Cust. He's one of the grandest old men in Europe. Put business out of your mind today and let us entertain you. I give you my word you won't regret it.'

'*S'il vous voulez*,' she surrendered. 'You are such a tempestuous person. It is difficult to refuse you, and that business lunch, it would have been boring anyway.'

'Page,' Gregory beckoned, 'tell the operator to get me Claridges.' Then he turned to Sabine. 'What's your friend's name? I'll make your excuses for you—a little taxi accident in Bond Street this morning—I think. Nothing serious but you're a bit shaken and resting now until you've recovered from the shock. How'll that do?'

She shook her head. 'No. Your powers of invention are quite marvellous but I will speak myself.' She turned and followed the boy away to the telephone booth.

Gregory smiled with self-congratulation as he watched her take the call. He had failed in a quick attempt to find out with whom she had meant to lunch, but he had achieved his main objective in making his presence there seem accidental and securing, at all events, an hour or two of her company for himself. When they walked into the lounge Sir Pellinore was already there; and rose to meet them.

'I'm sure you won't mind,' Gregory said, 'but I've brought a friend, whom I had no idea was in England until I ran into her here five minutes ago. I couldn't possibly let the opportunity slip so I've asked her to join us. This is Sir Pellinore Gwaine-Cust, a very old friend of mine, Mademoiselle Sabine . . .' he paused, remembering that he was not supposed to know her other name, and looked away with an excellent imitation of slight embarrassment.

'Szenty,' she added calmly.

Gregory repeated the name.

Sir Pellinore bent over her hand, 'Mademoiselle Szenty's presence could never need an apology. On the contrary I consider it a very great piece of good fortune that anyone so lovely should consent to grace the table of an old man like myself.'

As they passed up the steps to the restaurant he murmured her name again. 'Surely you are Hungarian. There was a Grof Szenty whom I knew long ago. A delightful feller; a Captain in one of the crack regiments of the old kingdom, who used to bring his horses over, and came within an ace of winning the cup for jumping one year at Olympia.'

'But, of course,' she smiled, 'that was my father. He would be about the same age as you.'

'By jove now! Is he . . .' Sir Pellinore hesitated.

She shook her head. 'No, he was killed on the Russian front in the early days of the war.'

Sir Pellinore nodded sadly. 'That damnable war. It robbed me of my only son and countless dear fellows of both our generations. As I watched them go under one by one I thought that I would not have a single friend left in the world by the time it was over.'

Gregory tactfully turned the conversation to the ordering of the meal and then said quietly: 'Mademoiselle Szenty tells me that she is now in business.'

'Indeed?' Sir Pellinore looked up. 'Well, most of us have had to come to it, and perhaps that's not a bad thing in a way, but I hope the estates still remain in your family my dear. That beautiful old castle upon the River Theiss which I remember well. I went out to stay there once with the Count, your father, for the shooting. You have the finest partridge shooting in the world in Hungary.'

'But how interesting,' she smiled, 'that you should know Schloss Scány. When were you there?'

'Nineteen seven, no nineteen eight it must have been, I think.'

'Ah, that was before I was born, so you would not have seen me, even as a baby. I remember it well, of course, although we had to leave it when I was nine.'

'You *have* lost it then?'

'Yes. All our money went in the deflation and for a little time my mother and I were almost paupers living in a back street in Pest.'

'Your luck's turned since though I gather.' Gregory smiled. 'How did you come to go into business?'

'It was through an old friend of my mother's. The man whom you saw me with at Deauville. He is very rich and very generous. He was in Budapest in 1922 and he took us from the slum where we were living, gave my mother a very nice allowance, and sent me to France and England to be educated. We owe him everything, and when he offered me a position in a French firm in which he was interested, a few years ago, I was very happy to take it.'

Gregory nodded. Philanthropist seemed a strange role for Lord Gavin Fortescue but obviously the man had his reasons for displaying this unusual generosity. Even at the age of twelve or thirteen, Gregory thought, Sabine must have displayed promise of unusual beauty. Lord Gavin had evidently decided to invest a fraction of his surplus millions in tying the mother and daughter to him by bonds of gratitude with the idea that the girl would prove useful to him later on. Doubtless it was true that she had been glad to accept a well-paid job in this Paris firm which Lord Gavin had acquired, with his usual far-sightedness, in preparation for his vast smuggling campaign; probably soon after England went off gold and brought in Protection. Later, of course, she would have found out that the business was not all it appeared at first sight but her position would have made it practically impossible for her to quarrel with her benefactor.

'Is your mother still alive?' he asked after a moment.

She nodded. 'Yes, and she lives now, not as in her youth of course, with a great household, but in every comfort. While I was at school and finishing she had quite a pleasant little apartment in Buda, but since I have been in business, and my salary is a very generous one, I have been able to rent a nice house with a pretty garden for her just outside the city.'

Gregory saw that his surmise had been correct. If Sabine

quarrelled with Lord Gavin now her fine salary would cease immediately and the old lady, who doubtless adored her creature comforts, would be faced with poverty again.

The lunch proved a cheerful and successful meal. Just before it was over Gregory smiled into Sabine's eyes and said: 'Now, what for the afternoon? How would you like me to motor you down to Hampton Court or somewhere where we could have tea on the river?'

'I am sorry,' she said gravely, 'but that is quite impossible. I have my business to attend to. A buyer from one of the big Kensington stores meets me at the Royal Palace Hotel at half past three.'

'Put him off; like you did the other fellow.'

'No, I cannot. It is the same man. When I telephoned before lunch I made this new appointment.'

'How about tonight. Will you dine with me?'

'No. Unfortunately I am engaged once more.'

'Tomorrow then?'

'I return to France. This is a flying visit only.'

Gregory suppressed a grin, knowing that it was probably a flying visit in more senses than one. 'But I can't let you go so soon,' he protested. 'How about tea after you've seen this fellow?'

'Yes. That I can manage—if you wish.'

'Fine. I'll run you down to the Royal Palace then and pick you up afterwards. Say four o'clock—how would that do?'

'Nicely, I t'ink. My business should not take more than half an hour.'

They sat over their liqueurs for a little, then Sir Pellinore expressed his intention of leaving them, yet from his excuses made them both believe that he did it with regret.

As they thanked him for the meal he took Sabine's hand and said with unusual seriousness: 'My dear, as an old friend of your father's I want you to extend the privilege of your friendship to me too. I live at number 64 Carlton House Terrace. Any time you are in England my house and my servants are entirely at your disposal so please do not hesitate too ring me up, either day or night, if I can be of any service to you.'

A warm smile lit her limpid eyes. 'Such hospitality makes me think of Hungary. I mean, not all English people are so very kind to strangers.'

'That is true I fear. Nevertheless we can prove good friends on occasion. Strangers here sometimes have little difficulties with the authorities and I am in the fortunate position of being able to smooth such things over.'

'I will not forget, Sir Pellinore,' she promised, and a few moments later she was seated beside Gregory in a taxi on the way to Kensington.

He dropped her at the hotel and took the taxi on to his rooms in Gloucester Road. There he pressed a five pound note into Rudd's hand and told him to go out and buy flowers, fruit, cakes and all things requisite to entertain a lady. 'And if you give away by so much as a blink of an eyelid that you've ever seen her before I'll wring your neck my lad,' he ended gaily.

'It ain't the popsy we seen with old monkey-face in that car on the Calais road, is it sir?' Rudd asked with quick interest.

'It is, my boy, and you'll kindly refrain from referring to her as a popsy, unless you want to take a journey in a hearse.'

'No offence, sir, but my! Ain't you the lucky one, and no bloomin' error. Think she'd like eclairs for 'er tea?'

'Yes, eclairs and lots of other things. Go on now, get out and buy them. We'll be back in half an hour.'

Gregory cast a hasty glance round the comfortable book-lined room, straightened the cushions on the settee quite unnecessarily, and then dashed out to get his car.

By four o'clock he was back again in it, outside the Royal Palace, ready to pick up Sabine.

She did not keep him waiting long and soon appeared with a short tubby little man to whom she said good-bye on the pavement. Gregory studied his face carefully and felt quite sure that he would know him again; but the chances were that the fellow was some quite innocent buyer who had no idea whatsoever that he had just been purchasing a line of contraband.

As soon as Sabine was in the car Gregory let in the clutch and headed west but a few hundred yards farther on he turned it, dexterously avoiding an omnibus, and shot down Gloucester Road.

'Where are you taking me?' she asked, 'or is this a better way to avoid the traffic before we reach again the West End?'

'I propose to give you tea in my rooms,' he smiled. 'Any objection?'

She hesitated. 'Is it your custom to take a lady to your apartment on so brief an acquaintance?'

He laughed. 'No, but ours is hardly an ordinary acquaintance. After all, we shared a bedroom and bathroom for the night in Deauville, didn't we, so surely you're not going to kick at having tea in my sitting-room. We'll be more comfortable there than in the crowded lounge of some hotel.'

'Perhaps, but did you not warn me that when that night was over you would become the Big Bad Wolf? And now it seems you propose to take me to your cave.'

'Here it is,' he said, pulling up, 'and it's a very nice cave although it doesn't look much from the outside.'

Sabine got out and stared for a moment at the grimy three-storey house, one of a block of twenty or more, with its little grocery shop on the ground floor abutting on the side-walk. 'You live here—no!' she said in considerable surprise.

'Yes. Queer-looking place, isn't it, but my soldier servant who went all through the War with me, and saved my life more than once, owns it. His wife left it to him and this little bit of property is about the only thing he's got. I occupy the first floor and pay my rent regularly, which is more than most of the other tenants do, as they're poor students studying at the university round the corner. If I cleared out the poor chap might go broke and have to sell the place. That's why I stay on.'

She regarded him doubtfully for a moment and then she

smiled. 'I pay you a great compliment, for I do not t'ink that I would go into such a place with any other man that I had known only for so short a time but, you see, I trust you.'

He opened the side door with his key and as she preceded him up the rickety stairs he thought, 'She trusts me, and I'm spying on her, ferreting out her affairs. What a rotten swine I am when one comes to think of it, but it's that devil Gavin Fortescue we're up against and we've got to save the country from unprincipled blackguards like him. I'm only using her as a stalking horse, after all, and somehow or other I'll have to get her out of it when the crash does come, else I'll never be able to look at myself in my shaving mirror any more.'

'But how lovely!' Sabine exclaimed as he threw open the door of his sitting-room and showed her in. The room was unexpectedly gay and cheerful after the blackened exterior of the house and Rudd had done his duty nobly at the florists by spending lavishly on flowers.

Gregory guided her to the settee, stacked cushions round her and threw one at her feet. 'A cigarette,' he laughed, proffering an onyx box, 'then tea.'

They had hardly settled down when Rudd came in wheeling a dumb waiter with half the contents of a baker's shop spread out upon it.

'*Mon dieu!*' she exclaimed. 'Do you expect me to eat all this—or have you a party of twenty people coming?'

'No, it's just Rudd,' he laughed. 'Rudd's fond of cakes and he gets all the ones that we can't eat.'

' 'Arternoon, Miss,' Rudd said with a sheepish grin. 'You won't take too much notice of Mr. Gregory, I hope. He's always been a one what likes a leg pull.'

She smiled up at him, pulling off her hat and throwing it carelessly on to a chair. 'But you are a genius, Mr. Rudd, to provide so heavenly a tea. Look now at those eclairs. I am greedy for eclairs always and shall not leave you a single one.'

Rudd almost blushed with pleasure. 'That's the way, Miss. It's a real pleasure to find for a lady what likes it when you do your best.' He backed out of the doorway with a smile.

'I understand now why you live here,' Sabine said, nipping off the end of one of the eclairs with her small white teeth. 'He is a character, that one, and I would bet, your devoted slave as well.'

Gregory nodded. 'Yes, he's one of the very best and I'm a stupid sentimental fool but I'd go through hell to pull him out of a hole.'

'I believe that. You persuade yourself always that you are hard, hard as iron nails, yet for your friends you are, I think, supremely good.'

He looked at her for a moment searchingly. 'And do you count me a friend of yours, Sabine?'

'Yes. You are my friend, although why I do not know.'

'Do we ever know these things?' He shrugged. 'Does it matter. We're a short time living and a long time dead. Believe me, *I am* your friend and that's why I wish to God you were out of all this.'

'By this—you mean what?' Her eyes clouded quickly.

'I don't know,' he lied, 'only that you're mixed up in some way with a pretty nasty crowd. You'll remember, no doubt, that the last time we were together, and I left you to get my car in the Guillaume le Conquérant at Dives I was unavoidably detained; so I was unable to run you back to Deauville after all or even send you my apologies. I suppose you know what happened to me?'

Sabine began to giggle; then she suddenly lay back and gave way to a fit of helpless laughter.

'Go on! Laugh away,' Gregory chid her in mock anger, 'but it was devilish painful at the time.'

'Forgive me,' she sighed, struggling to regain her breath. 'Of course I know and I was miserable until I learned that no serious harm had been done you. The Big Bad Wolf walked into the Tiger's den and got more than he bargained for—*n'est pas?*'

Gregory shrugged. 'I'm not grumbling. Your elderly friend sent me a note to the *Normandie* saying that he'd make trouble for me if I didn't send you back to him immediately after

allow a plea that Gavin Fortescue had been a benefactor to her and her mother as sufficient excuse for becoming a member of his criminal organisation and would pass sentence upon her.

The thought of her as a female convict, in rough clothes, serving a sentence among thieves, prostitutes, and child-beaters, was absolutely unbearable to Gregory and momentarily it overbalanced his usual astute judgment of the best way in which to handle a situation..

She did not show him by the flicker of an eyelid that he had blundered, but listened to all he said with grave attention and apparent gratitude; yet she would not commit herself to following the line of action he urged upon her, saying that she must have time to think it over.

Feeling he had gained ground, and that at least she would not commit herself further for the time being, he mixed some cocktails and asked what she intended to do that evening.

'I do not know—now,' she replied slowly.

'Why not dine with me then?' he suggested. 'Let's go gay. We'll forget all this until you've had time to sleep on it.'

To his immense relief she consented, and so it was agreed that she should take a taxi back to the Carlton while he changed into evening clothes, and that he should pick her up there at eight o'clock.

He had no hesitation in letting her go. They kissed again and clung to each other as though they were parting for a period of years although they were to meet again in a little over an hour.

It was only when he was in his bath that doubts about the wisdom of his action began to assail him. She had been so quiet and said so little while he had been pressing arguments upon her to cut clear of the mess she was in before it was too late. She had promised nothing and he really knew so little of how deeply she might be implicated in Lord Gavin's plans. What if he had failed to convince her of her danger and she gave him the slip. Knowing now, from his own admission, that he was working with the police, she would avoid any place where she feared he might find her. It might be weeks or months before she visited Quex Park again, and that was the only place from which he could hope to pick up her trail if she once abandoned the Carlton.

He began to dress with feverish haste, frantic with anxiety now that he had given himself away, lest she might disregard his warning and yet be compelled, from the nature of her activities, and the knowledge of his intentions, to sacrifice their overwhelming attraction for each other and disappear altogether.

By the time he was ready to telephone a cab his face was dark with anger. An inner voice kept telling him that he had acted like a lunatic. He had been mad to let her out of his sight for a second and utterly insane to confess that he was working with the police. How could his prayers that she should cut adrift from Lord Gavin possibly have any effect when she was so deeply involved. If only he had held his peace he could at least have followed her up quite easily, or even kept in touch with her by arrangement, as long as she had no suspicion that he was spying on her. Then, he would have been at hand to warn her just as the police net was about to close and perhaps be able to help her in escaping its meshes. Now, he had spiked his own guns by blurting out a premature warning. The sort of folly of which any callow youth, bitten by his first calf love, might have been guilty. He let out a peculiarly blasphemous and quite unprintable Italian oath as he bounded down the stairs.

On the way westward in the taxi he only paused long enough to buy her a great spray of orchids and a button-hole for himself. Then, immediately he reached the hotel, he dashed straight to the desk and asked the clerk to telephone her room.

A moment later his worst forebodings were realised. The bland young man behind the reception counter shook his head. 'I'm sorry, sir, Mademoiselle Szenty left here half an hour ago.'

'For good?' snapped Gregory.

'She took her luggage with her.'

'Did she leave an address?'

'No sir, but if you're Mr. Sallust she left a letter for you.'

'I am. Let's have it please.' With swift fingers Gregory tore open the blue envelope and read the few lines upon the single sheet:

My dear,

You work for the police. To confess it, because you hoped to save me, that was generous of you, but if you had known me better you would never have done so. How is it possible that I should ever betray the man who has been so good to my mother and myself?

That you should be engaged in this work is tragic for me. I liked you so very much, but now we must put our brief hour behind us because it is impossible for us ever to meet as friends again.

Sabine.

For a moment Gregory regarded the big box of orchids which he had bought for her a little stupidly. What should he do with them? Those gorgeous blossoms which he had hoped to see gracing her shoulder were useless now: nothing but a bitter mockery of a joy that might have been.

With an impatient gesture he thrust them over to the reception clerk. 'Flowers,' he said briefly. 'If you've got a wife or girl friend they may come in useful.' Then he turned angrily away.

To his surprise he found himself staring into Gerry Wells's freckled face. The young Inspector was standing there, clad in a neat dark-blue lounge suit, a black soft hat dangling in one hand and a walking-stick in the other. He was smiling broadly.

'Well, how's the amateur detective getting on?' he inquired cheerfully.

'He's not,' Gregory snapped. 'For God's sake let's have a drink. I've mucked up the whole darned business.' Then he led the way down the passage to the cocktail bar.

'Let's hear the worst,' Wells suggested when they were seated at one of the little tables with drinks before them.

'I met her here just before lunch,' Gregory tossed off his drink and ordered another, 'staged the party perfectly, brought old Sir Pellinore along so she shouldn't suspect I had any idea she was staying here. In the afternoon she met some buyer at the Royal Palace—then I got her along to my rooms. Everything was going swimmingly until after tea—then I lost my head and behaved like a stupid schoolboy.'

The Inspector chuckled. 'Doesn't do to mix pleasure with business, does it?'

'Dammit, you don't understand,' Gregory burst out. 'I'd rather lose my right hand than see her sent to prison; so I spilled the beans that I was working with the police and knew all about the smuggling racket. Then I begged and prayed of her to save herself by turning King's evidence. She wouldn't promise anything but said she must have time to think and promised to let me take her out to dinner if I called here for her again at eight o'clock. I was pretty well certain I'd persuaded her to come in with us; but when I turned up here a few minutes ago I found she had quit—and quit for good.'

Wells's eyes narrowed a fraction. 'What exactly did you give away to her during these empassioned moments?'

'Oh, don't fret yourself, passion or no I'm a cautious old bird. I only said we were on to Gavin Fortescue's smuggling racket generally. I didn't breathe a word about the secret base between Calais and Boulogne or Quex Park, so there's no reason to suppose that they'll abandon either of those hang-outs. She won't use the Carlton again, of course, and now she knows I'm a sort of unofficial policeman God alone knows if I'll be able to get in touch with her again at all.'

'I wouldn't worry about that.' The Inspector winked suddenly. 'We're not all quite nitwits, you know. I've had a couple of men following her all day, just in case you slipped up. She's on the road to Quex Park now, as I've just learned from one of the flying squad cars that's sitting on her tail, and as soon as I've had a bite to eat I'm flying down myself. When your man told me on the telephone, ten minutes ago, that you'd changed in a hurry to dash out to dinner, I had a hunch I'd find you here. I thought perhaps you might like to go with me—then—maybe you'll see her again this evening after all.'

13

Gregory Sallust Has Cause to Hate His Job

Gregory and Wells considered it unlikely that the smugglers would undertake any operations much before midnight, but Sabine would do the journey to Quex Park in a couple of hours and so should arrive there by a quarter past ten, or a little after. She might remain only long enough to make fresh arrangements then leave again by plane so, as it was essential to keep track of her, they decided to lose no time following her down into Kent.

They had spent barely a quarter of an hour in reviewing the situation, and Gregory reckoned that even allowing for a return to his flat and a scratch meal on the surplus of the supplies got in for Sabine's tea he could reach Croydon, where Wells's plane was stationed, by 9.30, if he was quick changing into more suitable clothes.

He left the Inspector to call at the Yard and go on down to Croydon ahead of him, then he secured a likely looking taxi and promised the driver double fare if they reached Gloucester Road in under twelve minutes. The man earned his extra money with thirty seconds to spare.

On arriving there Gregory sent Rudd for his car while he changed and ate simultaneously. Once he was out of his tails and clad in his battle equipment he sat down to the wheel of his long two-seater with Rudd beside him to bring it back. Taking the short cut across the river through Battersea,

Wandsworth and Tooting, he drove out to Croydon at a speed which shocked onlookers but was actually quite safe for a really expert driver.

Wells was awaiting him, now dressed in airman's kit, beside a single engine 120 h.p. two-seater Tiger Moth.

'Hello! Open cockpit,' said Gregory. 'Wish I'd known; I'd have put on warmer clothes.'

'You'll be all right,' Wells assured him. 'It isn't a long trip and there's a rug inside. Here . . .' he held out a flat neatly packed bundle with arm straps attached. 'Your parachute. It'll help to keep your back warm.'

'Parachute! What the hell do I want with a parachute?' Gregory grunted.

'Nothing, I hope, but I'm afraid you've got to wear it if you're coming in my plane. Government regulations.'

'Oh, well!' Gregory pushed his arms through the loops and fastened the gear about his waist, then climbed into the observer's seat. He never wasted his breath on unnecessary arguments when there was work to be done.

The sun had set at a little before nine. It was nearly dark now and the stars were coming out again for what promised to be another almost cloudless August night.

Gregory had flown a good deal in his time, but he had never quite got accustomed to the amazing speed by which one could cover an actual point to point distance by plane, as compared with road or rail. Twenty-five minutes after leaving Croydon he picked out the great mile-wide belt of trees which gave Quex Park such shelter, yet threw it up from the air in the flat surrounding landscape. Wells kept well to the south of it, passing over the little village of Acol, then veered northward towards the sea. After a moment a single beam of light showed in the fields to the east of the park and he came down towards it.

'I wasn't taking any chances this time,' he shouted back to Gregory as they bumped to a standstill. 'I gave orders for one of my men to show a light here—where you came down before.'

The torch had disappeared but a voice came out of the darkness: 'Mr. Wells?'

'Yes, Simmons, what's the latest?'

'Thompson reported twenty minutes ago, sir. There's nothing fresh, so he's gone back to watch the house again.'

'Good.' The Inspector smiled over his shoulder towards Gregory. 'We've beaten her to it then but she ought to be here fairly soon. Simmons will look after the plane while we go inside and give the lady a silent welcome.'

Gregory grunted non-committally as he climbed out. True, he wanted desperately to get in touch with Sabine again, but not when he was in the Inspector's company. Wells had quite enough evidence upon which to arrest her any moment he chose and Gregory knew that she was only being left at liberty so long as she might prove a useful lead to further evidence which would incriminate Lord Gavin. Once the net closed it would be beyond his power to help her.

It was a dark sultry night again; the very centre of the dark period between moons, which the smugglers were using for their operations. Hence, Gregory felt certain, their intense activity and swift journeying, which would continue for another forty-eight hours at least. After which, unless the weather broke, they would probably not run further cargoes until the moonless period in September.

With Wells beside him he made his way through the pitch-black wooded belt along the east drive to the fringe of the lawn, from where, knowing now the direction of the house, he could distinguish its outline among the surrounding trees less than a hundred yards away.

The hoot of an owl came from some bushes nearby and to Gregory's surprise Wells mimicked the cry in reply. Immediately there was a stirring in the shadows to their left and a figure tiptoed across the gravel path towards them.

'All quiet, Inspector,' said the newcomer in a low voice.

'Thanks, Thompson, you'd better stay here while we go round to the back of the house.' Keeping in the shadow of the trees they tiptoed down a narrow path through the shrubbery until they came out at the rear of the building. A light was burning in the scullery window where Gregory had attempted to break in the night before.

Wells moved along the wall of the house to the doorway and knocked gently on it. There was no reply. He knocked again, louder this time, and there was a sound of footsteps in the stone-flagged passage. The door swung open and Milly's slender form was revealed on the lighted threshold.

'Hullo,' she said in pleased surprise. 'I didn't expect to see you so soon again.'

'Nor I you. I thought you'd be in bed by this time.'

'It's not very late, only just ten, although often I go to bed earlier and listen to the wireless.'

'I like the wireless too,' he smiled, 'but I don't often get the chance of listening to it in bed.'

Gregory, growing impatient at this unimportant conversation, stepped forward out of the shadows and she started back, realising his presence for the first time. He had seen her the night before, but she had not seen him as she had been walking in her sleep. Wells introduced them.

'Won't you both come in?' she said. 'Perhaps you'd like some supper. I ought to have thought of that.'

'No; thanks all the same.' Wells shook his head. 'We fed less than an hour ago, and we'd better not come in, I think, in case somebody comes along to this wing of the house. Our presence might take a bit of explaining as your aunt's not supposed to have visitors.' There was marked regret in his voice as he added: 'We only knocked you up to let you know that some of the people we're after will be here again tonight. Nothing unusual's likely to happen, but I thought it would be a bit of a comfort to know we were close handy here, keeping an eye on things.'

'That *was* nice of you.' She smiled up at him. 'We knew they were coming though. The foreign lady telephoned only a few minutes ago to say that Aunty was to get her some supper. I was just going out to tell your man about it when you turned up.'

'D'you know where she telephoned from?'

'Canterbury. She didn't speak herself. It was a man at some garage who rang up for her.'

'She'll be here pretty soon then?'

'I expect so, but there'll be time for you to have a quick cup of tea, if you'd care to come in for a moment.'

'Better not.' Wells shook his head again. 'Although I'd like to. We'll get back to the bushes I think. Remember me kindly to your aunt.'

'All right. Will I be seeing you again tonight? If so, I'll—well I might stay up for a bit.'

'I'm afraid it's rather unlikely so I'd hop off to bed if I were you. Happy dreams.'

'Same to you. That is if you get any sleep—as I hope you will. Good night.'

When the two men turned away she stood at the half-open door reluctantly watching Wells's retreating back as he disappeared beside Gregory round the corner of the house.

Ten minutes later, from their cover among the bushes, they saw the glimmer of lights between the trees, and the big limousine that Gregory had seen set out for London the night before, roared up the drive with a single dark muffled figure seated inside it.

'Gavin's not with her,' Gregory whispered, as he saw Sabine descend from the car. 'I wonder where he's got to.'

'Lord only knows,' Wells muttered. 'He left the Carlton shortly after midday. I had a man tailing him, of course, but the fool mucked it when they were caught in a traffic block. When I last heard our people hadn't yet been able to pick him up again.'

Lights appeared in the downstair windows of the main part of the house and they guessed that Sabine had settled down to her supper. Meanwhile, they remained behind the bushes; Gerry Wells with the trained patience of a man who spends many hours of his life waiting perforce for things to happen, but Gregory fidgeting a little after the first half hour, wanting to walk up and down to stretch his limbs and wondering if he dare light a cigarette, but deciding against it.

An hour crawled by; then the lights in the downstair rooms went out and fresh lights appeared in one of the upper windows. Another twenty minutes and those went out as well.

'We've come on a wild goose chase,' muttered Gregory, half glad, half angry. 'There's nothing doing here tonight after all. Evidently she only cleared out of the Carlton in order to get away from me; and decided to sleep here.'

'Maybe you're right,' Wells replied noncommittally, 'but don't forget the telegram. From that it looked as though they were on the job tonight as well—didn't it?'

'Perhaps, but they may have a dozen hide-outs and rendezvous as almost all the numbers in the damn thing were different.'

'Sssh, what's that?' Wells caught Gregory's arm and pressed it. The faint low note of a motor engine came clearly to them in the silence. They glanced upwards, half-expecting the approach of a plane, but a moment later realised that a car had entered the west gate of the park a quarter of a mile away. Then they caught the gleam of its headlights flickering through the trees.

It was a long powerful sports model with two men in its bucket seats and it did not stop at the front of the house but went straight round to the garage.

Gregory and Wells slipped through the fringe of trees in order to get a view of the new arrivals but by the time they had reached a point from which they could see the garage the headlights of the car had been switched off.

A torch glimmered in the darkness. By it they could see that the big doors of the garage had been closed upon the car; then the light moved towards them and there was the sound of approaching footsteps. They shrank back into the blacker shadows. The two men passed, the nearest dragging one of his feet a little, and crossed the lawn to the shed that housed Lord Gavin's plane.

A bright light inside the hangar was switched on. In its

glare the two figures, in airman's kit, stood out clearly, one nearly a head taller than the other.

'The Limper,' Gregory whispered. 'How I'd like to get my hands on the brute's throat. He might have blinded me with that bag of pepper he threw in my face at Dives.'

The plane was run out on to the lawn, the lights in the shed switched off, and the two men boarded the machine. The engine roared and spat; then the plane glided forward.

'Come on,' snapped Gregory. 'We've got to run for it or we'll lose them.'

Almost before the plane was in the air Gregory and Wells were sprinting across the soft springy turf behind it. They dived into the belt of trees and stumbled forward tripping and jumping over vaguely seen patches of undergrowth. Then the darkness of the thick leafy branches above blacked out everything.

Stumbling and cursing they blundered on from side to side between the tree trunks until they reached the meadow, then raced on again, heads down, towards the east gate of the park. Breathless and panting they tore across the field to the spot where Simmons was waiting beside Wells's plane. The roar of its powerful engine shattered the silent night and Gregory was only settling in his seat as it sailed into the air.

They knew from the sound of the other machine, before Wells's engine had been turned on, that it was heading south-westward and took that direction. By the time they were up two hundred feet Gregory was scanning the starry sky with his night glasses.

'Got 'em . . .' he shouted down the voice pipe a moment later, '. . . little more to the south. Towards that very bright star low on the horizon.'

The plane in front was climbing and for a few moments Wells flew on at five hundred feet to make up the distance. Both planes were flying without lights and it was difficult to pick up their quarry, but soon, with the aid of Gregory's shouted directions, he caught sight of it.

Five minutes after taking off they picked up the few scattered lights of late-workers or pleasure parties in Canterbury, upon their right, but after that, flying south-west by south, they passed over a stretch of country containing only small villages, from which the glimmers of light were few and far between at this late hour.

Another five minutes and on their left they sighted another little glimmering cluster far below them which both knew, from their course, to be Folkestone. After that the country seemed to become blank and lightless; for once they had passed over the Ashford-Folkestone road they were above the low sparsely inhabited lands of the Romney Marshes.

Wells had climbed to two thousand feet, but the leading plane was just as fast a machine, and flying at a still greater altitude. For three hectic minutes, while Gregory frantically searched the sky with his night glasses, they lost sight of it but, keeping to their course, they flew on over the deserted, lightless, marshlands until a star blacked out for an instant and enabled them to pick up the trail again.

An intermittent revolving beam showed as a pinpoint miles away to their left, and Gregory knew that they were now opposite the Dungeness light. A moment later Wells shouted to him and pointed downwards straight ahead. Two rows of lights were just visible, forming a 'T' in the blackness of the marshes. The other plane was descending towards them and Wells swerved away to the westward in order to avoid being spotted from below. The roar of his engine would, he knew, merge into that of the other plane as long as it remained in the air. He flew on until he was almost over Tenterden, climbing all the time, then turned and came back again to the south-east, climbing still. He was now at five thousand feet when, flying seaward, they passed again the tiny 'T' of lights below.

'Got them,' he yelled to Gregory through the voice pipe.

'But they'll hear us if we fly lower; and away from the "T" of lights it's too risky to make a landing,' Gregory shouted back.

'You'll make the landing,' Wells bawled. 'What's your parachute for, man! Out you go.'

'Not likely,' Gregory bawled. 'Never made a parachute jump in my life—not going to start now. Think I'm going to risk my neck?'

'Dammit, you must,' yelled the Inspector as he banked, circling still higher, over the secret landing ground. 'We'll never find this place in daylight. It's our one chance to register their base. You've got to do it: don't let me down.'

Gregory stared over the side of the plane at the little cluster of lights seeming now so infinitely far below. He was no coward in a fight. All his life he had taken a grim delight in facing odds and winning through where battle with other human beings was concerned—but this was different. To jump from the safety of the plane into thin air with the horrible uncertainty as to whether the parachute would open, or if he would be dashed, a bleeding mass of pulp, on to the distant ground. Was the risk worth it? Why the hell should he? And then the heart-shaped face of Sabine came clear before his eyes.

'If I do, will you let Sabine out?' he cried.

'I can't. You know I can't.' Wells's voice just reached him above the roar of the engine, angry at this frustration when he was so near securing evidence of real importance.

'You must.' Gregory's voice pierced the wind and thunder of the engine; 'otherwise I won't play.'

'Will you—if I agree?' Wells shouted.

'Yes, damn you!' Gregory screamed back.

'I can't speak for my superiors,' bawled Wells.

Gregory was already fumbling at his back, seeing that the parachute was in position. He stood up uncertainly swaying as the plane soared through the air at 150 miles an hour. 'You've got to let her off,' he thundered, leaning over Wells's shoulder, his mouth close to the Inspector's ear.

'Go on, I'll do my best,' Wells turned his face up, shouting, 'won't arrest her myself anyhow.'

Gregory peered over the side again. The thought of leaping into that black immensity of space made his heart contract but he climbed out on to the fuselage. The wind rushed past him tearing at every corner of his garments as though it would strip him naked. For a second there was an awful pain which stabbed him in the pit of the stomach. He felt sick and giddy as he clung on with all his might to prevent the force of the blast ripping his clutching fingers from their precarious hold. Then he took a breath—screwed his face up into a rueful grin—and jumped.

14

By the Brown Owl Inn on Romney Marshes

As Gregory leapt the body of the plane seemed to shoot up like an express lift behind him. He felt himself gripped and twisted as though he was a straw in a tempest; then hurled violently downward. The plane roared away into the darkness above him.

His last thought before going overboard had been: 'Mustn't pull the rip cord until I'm clear of the plane.' He knew little enough about parachute diving, but he'd heard somewhere, back in the war days, before it became a sport and when it was only undertaken as a dire necessity, that many a stout fellow had come to grief because he'd opened his parachute at the moment of jumping and it had caught in the fuselage of the machine, tearing the fabric and so making it useless or hanging the miserable parachutist.

He had not realised that in such cases the machine, crippled and often burning from anti-aircraft shell or the enemy's inflammatory bullets, was falling too and that the wretched pilot might be a moment or more before, dropping with greater speed, he could get any distance from the wreckage; whereas in a normal jump, such as he had just made, he had been torn away from the fast-moving plane in a fraction of a second.

His fear, that if he had his hand on the rip cord the shock of the jump might open it immediately, had caused him to stretch his arms out sideways so that he could not possibly pull it inadvertently. Now, as he was flung face downwards by the rushing air current, his arms were forced back behind his shoulders and he was hurtling earthwards like a diver who has taken a fancy jump from a springboard, head foremost into the sea. The wind had ceased to turn him but seemed instead to be rushing upwards as he plunged down into the awful void.

Nearly a mile below him lay the earth; pitch black and terrifying; the friendly trees and inequalities of surface which formed its landscape blotted out by the midnight gloom. Not a light was to be seen in any direction, except the little 'T' of flares which now appeared to be some way towards his right as he shot earthwards.

With horrifying rapidity the 'T' grew larger. By a stupendous effort he forced his right arm inwards to grab the rip cord. The wind, tearing at his left as at some fin, instantly flung him over on to his back, and then, to his utter horror, he began to spin like a top.

His fingers were numb from the icy blast of the rushing air. He had an awful moment when he feared that they would no longer have sufficient feeling left in them for him to use them. Cursing himself for a panicky fool he tried to snatch comfort from the thought that plenty of people who did this thing for fun took extra pleasure in waiting until the very last moment before opening their parachute and that he must have a long way yet to drop.

It seemed an age since he had sprung off the plane; an eternity since he had begun his fight against the up-rushing air to force his hand into the ripcord. At last he found it and, half-choking from relief, jerked it with all his might.

Nothing happened. He pulled again but the cord was hanging loose now in his hand. Still nothing happened. He made a desperate effort to force his head round so that he could look over his shoulder. The movement flung him out of his spin and he was facing the earth head downwards again. The 'T' of flares was much bigger now. It seemed like some fiery group of stars rushing up out of the darkness which would roar past him over his right shoulder with the speed of an express train at any second. But it wouldn't—he knew that. When his right shoulder came level with the flares he would hit the earth. It would be as though some giant, greater than any fabled hero, had flung the whole world at him. He would be broken, burst, shattered into a thousand fragments by that appalling impact.

Almost sick with horror, he pulled and pulled at the useless rip cord, while he alternately cursed his utter folly in flinging himself to his death and gasped breathless prayers to God to save him.

Time ceases to exist at such awful moments. He was still plunging downwards at a fantastic speed and had virtually given himself up as finished when, without a second's warning, his arms were nearly torn from their sockets and a violent jerk at the belt round his middle drove the breath out of his body.

He had forgotten that a short interval must elapse between releasing the parachute and its opening to its full spread when it would arrest his headlong descent. Now, as that thought flashed into his agonised mind, he could still hardly believe that the safety device had begun to function efficiently the second he had pulled the cord.

His feet sank down lower than his head and before he knew quite what had happened he was standing upright, swaying a little from side to side, his long legs dangling.

Almost collapsing with relief he found he could look upwards and saw the dome of the fully opened parachute like a great dark mushroom against the starlit sky above.

For the first time since leaving the plane he was able to gasp in a full breath and look about him consciously. The 'T' of flares towards his right was still larger now but only the blackness of the land below had caused him to think he was so near it. His terror had been engendered by his complete inexperience; for he had made a good take off, although he had lost some seconds before being able to pull the rip cord, but when he had done so the parachute had opened perfectly normally.

The swaying motion increased, until he was covering an arc of about thirty degrees; as if he were the pendulum of some huge clock. He knew he should try to check the movement, otherwise he might make a bad landing, but he did not know how to, not realising that a pair of ropes now dangling one at each side of him were for that purpose. Apart from the fear that he might suddenly be swung into a tree he found the motion rather enjoyable. The lights were now rising gently towards his right, but he did not seem to be coming any nearer to them, and he judged that he would make his landing quite a long way from the smugglers' secret base.

As they came low on the horizon it warned him that he was nearing earth and he gathered his muscles taut together, so that as his feet touched he might spring into the air again, in order to reduce the force of the impact. A faint shimmer showed to his left and he realised that it was the reflection of the starlight upon a winding creek of water. Next moment the flares disappeared from view; blotted out by an unseen crest. Then his right foot hit something with a thud and instantly he was sprawling on the ground with every ounce of breath knocked out of his body.

He clutched wildly at the grass as he felt himself moving still, but sideways now, dragged by the parachute. Bumping over a ditch he was pulled into some low bushes. There was a sharp crackling as the dry twigs snapped and he thrust up his arms to protect his face, then the dragging ceased, for the parachute had sunk to earth.

For a moment he remained there, bruised and breathless, then he struggled into a sitting position and wriggled out of his harness. Only a dull glow, coming from over a crest of rising ground to the north, now indicated the smugglers' landing place. He stood up and pulled his big torch from his pocket then cursed aloud as he found that his fall had broken the bulb. He had meant to bundle up the expensive parachute and hide it somewhere but time was precious and he dared not waste it fumbling round for something that he could not see. Except for the lighter patch of sky low on the horizon to the northward, caused by the flares and the faint starlight, the whole countryside was shrouded in darkness. Abandoning the parachute he set off towards the north. Only the deeper patches of blackness indicated the taller grass and low bushes when he was almost upon them while there was nothing at all to show the frequent ditches which intersected the marshes.

Pressing forward warily, he stumbled at almost every step, and was compelled by some obstacle to alter his course every ten yards or so. He thanked his gods at least that it was August. Most of the smaller water courses now had dry beds and the marshland squelched under foot only in the lower places. To have attempted to cross this wild country in winter would have been impossible; he would have been bogged for a certainty.

As it was, he had to cross two creeks; stagnant, scummy bands of water with muddy bottoms which dragged and sucked at his boots when he floundered through them and thrust his way among the tall knife-like reeds that fringed their banks.

It was a nightmare journey. Wet to the waist, tired, bruised and angry, he struggled onward; yet the glow from the flares seemed little nearer and the going so difficult he doubted if he had traversed more than half a mile in twenty minutes. Then he came to a wire fence, climbed over, and found a steep grassy bank, up which he crawled on all fours. The top was level; next moment he tripped over a sleeper and came down heavily between two railway lines.

Picking himself up with renewed curses, he found he could now see the flares some distance away on the far side of the embankment, and turned northwest along it.

Knowing how quickly the smugglers completed their operations, he began to hurry; fearing that with all the time he had lost plunging into ditches and over tussocks of coarse grass he would be too late to find out what was going on.

He had barely covered another two hundred yards when he caught the sound of a train puffing up behind him from Dungeness and, jumping off the permanent way, slid down the bank to conceal himself while it passed.

A short goods train of no more than half a dozen closed wagons rumbled by shaking the embankment. The sparks from its engine and glare of the furnace temporarily lit up a small section of the surrounding country.

When the train had gone past Gregory stumbled on to the permanent way again and set off after it. To his surprise he saw it pull up ahead of him, opposite the flares, so he broke into a jog trot, spurred on by the thought that his gruelling experiences of the last hour might, after all, have been well worth while.

Five minutes later he was within fifty yards of the train's rear wagon and, slipping down the far side of the embankment, he crawled along under its cover still nearer, until he could see by the bright light of the landing flares the business which was proceeding. Beyond the flares were a couple of big planes and the smaller one in which the Limper had arrived from Quex Park. The others had already left and big stacks of boxes at intervals on a level stretch of ground showed where they had unloaded their cargoes. One of the large planes took the air as he watched and he was able to see enough of it to recognise it as a 240 h.p. twin-engine de Havilland Dragon, which would normally carry eight passengers, but in their place was capable of transporting about half a ton of cargo.

From the sound of the engine, as the plane circled in the air, he knew that something of its cruising speed, which should have been 140 m.p.h., had been sacrificed by the appliance of the latest silencing devices, so that the noise of even a fleet of these machines, crossing the coastline at six thousand feet, would barely be noticeable and certainly not sufficient to attract undue attention.

At the bottom of the embankment he wriggled through the

fence and found a dry gully which offered such excellent cover that he determined to risk crawling even nearer; soon he was crouching in it no more than twenty yards from the landing ground.

About forty men were working with frantic speed unloading the goods train; pitching dozens of wooden boxes from it down the embankment. They had already cleared the first three wagons and, while a number of them attacked the rest, the others went off to the dumps which had been unloaded from the planes, then began to carry the boxes towards the empty wagons.

For ten minutes Gregory remained a silent spectator of their intense activity. By the end of that time the contraband cargo had all been loaded on to the train, the wagons relocked, the last big plane was gone, and all the flares except one had been put out.

The train moved off and, rapidly gathering speed, disappeared in the direction of London. The men then flung themselves upon the great higgledy-piggledy pile of boxes which had been thrown out of it, and started to hump them across the landing ground, disappearing into the belt of shadows beyond which the flare did not penetrate.

'What now?' thought Gregory. 'My luck's been in so far and I'm not chucking up till I find out what they do with the stuff.' Crawling back by way of the ditch, he began to make a detour outside the lighted patch of ground and, after going a hundred yards, he stumbled through some low bushes, up a small bank and on to a road. Having crossed it, he slid down the slope on the other side and proceeded to follow the line of the lane, which curved slightly. The flare was some distance away, but he could hear muffled voices carried on the night wind to the front of him and, a moment later, came upon a thick hedge which barred his passage.

Scrambling up the bank again he got round the corner of the hedge and saw that it hid the kitchen garden of a solitary house, which loomed up before him, abutting on the road. A faint square of light filtering through a heavy curtain marked one of its downstair windows.

He got down on his hands and knees and crawled forward under cover of the hedge which here fringed the roadside. The voices of the men grew louder as he advanced and then he saw the dark outline of a lorry. There were others behind it and on these the men were busily loading the boxes that had come off the train.

From this new position he could see some of the smugglers in the distance, silhouetted against the light of the flare, as with the boxes on their shoulders they trudged in Indian file across the grassland. Suddenly the last flare was put out and two minutes later the loading of the lorries was completed. The men climbed into them and the lightless convoy set off in the direction of New Romney.

One by one they crawled past Gregory, where he crouched in the shadows, and shortly after the last one had disappeared a sudden vibrant hum, which grew lower and then receded, told him that the Limper had departed unseen in his plane. The rumble of the lorries faded in the distance and an utter silence closed down upon the deserted stretch of country. Not a sign or sound remained to show the illegal activity which had been going on there so recently.

Gregory came out into the lane and tiptoed along it towards the front of the silent house. The light in the ground floor room had gone out but there was now one showing in a front window upstairs. The heavy curtains had been carelessly drawn and a bright ray filtered through between them. The window was too high for Gregory to see into the room, but a wooden sign above the doorway of the place showed that it was a wayside inn and, by the light which came from the crack between the curtains he was just able to make out the lettering upon it. Thankful that he would be able to find the place again in this desolate stretch of country he read the faded lettering on the weatherbeaten board. It was the Brown Owl Inn and he knew that it must lie within a few hundred yards of the railway line south of Romney.

Turning away, he walked up the road for a hundred yards and lit a cigarette. He was unutterably tired and now he had to trudge he didn't know how many miles before he could get a lift into Ashford. That seemed the nearest place where there would be any chance of his picking up an early train. He could sleep there, of course, or knock up some pub which he might pass on his road, but that did not fit in with his way of doing things. Wells would be anxious about him and eager to hear the result of his night's work. The extra hour or two in passing on the information he had secured might make all the difference so, tired as he was, he hardly thought of bed, but determined to get back to Quex Park at the earliest possible moment. Chin down, and in his long loping stride, he set off up the road inland.

15

Glorious Day

Inspector Gerry Wells was the lucky one this time. He very definitely had the soft side of the deal and, while the wretched Gregory was still hurtling through the air in fear of an imminent and horrible death, the Inspector turned his plane north-westward heading back towards Thanet. He was not risking any more night landings in the fields outside Quex Park without adequate reason so he came down on the well-lit landing ground of the Royal Air Force Depot at Manston, about midway between Quex Park, Margate and Ramsgate. Having presented his official card to the officer on duty, the courtesy of accommodation for his plane was extended to him and he managed to get a lift in a car to Margate where, feeling that he had earned a comfortable night's rest, he went straight to the Queen's Highcliffe Hotel.

One of the hotel guests had had to return to London suddenly that evening because his son had been taken dangerously ill. It was only this fortuitous chance which enabled the night porter to give the detective a bed at the height of the August season with every room booked for a month ahead.

Early rising was a habit with Gerry Wells. He was as fit as a fiddle in wind and limb and a few hours of deep healthy sleep were all he needed to prepare him for another almost indefinite period of activity.

Splashing in his bath at half past six he only controlled the impulse to burst into song at the thought of the other guests who were still sleeping. He was not unduly worried about Gregory because he knew the care with which service parachutes are packed and inspected; it never even occurred to him that the great silk balloon might fail to open.

He thought that Gregory might perhaps have had a bit of a shaking when he landed, owing to the fact that he had never had any instruction in parachute jumping, but Mr. Sallust was a tough customer to the Inspector's mind and, therefore, should come to little harm. Moreover, Wells had made certain that his unofficial colleague would drop well away from the smugglers' base so there was no likelihood of his descending in the midst of their illegal activities and being bumped on the head for his pains.

As the Inspector rubbed himself vigorously with his towel his thoughts turned to Milly Chalfont at the Park. What a delightful little thing she was, so slight and graceful, so utterly unspoiled, and so friendly too in spite of her apparent shyness. Gerry was rather a shy fellow himself where women were concerned and although he could admire Sabine as a work of art he would have been terrified of having anything to do with her outside his official business.

While he dressed he reviewed the situation and found it good. His investigation had progressed by leaps and bounds in the last forty-eight hours, thanks of course largely to that lean, queer, cynical devil, Gregory Sallust, but Wells had no stupid pride about the matter. It was his job to run Lord

Gavin's crew to earth and he was only too grateful for any help which might be given him. He assumed, quite reasonably, not knowing what a tiger Gregory could be when he had got his teeth into a thing, that his ally, stranded in Romney Marshes, would spend the night at some local inn, whether he had secured any information or not and, therefore, it was most unlikely that he would put in an appearance again much before midday. There was nothing Wells could do to further his inquiry until Gregory turned up and the golden August morning lay before him. His thoughts gravitated again towards Milly and Quex Park. Had Sabine spent the night there or gone off again after all? In any case it obviously seemed his business to go over and find out.

After an early breakfast he paid his bill and left the hotel. Crowds of holiday makers had risen early too. Family parties, the children with their spades and pails, the elders with their towels and bathing costumes slung across their shoulders, were already making their way from boarding houses and apartments down Petman's Gap to play cricket on the sands, or bathe in the shallow waters of the low tide, which sparkled in the sunlight, ebbing and rippling in little chuckling waves a quarter of a mile away from the tall white cliffs. Gerry Wells watched them with a smile. He liked to see people happy, but he wondered what they would think if they knew of his last night's adventure. That he was a Scotland Yard man they might credit easily enough; that he was on a special inquiry and had been allotted an aeroplane to undertake it, would cause interest and a pleasant feeling that they were in the know about the police not being such a slow-witted lot
some people were inclined to think; but if he had
that this international smuggling racket
more important than anyone could su
to dangerous criminals and agi
night, and so evading
that bombs and
lead to

tower over there too,' she glanced towards their left where a tall brick building crowned a low fenced-in mound that rose from the grass land. 'The old gardener told me that Major Powell-Cotton's father was awfully keen on ships and things; so he used to signal from it to his friends in the navy when they sailed across the bay. The sea is hidden from us here by the trees but it's only a mile away.'

'I see he made a collection of old cannons too,' Wells remarked, looking at the six-deep semi-circle of ancient guns which occupied the mound.

'That's right. Some of them came from the *Royal George*, I'm told, and the little baby ones were taken from Kingsgate Castle. The mound itself is an old Saxon burial ground, raised in honour of some great chief, and it's supposed to be the reason we have a ghost here. She's called the White Lady and walks along a path through the woods behind the tower at night, until she reaches the mound, then she disappears. They say she's the chief's young wife and she haunts the place where he was buried.'

'Ever seen her?'

'No, and I don't think anyone has for a long time now; all the same I wouldn't walk along that path at night for anything.'

'Not if I were with you?' Gerry asked, smiling at her.

She blushed a little. 'Well, I might then—that would be different.'

A few moments later they reached the park gates and took the by-roads through the open cornfields towards Manston. They were silent for a good portion of their two-mile walk but strangely happy in each other's company.

At the aerodrome a friendly artificer lent Milly a flying coat and she was soon installed in the observer's seat of Wells's Tiger Moth, a little scared, but even more excited at starting on her first flight.

For nearly an hour they cruised over eastern Kent, first along the northern shore over Birchington, Herne Bay and Whitstable, then south-east to Canterbury, where the towers of the ancient cathedral, lifting high above the twisting streets of the town, were thrown up by the strong sunlight which patterned the stonework like delicate lace against the black shadows made by its embrasures. Ten minutes later they had reached the coast again and were circling over Hythe on the southern shore of the county. Turning east they visited Sandgate, Folkestone and Dover, flying low round the tower of the old castle upon its cliff, while below them the cross-Channel steamers and the destroyers in the Admiralty basin looked like toy ships that one could pick up in the hand and push out with a stick upon a voyage across a pond. Away over the Channel the white cliffs of Calais showed faintly in the summer haze. From Dover they sailed on to Walmer, Deal and Sandwich, then across Pegwell Bay to Ramsgate, and completed the circle of the Thanet coast by passing low over the long beaches of Broadstairs, Margate and Westgate, where the holiday crowd swarmed like black ants in their thousands and countless white faces stared up towards the roaring plane, waving hands and handkerchiefs in salutation as it soared low overhead.

'Well, how did you like it?' Gerry Wells turned to glance over his shoulder as he brought the plane to a halt once more on the Manston landing ground.

'It—it was fine,' Milly said a little breathlessly. She had feared that she might be air-sick, but the thrill of watching the tiny human figures in the sunlit fields, and town after town as they circled above them, with some new interest constantly arising out of the far horizon had made her completely forget her fear after the first few moments. Her cheeks were glowing now with a gentle flush from the swift wind of their flight and her blue eyes were sparkling in her delicate little face with happy exhilaration.

As Wells helped her out of the plane he had not the least twinge of conscience at having neglected his duties for an hour or so to give her the experience. He had no regular hours and his work often kept him up all night so he felt perfectly justified in taking this little break which had given Milly and himself so much pleasure.

Having seen his plane into its borrowed hangar they set out again for Quex Park and arrived back at the east gate by half past eleven. Their friendship had now grown to such a state that talking no longer proved a difficulty and Milly was giving him an account of her childhood which, although utterly lacking in all interest for most people, he found quite absorbing.

When they reached the house they went into Mrs. Bird's sitting-room and found a lanky, unshaven, bedraggled figure lounging in one of the worn arm-chairs. It was Gregory and he was in none too good a humour.

He smiled at them with a cynical twist of his thin lips. 'Well, you had a good time I hope? Thinking of settling down in Thanet for a holiday?'

Gerry Wells raised his eyebrows. 'So you're back already? I hardly thought you'd be likely to get here before midday.'

'It's lucky I'm here at all,' snapped Gregory. 'Having risked my neck with that blasted parachute of yours. Still, I've been kicking my heels here just on two hours, while you've been disporting yourself, I gather, with the intention of showing Miss Chalfont what a mighty fine pilot you are.'

Milly went crimson. 'I—I think I'd better go and find Aunty, if you'll excuse me,' she murmured uncomfortably, all the gaiety gone out of her pretty little face.

'Run along, my dear,' Gregory said more amiably. 'It's not your fault if our heroic policeman decides to take time off to amuse himself—and I'm not his boss anyway.'

Wells drew his shoulders back a little as the girl fled from the room. 'I take what time off I like, Mr. Sallust, but don't let's quarrel over that. Did you have any luck when you landed?'

Gregory shrugged. 'As I survived the ordeal it was almost inevitable that I should. Their headquarters down there is a little place called the Brown Owl Inn. It's miles from anywhere—in the middle of the marshes—but near the railway.

line running from Dungeness to Ashford. I had to stagger a mile through every sort of muck before I got near enough to see what was going on and by that time most of the planes had dumped their stuff and got off again. The interesting thing is, though, that while I was there a goods train came in from Dungeness and unloaded several hundred wooden cases, then the cases the planes had brought were loaded on to it instead, and it puffed off, presumably to London. Afterwards the stuff from the train was loaded on to a fleet of lorries which duly trundled away inland; all the gang who had handled both sets of goods going with them. The two different lots of cases, which were swapped over, had exactly the same appearance, by the way.'

Wells's eyes brightened. 'I think I get the idea. They're probably shipping cargoes of non-dutiable goods in a small freighter. Those would be cleared by the customs without any charges in the normal way, of course, then consigned to London by the railway. But they must have got at some of the railway people to halt the goods train for a few moments near their secret landing ground; then the contraband that the planes bring over is substituted for the non-dutiable stuff and delivered in London without any questions being asked.'

'That's about it,' said Gregory, 'though why they should bother to make the exchange I don't quite see.'

'I do,' Wells grinned. 'A fleet of lorries anywhere near the coast at night might quite well be pulled up by one of the preventative men. By using this method they eliminate that risk and get the contraband straight through to London. The thing we've got to find out now is the address where the goods are to be delivered at the other end—after they leave the London goods depot.'

Gregory produced the carefully folded form of the stolen telegram, addressed to Corot, from his pocket and spread it out although he knew its contents by heart now. 'Look,' he said, 'at the last two lines, "*Seventh*", that was yesterday, 43 47, "*Eighth*", that's today, 43, *again* 47. From the repetition of the numbers it looks a reasonably safe bet they mean to use the same landing ground to run another cargo tonight; but we're not having any funny business with parachutes this time. We'll fly over to Ashford this evening, hire a nice safe car there, park it somewhere where it won't be noticed a few hundred yards from the Brown Owl and see what's doing. Maybe, if the luck holds, we'll be able to secure the information you want.'

'Fine,' Wells agreed. 'We'll have to get on that train somehow, if it's only for a moment, so that I can get the address to which the goods are being forwarded in London.'

The next move having been arranged, Gregory decided to go in to Margate. It did not trouble him that the room Wells had occupied at the Queen's had probably already been let again, owing to the holiday rush, as the proprietors of the St. George's were old friends of his and he felt certain that, however full up they were, they would fix him up with a bath and a bed for the afternoon. Margate too was more convenient than Birchington for Manston Aerodrome, so it was agreed that Wells should pick him up at the St. George's, before going out there, at seven o'clock.

As Gregory stood up Mrs. Bird came in. 'You'd better make yourselves scarce now you two,' she said. 'That Miss Szenty is a proper lazy one, lying abed there and wasting all this lovely morning, but I've just taken her breakfast up so she'll be down shortly, and you don't want her to see either of you about the place. She says she'll be staying here for the next few nights so you'd best watch out when you visit us again or you may run into her in the garden.'

'Thanks, Mrs. Bird. I'm just off,' Gregory told her. It was some small comfort to be reasonably certain that he would be able to find Sabine there if an emergency made it necessary for him to get hold of her in the next day or two. Tired as he was, he wished desperately that he could remain and see her when she came downstairs, if only for a few moments, but he dared not risk it. His previous blunder was still fresh in his mind. It was a hundred to one that she would take to flight again the second she got rid of him and, in addition, it would give away the fact that the police knew Lord Gavin to be the tenant of Quex Park.

'Coming, Wells?' he said abruptly.

'Not your way,' the Inspector answered with a shade of embarrassment. 'As I'll be at a loose end till this evening I thought of spending the afternoon in Birchington.'

'Take her to lunch at the Beresford,' suggested Gregory with a cynical twist of his lip. 'Be careful you don't get run in for cradle snatching though.'

Gerry Wells flushed angrily. He saw no reason why he should deny himself the pleasure of remaining in Milly's immediate vicinity, and asking her to lunch with him had been the very thing he had had in mind, but before he could think of an appropriate retort Gregory had turned his back and slouched out of the door.

'He's a rum one and no mistake,' murmured Mrs. Bird gazing after him resentfully.

'Oh, he's all right,' Wells shrugged. 'Bitter at times as though something had hurt him once, right inside if you know what I mean, but there's something about him that one can't help liking, all the same.'

Milly accepted the Inspector's invitation joyfully and they lunched together at the hotel. An hour later they were bathing in the west bay beyond the town. The tide was in now but a narrow strip of golden sand enabled them to sun themselves afterwards and Wells thought it altogether the most delightful day he had ever experienced.

He would have like to linger on the beach indefinitely but his sense of duty to be done did not allow him even to consider such an attractive prospect, so, a little after six, he set off again and by seven he had collected Gregory from the St. George's Hotel, shaved now and refreshed from his bath, sleep, and an excellent dinner. An hour later, having made the hop to Ashford in Wells's plane, they were running out of the town in a small hired car towards the scene of Gregory's adventures on the previous night.

By the time they had completed their fifteen-mile run the

sun was setting and soon twilight obscured the more distant prospects across the low-lying marshland. They pulled up at the Brown Owl Inn and went inside for a drink; just as though they were a couple of ordinary motorists.

It was a tiny place, much smaller than it had seemed to Gregory when half-obscured by semi-darkness the night before, and boasted only one small parlour which served the purpose of saloon, private bar, lounge and tap-room, all in one. A big red-faced man, who seemed to be the owner of the place, as well as barman, served them. His manner was surly and off-hand so they failed to draw him into conversation, as they did not wish to arouse his suspicions by forcing themselves upon him and appearing too inquisitive.

Gregory, never at a loss for a plausible lie, said that they were employed by the Ordnance Department, and had to spend the night at Lydd, the Artillery depot, in order to witness some experimental firing with a new gun which would take place early the following morning.

The landlord listened to their statement with a nod of his head but made no comment on it. He had accepted a drink for politeness' sake, but lounged there behind his bar, stolid and apparently uninterested in their business.

Wells stood another round of drinks then, as an old grandfather clock in the corner of the low room chimed nine, he said to Gregory: 'We'd better be getting on I think,' so they went out to their car and drove away.

Gregory pointed out the actual landing-place of the smuggler planes as they passed it in the car just after leaving the Brown Owl. It was a long flat stretch of grassland about three hundred yards wide, between the railway embankment and the road. The place showed no trace of occupation in the evening light and they thought it better not to make a closer inspection of it in case they were observed from the windows of the inn.

The Inspector asked Gregory if he thought he could find the place again where he had abandoned the parachute; so that they might try and retrieve that expensive piece of Government property before darkness set in.

'Drive on for another half-mile or so towards the coast,' Gregory suggested, 'then we'll have a look round and see if we can spot it. We've got to park the car somewhere well out of sight, anyway.'

A few moments later they found a grassy stretch to the left of the road, over which they could drive the car for fifty yards, and they pulled up between two low mounds where there was little chance of it being discovered after nightfall.

Gregory got out and, scaling the fence, ran up the railway embankment. The landscape was dusky now in the fading twilight but, almost at once he saw a grey blob, a little to his right on the far side of the railway. It was the parachute; its tangled cords and material draped over some low bushes.

Calling Wells he set off towards it; marvelling at the ease with which he could cross the tricky country compared to the frightful time he had had when blundering over it in pitch darkness.

They bundled up the parachute and got it back to the car, then settled down to wait, knowing that there was no prospect of the smuggler fleet arriving for another two hours at least.

Fortunately they had brought some sandwiches with them and, sitting on two tussocks of coarse grass, they made a leisurely meal which whiled away a fraction of the time before them.

The night had now closed in and the time of waiting seemed interminable but they had known that they would have to face it if they were to see the landing place by daylight. Gradually the hours dragged themselves along until, at half past eleven, they decided to leave the vicinity of the car and conceal themselves somewhere nearer to the landing ground, so that they would be able to overlook it.

They walked back past the inn, where a single light was still burning in one of the windows, and a few moments later discovered the bushes into which Gregory had blundered the night before. Following these they arrived at the gully under the railway embankment, where he had lain hidden, and decided that it was as good a spot as any from which to observe the operations of the smugglers.

They had been settled down there for about twenty minutes when they caught the noise of a car approaching from inland down the lonely road. It halted outside the inn and soon afterwards the shadowy figures of a little group of men appeared on the landing ground. There was a hissing sound and suddenly a bright flare lit the scene, then the watchers saw that the men were planting big acetylene cylinders in the 'T' shaped formation, to indicate the direction of the wind. A few moments more and all the flares were burning brightly.

Wells and Gregory sat tight, knowing that no time would be wasted now the flares had been lit and, within a few moments, they heard the roar of an aeroplane engine as it approached from the north-west.

The plane landed and they recognised it as the four seater which both of them had seen leave Quex Park on the previous night. A tall figure descended from it and limped up to the men by the flares. Evidently it was the Limper's business to see each cargo safely landed and sent on to its unknown destination.

Next, there was a rumble on the road. Gregory and Wells could not see them but, as it ceased somewhere beyond the inn, they guessed that the fleet of lorries had arrived with the crews who would hump the illicit cargo, and about thirty more men came on to the ground in groups of twos and threes. A new note now came from high up in the sky to eastward, a steady drone which rapidly grew louder, then one by one the de Havillands, lightless but obviously well-practised in making night landings at this secret base, came bouncing forward out of the heavy darkness to land in the glare of the flares.

A group of men ran over to each plane as its propellers ceased to twinkle and began to unload its cargo with well-drilled precision. Then, as the last plane landed, there came the puff, puff, puff of the midnight train, and the earth quivered below the embankment until its driver brought it to a standstill.

Wells touched Gregory upon the elbow and began to back away down the gully. Gregory followed, and when they were out of earshot the Inspector whispered: 'We've got to get over the bank—far side of the train—so they can't see us by those beastly lights. Then we'll try and get into one of the wagons unobserved.'

Climbing the wire fence, they crawled up the steep slope, crossed the permanent way on hands and knees, slid down the other side, and made their way back to the place where the train was standing.

Intense activity was now in progress on the far side of it. The men were hurling out the boxes from its foremost wagons. Wells scaled the bank again and slung himself up on to one of the rear trucks but found it padlocked. Gregory tried another with the same disappointing result. Dropping off, the two men conferred again in whispers.

'They won't unlock the doors of the vans on this side,' Gregory muttered.

'No. Got to take a chance on being spotted and reach the boxes,' Wells replied. 'Come on, let's get beneath the train and wait our opportunity.'

They crawled between the wheels, Wells leading, then a little way along, until they were below some couplings where two of the vans were hitched to one another. The smugglers were hard at work unloading within a few feet of them. The planes which had first arrived, now emptied of their cargo, were already leaving.

One of the wooden cases, which the smugglers were pitching out of the wagons, caught in the rough grass only about a third of the way down the embankment. Wells craned his neck to see the markings on it but the side towards him was in deep shadow. He poked his head out from below the train and took a quick glance round. The men were sweating and cursing as they heaved other cases down the bank. Speed seemed to be the essence of the whole operation and they evidently knew it. The drill, as the Inspector saw it, was that less than half an hour should elapse between the lighting of the flares to show the landing ground, and their extinction; while the train paused on its journey for about seven minutes only.

Gerry Wells decided to take a chance. Praying to all his gods that if the men saw him in the semi-darkness they would take him to be one of themselves, he slipped out from beneath the train and, drawing himself upright, launched himself upon the stranded case. As he heaved it up to throw it down among the rest, he tried to read the big label which was tacked to its top, before it left his hands.

'Hi!' a shout came out of the darkness in his rear. 'What's that feller doing there?' It was the driver or the fireman who had witnessed his sudden appearance from underneath the train.

Instantly the mob of workers dropped their cases and turned towards him. Next moment a new voice called from the bottom of the embankment. 'You there—come here—else I'll plug you.'

A torch flashed out, and Gregory, who was still concealed under the train, an immobile witness of the scene, saw that the order came from the Limper.

For a second Gregory's hand closed on the butt of his automatic, but this was England. If he shot the fellow all sorts of unpleasantness would result. He shifted his grip swiftly to his torch instead and silently drew himself up between the two coaches. Then, before Wells had time to answer, he flung it with all his force and unerring aim straight at the Limper's head.

'Run, man!' Gregory shouted, as the torch struck the Limper full on the forehead. 'Run!'

The Limper went down under the impact of the missile. Wells leapt on to the permanent way, but the man who had first spotted the Inspector sprang from the step of the engine cab and grabbed him round the waist.

Next moment the Limper was on his feet again, yelling

blasphemous instructions to his men as half a dozen of them closed in on Gregory.

He laid one of them out with a blow behind the ear and tripped another who went plunging head-over-heels down the embankment.

Wells had torn himself from the grip of the man who had jumped off the train and turned to Gregory's assistance, but below them now the smugglers were running from all directions, throwing themselves over the fence and scrambling up the bank. The Inspector hit out valiantly but he could not reach Gregory, who had been dragged to the ground. A second later he too was hurled off his feet by the rush of a dozen brawny ruffians. He went down with a thud, one of the men kicked him in the ribs and another, kneeling on his back, pinioned his arms behind him.

16

Hideous Night

Bruised and half stunned from their desperate struggle the two men were lugged to their feet and thrust down the bank. Half a hundred threatening figures milled round them, their scowling faces lit by the glare of the torches. Pilots, loaders, and the men off the train—all left their jobs to crowd about the captives. Every man on the secret base arrived at the scene of the excitement where they jostled together muttering hoarse questions.

A tall figure elbowed his way through the press. 'Silence!' he thundered. 'Stand back there. I'll attend to this.'

It was the Limper. The men gave way before him, forming a semi-circle, while he stood in its centre glowering at the prisoners, a little trickle of blood oozing from his forehead where Gregory's torch had cut it.

'You, you, you, you,' he jabbed his finger at four husky fellows, 'take these birds over to the inn. The rest of you get back to work. This upset's put us two minutes behind schedule. You've got to make it up. To work! Like blazes now!'

The four men thrust Gregory and the Inspector forward. The Limper followed close behind with the sharp warning: 'No tricks now. I'll shoot you in the back the instant you try anything.'

The breath having been kicked and beaten out of their bodies they were in no state at the moment to do more than stagger along between their captors; even if they had been mad enough to think of attempting a breakaway.

At the inn they were dragged into the little bar parlour and the door slammed to behind them. The fat landlord was still behind his bar and the handsome knife-thrower of Trouville, now in airman's kit, leaned against it drinking a tot of brandy.

'*Q'est-ce qu'il-y-a,*' he exclaimed, as the others tumbled into the room.

'Spies,' snapped the Limper. 'Caught trying to board the train. Preventative officers I expect; we'll soon find out.'

The Frenchman evidently understood English. An evil little smile twitched at his lips. With a single jerk he drew a murderous-looking knife from his sleeve. '*Espions, hein,*' he murmured. '*Ca s'arrange trés simplement.*'

'Stop that, Corot.' The Limper jerked his hand out swiftly at the Frenchman's knife. 'This is not the place. Now you,' he swung on Gregory, 'what's your little game?'

Gregory pulled himself together as well as he could with the two thugs still hanging on his arms. 'What's yours?' he blustered, 'that's more to the point. We've got no game. We were just lost in the marshes. Seeing the lights we came over to ask if you could put us on our road again; but before we had time to open our mouths we were set upon.'

'That's a lie,' said the landlord, leaning forward over his

bar. 'The two of them were here at nine o'clock. Said they were attached to the Ordnance Department and on their way to spend the night at Lydd.'

'So we were,' Gregory protested hotly, 'but our car broke down and we tried to get back here to telephone. We took what we thought was a short cut and lost ourselves. We've been tumbling about in dykes and ditches for hours.'

'That's so,' Wells affirmed, glaring with feigned indignation at the Limper. 'You may be the boss of this gang of railway workers, employed on special night construction that's being kept dark by the Government for some purpose, but that doesn't give you the right to manhandle people. If you don't let us go at once I'll report this matter to the police.'

It was a gallant attempt to persuade the Limper that they had no idea of his real business; but at the sound of Wells's voice Corot took a few mincing steps forward, peered into the Inspector's face, and then began to laugh; a low unpleasant chuckle.

'What's bitten you?' the Limper asked him.

He shrugged. '*Tiens! C'est ce scélérat de Scotland Yard avec qui nous nous sommes brouillé à Trouville.*' Then he turned, stared at Gregory for a moment and added: '*Et voilà l'autre.*'

His knife slid out again. With a vicious snarl he raised it remembering how Gregory's intervention had prevented his attack on Wells succeeding the last time they had been face to face.

As the blade flashed high above Corot's head Gregory jerked himself backwards but, before the knife came down, the Limper grabbed the Frenchman's arm.

'Not here,' he said sharply. 'Your planes are leaving. Get back to them and see them home. I'll handle this and I'll see these two never worry us again. I'll croak the two of them before morning but it's got to be done in the proper way; so there's no trouble for us afterwards.'

Corot's handsome face went sullen, like that of a greedy child who has been robbed of an entertainment, but he shrugged, spat on the floor at Gregory's feet and, turning, slouched out of the inn.

'Search them,' snapped the Limper, raising his automatic a little, as an indication that he meant to shoot if they tried to break away, while his four henchmen ran through their pockets.

Pistols, night glasses, torches, letters and money were piled upon the drink-puddled bar. When they were held firm again the Limper glanced through the papers; then stuffed them in his jacket.

'Quick march now,' he ordered. 'Take them to my plane.'

The prisoners were hustled out into the night and across the grass. The smuggler fleet was leaving; only four planes remained now upon the landing ground. The men were busily transporting the cargo from the railway embankment to the fleet of lorries beyond the inn; the train had gone.

A four-seater monoplane stood a little apart from the big de Havillands. The Limper scrambled into it, dived down to a locker near the floor, and pulled out some lengths of cord. 'Truss them up,' he said, 'then push them into the back of the plane.'

Gregory and Wells were securely tied hand and foot; then bundled in behind. One of the men got into the plane with them and the Limper went off to supervise the departure of the convoy. At short intervals the other planes roared away into the air. The landing ground was now in darkness and the lorries began to rumble down the road; the smugglers had disappeared when the Limper returned and climbed into the pilot's seat.

He slammed the door and pressed home the self-starter. The plane ran forward, bumped a little and lifted, then with a steady hum it sailed away lightless into the night.

Gregory was hunched on his side in a back seat but his face was turned towards one of the windows of the enclosed plane and he could see a good section of the sky. After they had been flying for a few moments he managed to pick up one of the major constellations, and knew, from its position, that they were flying in a north-westerly direction, towards Quex Park. His agile mind began to conjure frantically with the possibilities of drawing Mrs. Bird's attention to their wretched plight so that she could secure help.

Mrs. Bird and Milly would be in bed by now though, he remembered, as it was well after midnight, probably somewhere near one o'clock. The Limper would certainly do nothing to rouse them from their slumbers and he had spoken of seeing to it that his prisoners were both dead before the morning.

Gregory had faced death many times, but on those previous occasions his hands had been free and generally there had been a handy weapon in one of them. This was a different business altogether. They were trussed like Christmas turkeys for the slaughter and must depend upon their wits alone to save them.

As they were not gagged, they could, of course, scream in the hope of rousing Mrs. Bird but, whereas a few nights before she might have telephoned the police at once upon hearing shouts for help, she would now more probably wait to investigate the matter or see what happened next, knowing that Wells and his men had the Park under observation.

What about Wells's men who would be watching the place? They would be certain to appear on the scene if they thought murder was being done, but unfortunately both of them were stationed outside the Park gates, and it was nearly a mile in width. Would the most lusty shouts carry half that distance? Gregory doubted it; moreover, it seemed certain the Limper would shoot them out of hand if they bellowed for help. They would be dead long before anyone arrived upon the scene.

The situation began to assume a far grimmer aspect in his mind. From the moment when he had gone down under the rush of men, every second had been occupied until now, so he had not had a chance to realise the full danger in which they stood. No one except Wells and himself knew of the secret landing ground at Romney Marshes, or what their intentions had been when they left Quex Park, so no one would worry about them if they failed to turn up until a day or two, at least, had elapsed without news of them. Then the police would begin to wonder where Wells had got to; but that was little comfort if they were to be killed before morning.

The plane banked steeply and began to descend. Beads of perspiration broke out on Gregory's forehead. 'We're there already,' he thought, 'this plane must be a mighty fast one, or else it's just that time rushes by when you need it most. And I've thought of nothing. We may be for it now any moment—once we land. By Jove! this is tougher than anything I can remember.'

They scarcely felt the bump as the Limper landed the plane and it flashed through Gregory's mind that the fellow was a first-class pilot. The engine ceased to hum and for a moment there was dead silence then the Limper opened the door of the cockpit and wriggled out. The beam of a torch showed from near by and a new voice came out of the darkness.

'He's on his way over.'

'Good,' replied the Limper. 'I've got them both here. Get 'em out and bring 'em inside.'

The Limper's assistant pilot leaned over and grabbed Wells by the shoulders, hoisted him up and pushed him head foremost through the door, where two other fellows seized him and pulled him to the ground. A minute later Gregory was bundled out beside him.

He wriggled his head and looked around. A gentle wind was blowing which brought with it the salt tang of the sea. No lights were to be seen anywhere, and no dark groups of trees, such as he had expected, broke the starry sky line in any direction. Perhaps he had been wrong about their course being to the north-eastward; at all events it did not seem as though they had landed in Quex Park.

Before he had further time for speculation the cords about their feet were undone and they were jerked upright. Limper's assistant pilot and the two new men pushed them forward, while he brought up the rear, lighting their way now and again with flashes from a torch.

After a few moments they came to a wire fence, through

which the prisoners were pulled, and then to a steep embankment. On its flat summit they tripped and stumbled across a double railway line, slid down the further bank across another fence, and so into a field. They tramped on for two hundred yards, slightly down hill, then came to a wooden paling. One of the men unlatched a gate and the party tramped up a brick pathway, through a kitchen garden, to a small dark cottage.

Round at its side a chink of light showed beneath an ill-fitting door on which the Limper gave three single and then a double rap. It was pulled open by a seedy-looking man in corduroy trousers who, judging by his cauliflower ears and broken nose, might at one time have been a pugilist.

The room had an old-fashioned fireplace and oven let into one wall and a smaller room which led off it, barely larger than a cupboard, was obviously the scullery; otherwise the place was furnished as a living-room although it probably served the purpose of kitchen as well.

The man with the cauliflower ears shut the door after them and bolted it quickly, then he shot a shifty glance at the two prisoners, and asked somewhat unnecessarily and, Gregory noted, ungrammatically: 'These them?'

'Yes,' said the Limper, signing to the others to stand Wells and Gregory at the farthest end of the room up against the white-washed wall. Then he lowered himself with a sigh into a worn saddle-bag arm-chair.

When they had faced each other at the Brown Owl Inn Gregory had still been half-dazed from the blows he had received in the scrap so this was the first opportunity he had really to study the Limper. The man was obviously a much better type than the average professional crook. He had good grey eyes under straight rather heavy brows and a direct glance with none of the apprehension about it noticeable in that of the flashy 'con' man who is always anticipating a detective's touch on the shoulder. The Limper did not boast an Oxford accent but his voice was an educated one and had a crisp note in it which comes from the habit of command. Only the thin, discontented mouth, which turned down a little at the corners, betrayed a certain hardness in his nature and, perhaps, explained his choice of occupation. Gregory summed him up as the product of one of the lesser public schools, who had slipped up somewhere, perhaps in business, or possibly in one of the services. At all events he did not look at all a killer type and Gregory racked his wits for a good opening, whereby he might possibly arouse sympathy, but Wells forestalled him.

Although he was a younger man than Gregory his professional duties had brought him into quite as many rough-houses and was a courageous fellow; but his thoughts during the brief journey in the plane had been far from comforting.

He knew, although Gregory did not, that his Superintendent would have his report on Gregory's operations the night before by now, and be aware that they had both set off again for the Brown Owl Inn on Romney Marshes. His people would, therefore, become very active indeed if they did not hear from him again by midday, but that was little comfort if they were both to be wiped out in an hour or so. He took the bull by the horns and began to lie like a trooper.

'I think this has gone far enough,' he said evenly, 'unless you want to make things far worse for yourself. We've been on your trail for days and we know all about you. Headquarters have got all your addresses so they can pull you in any time they want to, and if my report's not in by six o'clock in the morning the Flying Squad will be out on a round up. It's no good thinking you'll get away by crossing the Channel in your plane either, because the French police have got a line on your outfit the other side, so you'll be pinched on landing.'

The Limper stared at him with open disbelief. 'That's a pretty story, Inspector, but I'm afraid it won't wash. Even if it were true there's nothing to stop me avoiding any net you may have spread by flying to Holland after I've settled your business.'

'Perhaps, but they'll get you in the end, don't you worry.' Wells leaned forward impressively. 'They'll get you, and you'll swing for it as sure as my name's Wells, if you do us in.'

'It doesn't rest with me,' the Limper shrugged, 'so you might as well save the argument. I brought you here under instructions, that's all, and the Big Chief should be here at any moment. It's for him to say whether you go down the chute or if he can think of other means of silencing you.'

There was a horrid silence which lasted nearly a couple of minutes while the Limper pulled out a cigarette and lit it. The men who had met them on the landing ground, the extra pilot, and the ex-pugilist still held Gregory and Wells against the wall, although their arms remained tied behind their backs.

Suddenly the three single raps, followed by two quick ones, came upon the wooden door again. The Limper rose, pulled back the bolt and flung it open, revealing a strange little figure upon the threshold.

Gregory was expecting Lord Gavin Fortescue to put in an appearance after the Limper's last remark but Wells had never seen the Duke of Denver's abnormal twin before and greeted him with a fascinated stare.

Lord Gavin's small, perfect, childlike body was clad in a dinner-jacket suit. Over it he wore a black evening cape; the folds hid his hands resting upon the two sticks with which he assisted himself to walk; but it was his massive, leonine head that held Wells's attention. A shock of snow-white hair was brushed back from the magnificent forehead and beneath the aristocratic upturned brows a pair of pale magnetic soulless blue eyes, utterly lacking in expression, stared into his own.

Lord Gavin nodded slowly then sat down carefully in the arm-chair the Limper had just vacated. It was quite a low one yet his tiny feet, in their shiny patent shoes, still dangled an inch or so from the floor. 'The two gentlemen from Trouville,' he said softly. 'Inspector Wells and Mr. Gregory Sallust. You have been very indiscreet, extremely indiscreet.'

Gregory tried to step forward but the men held him back as he burst out: 'Now look here, Lord Gavin, your record's bad enough! You've been mighty lucky to get away with it so far but you'll tempt fate once too often. They know all about your little game at Scotland Yard this time so you'd better let us go, or else the charge against you is going to be a really ugly one.'

'When I wish for your advice I will ask for it,' said Lord Gavin smoothly. 'I was just saying that you have been very indiscreet. You were indiscreet that night when you followed little Sabine out of the Casino; you were even more indiscreet when you refused to take the warning which I sent you the following morning, and now . . .'

'How did you know that Sabine was with me that night?' Gregory interrupted. 'I've often wondered.'

'I saw you follow her out of the *salle de jeu* so I thought it possible that you were responsible for her not returning to me after her business was done. That unfortunate scar above your left eyebrow makes it tolerably easy to trace you and having given your description to my agents they very soon ran you to earth at the *Normandie*. My men confirmed my impression that Sabine was with you when they reported that she had left the *café* at Trouville in your company.'

Gregory forced a smile. 'Well, give her my love when you next see her.'

'Certainly, if you wish it. She will be most distressed to hear of your demise as she seems to have enjoyed her time with you in Deauville. As there will be no possible chance of her running across you again I must try to make it up to her in some way—another bracelet perhaps—sapphires, I think. Sabine likes sapphires.'

As Lord Gavin made no mention of their having met again in London Gregory assumed that Sabine had concealed the fact that they had spent a good portion of the previous day together. The brief silence was broken by Wells; who shot out suddenly:

'Cut out the talking and say what you mean to do with us.' The quiet manner of this sinister little man was beginning to fret the Inspector's nerves in a way which no bullying or bluster could have done.

Lord Gavin turned his heavy head slowly in Wells's direction and his pale eyes glittered for a moment. 'Surely there can be no question in your mind, Inspector, about my intentions regarding you. Both you and Sallust have pried into my affairs. You ferreted out the address of Sabine's firm in Paris: in consequence I have been compelled to close it. Not a matter for grave concern but an inconvenience all the same; and now it seems that the two of you have actually witnessed certain operations by my people south of Romney Marshes. You know too much. You have signed your own death warrants. There is no alternative.'

'But you can't kill us in cold blood!'

Lord Gavin shrugged. 'What is there to prevent me? My interests are far too great for me to jeopardise them just because the lives of two inquisitive young men are in question.'

'You'll hang for it if you do,' snapped Gregory. 'Scotland Yard knows what you're up to this time, I tell you. You can't murder us and dispose of our bodies without leaving any trace; sooner or later they'll get you for it.'

'It is most unlikely that they will ever get me for anything, but if they do they will never be able to pin your deaths upon me. Both of you *are* going to disappear and *without leaving any trace*.'

Wells grunted. 'Lots of people have thought they were so clever they could get away with murder—but it's not so easy.'

'Indeed?' A cold smile twitched Lord Gavin's lips. 'Do you know where we are at the moment?'

'Somewhere in Thanet.'

'No, we are a little to the south of Thanet, less than half a mile from the coast of Pegwell Bay. Does that convey anything to you, I wonder.'

'Only that it'll be useful to have the location of another of your bases when we're out of this,' said Wells doggedly.

'You will never be out of this, so the knowledge is quite useless to you and, whenever I wish them to do so, my fleet of planes will continue to land upon that beautiful stretch of ground called Ash Level, so convenient to the railway line which you must have crossed when you were brought here. It seems you do not know the peculiarities of Pegwell Bay.'

'It's very shallow,' said Gregory slowly. 'If I remember, the tide runs out for nearly two miles, and when it turns comes in nearly as quickly as a man can run. There are lovely sands too. I went for a gallop along them once when I was staying with some friends at Sandwich.'

'Excellent sands,' Lord Gavin nodded. 'That is, for the first half mile or so from the shore, but farther out there are certain areas which have cavities of water beneath them, although they appear firm and beautiful to the uninitiated. It is a dangerous thing to take a short cut across the big bay at low tide, particularly at night, if you do not know the location of the treacherous patches. People have died that way, just disappeared beyond all trace, their bodies being swallowed up by the quicksands.'

The muscles of Gregory's hands tightened, and he felt that his palms were damp; while Gerry Wells's freckled face went a perceptible shade paler.

Lord Gavin went on unhurriedly: 'That was the reason I had you brought here immediately my people telephoned to tell me that they had caught two spies. It is a great convenience that one of my bases should be adjacent to my private burial ground. The tide is running out. It will be low at six-ten this morning. A stone's throw from the cottage here we have the river Stour, which flows through Sandwich and empties itself into the sea by a deep channel in the bay. At five o'clock, while the tide is still running out, my men will take you in a boat down the river and out to sea; then they will throw you overboard in a place where it is too shallow for you to swim and which the tide will probably have left dry by the time you are engulfed in the sand up to your armpits. You have a little over three hours now to exercise your imagination as to what will happen after that.'

'God! you're not human,' Gregory gasped.

Lord Gavin wriggled forward in the arm-chair and shuffled to his feet. 'I am as the God you invoke made me,' he said with sudden venom and all the stored up bitterness of years seemed concentrated in his voice. His childish body shook with a sudden gust of passion and he spat out at them: 'You have had health and strength, been able to run and leap, and take your women, during your time. Now, your feet shall be tied by the grip of the sands and your great muscles will not help you. You chose to match your wits with mine, and I have proved your master. In your little minds you plotted to interfere with the work that I would do. All right then! You shall gasp out your lives repenting of your folly.'

Suddenly the storm passed and he went quiet again. 'You'll see to it,' he said softly to the Limper, and drawing his black cloak about him he left the cottage without another word.

As the door banged to behind him Wells let out a sharp breath. Little beads of perspiration were now thick upon his forehead. He had been in some tight corners before now, criminal dens in the East End where crooks would have given him a nasty mauling if they had suspected he was a policeman, but nothing to compare with this where he would lose his life unless he could think of a way out.

'Tie their feet again,' said the Limper, 'and push them in the scullery.'

His order was the signal for a fresh struggle. Gregory and Wells both kicked out with savage violence and tried to break away but their arms were still tied and they had four of the Limper's men against them. The uneven tussle could only end one way. The pugilist hit Gregory in the pit of the stomach; one of the others sloshed Wells on the side of the jaw. The Limper did not even need to go to the assistance of his underlings. The prisoners were forced down on the floor and their ankles tied again with thick cord. Then they were dragged across the room and laid out side by side upon the scullery floor.

Gregory had given up the fight before Wells, and as soon as he got his strength back he was thinking, 'If only they shut us in we'll cheat the devils yet. If Wells rolls over on his face I'll unpick the knots that tie his arms with my teeth. The rest'll be easy providing they don't hear us going out through the window.' But even as he was planning an escape the Limper's voice came again:

'Don't shut the door. Leave it wide open; so I can keep my eye on them in case they start any tricks.'

The ex-pugilist put a kettle on the hob and then produced a greasy pack of cards. He and his three companions sat down to a game of nap while the Limper picked up a tattered magazine and settled himself in the arm-chair to read.

A grim silence fell inside the cottage, broken only by an occasional murmur from one of the card players or the squeak of a chair as it was pushed back a little across the boards.

Gregory turned over twice to ease his position but each time he moved he saw the Limper glance up and stare in his direction.

For a quarter of an hour, that seemed like and eternity, he decided to try bribery.

Struggling into a sitting position he spoke softly to the Limper. 'Come here a minute will you.'

The Limper put down his magazine and walked over to the entrance of the cupboard-like scullery. 'What is it?'

'Just wanted a word with you,' Gregory said in a low tone. 'You're in this game for what you can get out of it—aren't you?'

'That's so,' agreed the Limper non-committally.

'Well, I don't know what Gavin Fortescue pays you but I'm a bidder for your services. I'm not a rich man myself, although I could raise a tidy sum, but there's a friend of mine who's next door to being a millionaire—Sir Pellinore Gwaine-Cust—you may have heard of him. He looks on me as a sort of adopted son and he'll honour any arrangement that I make without a murmur. Fix it how you like with the others, but get us out of this and we'll pay you £5,000, besides seeing to it that you get safely out of the country. It's Gavin Fortescue we're after and we can afford to shut our eyes to anything you've done if you'll give us a break. How about it?'

The Limper's mouth hardened. Its corners turned down more than ever; making his face suddenly grim and pitiless. He lifted his foot, planted it swiftly on Gregory's chest, and kicked him savagely backwards. 'Another word from you and I'll have you gagged,' he said contemptuously. Then he turned back to his arm-chair and magazine.

Gregory's head hit the stone floor of the scullery with a crack which almost knocked him senseless and made further thinking impossible for some minutes.

Gerry Wells had listened to Gregory's proposition with mingled hope and fear. He too had been revolving every possible approach in his madly racing brain; yet could think of nothing. Each time he tried to plan a line of action Milly's face appeared before his mental vision. Death might not be so bad—a decent death—but it was hard to go now that he had found her. She was so utterly different from other girls; so gentle and unspoiled and lovable. The sort that made a big fellow like him just ache to protect her, and she liked him, liked him a lot. He was certain of it. Not a word of any significance had passed between them but it was just the way she looked at him with shy admiration in her big blue eyes. He thought of the wonderful day they had spent together, their flight over Thanet in the morning and their jolly time on the beach in the afternoon; but he mustn't think of her now. It was utterly suicidal. He had got to concentrate on getting out of this ghastly mess he was in; and yet he could not. Every time he tried to reason or plan Milly's delicate oval face, crowned by its mass of golden hair, rose before him .

Time drifted on slowly but inexorably. The pain at the back of Gregory's head was less now and he was trying to formulate new plans. Threats had failed; bribery had failed. They were trussed like sacred offerings for the slaughter. What was there left? If Wells *had* sent in a report about the base near Dungeness, and the police went there, they would discover nothing. The places where the flares had been, a few tracks of aeroplanes, perhaps, and the marks of the lorry wheels in the dust of the road. But they wouldn't go there: why should they when the essence of the game was for Wells and himself to gather all the threads of the conspiracy together before the authorities acted? Even if they blundered, and made a premature mop up for some unknown reason, they might raid Quex Park and the Brown Owl Inn and the *Café de la Cloche* near Calais, but this other base at Ash Level, just inland from the southern arm of Pegwell Bay, was unknown to them.

How those three hours drifted by neither of them knew and both began to believe that the Limper had forgotten how time must be passing. At last he stood up and gave a curt order. The men came in and dragged them out of the scullery into the living-room again.

Their ankles were untied and they scrambled to their feet. The Limper produced his automatic. 'Understand now,' he said. 'The sands will swallow up a dead body as quickly as a live one. I'll be behind you while we're walking to the boat and if there's any attempt at breaking away I mean to shoot you.'

They were led out of the cottage and round the corner to its other side. Beyond, through the grey half-light that precedes the dawn, they could see a deep gully with muddy banks. In its bed a narrow stream was ebbing swiftly. They crossed it a little farther down by a plank bridge and came again on to the grassland, up a bank, and across the broad main road from Sandwich to Ramsgate. It occurred to both the condemned men to make a dash for it there. If they were shot down, well—better death that way than what awaited them; yet such is the instinct of all humans to cling to life up to the last possible moment that both hesitated, knowing the odds to be so terribly against them. Before either had decided to start kicking out they were across the road and had been pushed down the far embankment; to a place where the river appeared again having made a hairpin bend.

Here the channel was deeper and the stretch of water wider.

Swiftly and silently it raced towards the sea in an endeavour to keep pace with the out-going tide.

They were led along to a little wooden landing-stage, running out above the mud, at the far end of which a stout-looking rowing boat was moored. Another moment and they were hustled into its stern. Two of the men took the oars while the other two and the Limper crowded into the seats which ran round its after-part.

The Limper sat in the middle with his pistol drawn, Gregory and Wells on either side of him, and beyond each of them one of the other men, holding them firmly by the back of their collars in case they attempted to jump overboard.

The ex-pugilist, in the bow, cast off the painter and, without any effort on the part of the oarsmen, the boat was carried by the swift current towards the sea.

Dawn had broken and, as the boat emerged from between the two banks into Sandwich Haven on the southern portion of the bay, the captives saw the vast area of sand stretching before them. The river continued; its deep channel twisting and winding between the flat stretches which, at high tide, would be covered by the sea. Only the quiet splash of oars now broke the silence of the early morning. Not a soul was to be seen across all the wide expanse, or upon the steep cliff over a mile away to the northern extremity of the bay, although Gregory and Wells both searched them with frantic glances.

Another few moments and they reached the spot where the river met the outgoing tide. It was rippling gently along the golden sand, yet running out with such speed that every little wavelet broke ten yards farther to the seaward, leaving a fresh stretch of damp, faintly shining sand exposed to view.

The men pulled vigorously and the boat began to heave a little on the gentle swell. Wells's face was now a mask of whiteness in the early morning light while Gregory's eyes were deeply sunk in his face on which the tan showed unnaturally grey.

The Limper produced a pocket compass and, steadying

it as well as he could, took a rough bearing of Fairway Buoy which was just visible, a black bobbing patch in the far distance slightly to the right. Then he took a bearing of Bur Buoy; just as far away but almost directly upon the course which they were making.

'Turn her,' he said. 'We must do the job about fifty yards to the left from here.'

The men plied their oars again. The tide was now only a distant ripple so that its rapid approach was hardly perceptible. A few more agonising moments passed for the prisoners then the Limper jerked his head in Wells's direction.

'Undo his hands,' he said. 'If the sands shift and they're washed up later it'll look as though they were caught by the tide.'

The man obeyed while the Limper thrust his gun within two inches of Wells's mouth. 'Make a move,' he said, 'and I'll blow your head off.'

Gerry Wells's arms were free. His impulse was to lash out but his hands had been tied behind his back for over five hours. His muscles were cramped and stiff and when he tried to move he found that the effort only resulted in agonising pain.

The Limper gave a quick glance round. No boat was to be seen. There was no one on the shore. Full dawn had hardly come and the faint, still lingering, twilight must obscure their actions from any distant casual watcher.

'Over with him,' he grunted.

Too late Wells wrenched his arms forward. The man beside him stooped, placed a hand beneath his knees, and tipped him backwards over the gunwale.

The oarsmen were dipping their oars, keeping the boat more or less in position, so that it drifted only very slightly. The Limper jabbed his automatic against Gregory's face while the man beside him loosed his hands and pulled the cord away. Like Wells, his arms were almost paralysed from having been tied behind him for so long, but he jerked himself to his feet, his eyes wide and staring.

Gregory felt it well up about his thighs and, wriggle as he would, there was no way to free himself of it. The tiny particles formed a glutinous mud which would not even bear his weight, more or less distributed as it was. His knees were buried and it trickled over the hollows behind them. Wells had sunk up to his arm-pits.

Both of them visualised the awful moment when the sand would be above their chins, when they could no longer lift their arms and were dragged down by the constant sucking motion, so that the sand reached their lips and entered their mouths in spite of all their efforts, choking them as they sank.

They began to scream at the top of their voices, yelling for help with all the force of their lungs, but not a sound came back to them from the desolate wastes that spread upon either hand, and no human figure appeared upon the distant cliff tops.

17

The Raid on Barter Street

Both men had sunk up to their chests. Waving their arms frantically above their heads they bellowed for help, but the Limper's boat had rounded a bend in the creek, where it met the land, so that it could no longer be seen from the shore and there was now no soul within sight or hearing.

Their field of view had narrowed as they sank and their eyes were now no more than twelve inches above the sand. Facing inshore they could only just see the lower coastline to the south of the bay, where it runs along to Sandwich flats and golf course; while to the north the steep white chalk cliffs reared up, naked and distant. Squirming and twisting they caught glimpses of the sea behind them. It was no longer running out at a great pace for it had almost reached low water level. About two hundred yards away the little wavelets broke with a gentle hissing noise but, from the line of vision of the desperate men, they appeared to have increased to the size of Atlantic rollers, cutting off the view to seaward.

To their left the channel cut through the flat expanse of sand by the river Stour was still filled with deep, fast-flowing water, but their eye level was too low for them to see it, although it lay only some thirty yards away.

They ceased to shout, conscious that their cries for help were unavailing, and that every ounce of breath was precious in their fight for life. The constant strain upon their muscles was appalling; bent forward from their waists they clawed at the treacherous sand, churning it into liquid silt in their fierce endeavours to hoist themselves out of the horrid ooze that gripped them.

The quicksand seemed to have become alive; as though imbued with some evil spirit of its own. It sucked and chuckled as they fought it; creeping up about them with gentle uncheckable persistence.

Their legs and torsos were fast embedded in its stranglehold so that they could no longer move a muscle of their lower limbs. It pressed upon them from every side seeming to weigh a ton. Their arms and shoulders were now sodden with it from their struggle; weighed down so that they could only move them with great effort.

Wells had almost given up; buried to the armpits, his head thrown back, he moved his arms only sufficiently to prevent their submergence as long as possible, while the sweat of the terror of death streamed off his face.

Gregory was still fighting, against his better judgment, as the sands seemed to suck at him more fiercely with each new effort that he made; but he would not surrender life until the last breath was choked out of him by the gritty slime covering his mouth and nose.

It was then, when both men felt all hope was gone, that they heard the muffled drumming of a petrol engine rapidly approaching. Suddenly it ceased and a loud report, like the crack of a small cannon, shattered the silence.

They stopped struggling instantly and wrenched their shoulders round towards the left. Thirty yards away a group of men appeared to be standing knee deep and rocking gently in the sand. From them a long black snake-like rope was whizzing through the air: a life-line fired from a rocket gun. It twisted a moment overhead and then came hurtling down with a plop on to the sands between the two almost buried men; the lead disc at its end piercing the morass a good twenty yards beyond them.

With almost unendurable relief they grabbed the rope and held it. The gun was fired again and another life-line hissed through the air above them. Gregory could just reach it as it fell so he left the first for Wells. With their last remnants of strength, fortified by the frantic will to live, they hauled the slack end of the ropes in and coiled them round their bodies, beneath their armpits, by thrusting them through the unresisting sand which had welled up to their shoulders.

'Ready?' came a hail from the group by the rocket gun.

'Heave away,' shouted Gregory and the strain was taken up upon the ropes.

There followed the most ghastly struggle between the rescuers and those evil sands which were so loth to give up their prey. The imprisoned men thought that their bodies would be torn in half. They moaned in agony as the life-lines gripped them like wire springs about their chests; cutting into their bodies and forcing the breath out of their lungs. They were lying at an angle now, with their heads towards their rescuers, their shoulders only supported by the pulling ropes, their torsos and feet still buried deep in the shifting sands.

For what seemed an eternity they were stretched as though upon a rack, striving with the tired muscles of their legs for even a fraction of movement which would free them, but it seemed that they were too firmly embedded ever to be drawn out.

It was Gregory who, through a mist of pain, realised that

now their heads and shoulders were supported there was no longer any danger of their arms becoming permanently imprisoned if they chose to use them, so he plunged his hands down and began to heave out handfuls of the soft semi-liquid silt from in front of his chest.

Almost as fast as he relieved the pressure the sand seeped back, but the movement at least eased the weight from his chest a little and, when he lifted his head again, he found that he could see more of the men who were heaving on the rope. Their lower extremities were hidden by the gunwale of a boat which was just visible now above the flat expanse of sand. Then he remembered the creek and realised that the motor boat must have come up into it from the sea.

The struggle lasted for nearly an hour; the treacherous sands pulling and plucking at their victims' limbs until the very last moment, when they were drawn out with a sudden plop and dragged face downwards towards the boat.

Gregory was free ten minutes before Wells. As the life-line drew him over a steep bank of sand he slithered into the water. Then he was hauled aboard a big flat-bottomed speed-boat, where he collapsed on the bottom boards, unconscious.

When he came to Wells was beside him and their rescuers were applying restoratives. The ordeal had been such an appalling one that they were unable to speak and could not move a muscle without acute pain. Both of them lapsed into unconsciousness again as the speed-boat's engine began to stutter. With a puff of blue smoke in its wake it roared out to sea.

They were vaguely conscious of being carried up the steps of a stone pier and bundled into a car, then through the side door of an hotel and up the back stairs into bathrooms, where friendly hands relieved them of their sodden sand-loaded garments. Then came the glorious ease of relaxing their exhausted bodies in clear warm water.

Figures moved in a mist about them: skilful fingers tended their hurts, then there came the joy of fresh cool linen about their bruised bodies and a merciful darkness.

It was late afternoon when they were aroused from the

deep black slumber which follows intense fatigue, to find themselves in single beds in the same room, with Sir Pellinore Gwaine-Cust and Superintendent Marrowfat standing beside them.

'How're you feeling now, my boy,' Sir Pellinore inquired, his hand on Gregory's shoulder.

Gregory gazed round the strange room with a vacant stare. 'Where—where are we?' he asked after a moment.

'Granville Hotel, Ramsgate. By Jove you've had a gruelling. Wouldn't have been in your shoes for a mint of money—but you're safe out of it all now.'

'For God's sake go away and let me sleep again,' Gregory muttered.

'Sorry,' said Superintendent Marrowfat abruptly. 'We let you lie as long as we dare, but I must have any information you've got to give us. Come along, Wells, let's have your story.'

Gerry Wells moaned as he hoisted himself up against his pillows. His body seemed to be one large burning ache, and he felt that under a pair of strange pyjamas his back and chest were bandaged, although he could still feel the vice-like grip of the life-line round his body.

Slowly and painfully he told his superior of the evil chance that had brought about their capture the night before and of the manner in which they had very nearly lost their lives.

Gregory had been gathering his strength. He looked up at Sir Pellinore. 'What brought you on the scene so opportunely. If you hadn't turned up when you did we'd both be fiddling in heaven now—or stoking up the coals.'

Sir Pellinore grinned. 'No thanks to me, my boy. What women see in you I never could make out, but you've got to thank some hidden charm that you're here in bed in Ramsgate, and not a dozen feet under those ghastly sands by now. Sabine telephoned to me from Quex Park a little after midnight. She said they had caught you both and that Gavin Fortescue had just left for Ash Level. She seemed to know the drill too and gave a pretty good forecast of what they were likely to do with you.'

Gregory frowned. 'A little after midnight! Why the hell weren't you there before then! In a fast car you could have made that place in a couple of hours; whereas you took darned near six and very nearly turned up too late into the bargain.'

The fat Superintendent coughed. 'I'm afraid that's my fault, Mr. Sallust. Sir Pellinore got on to the Yard at once and they reached me at my home. We were down here by a little before three, so we could have raided that cottage, if we'd wanted to. But this thing's such a terrible threat to the well-being of the country we've just got to get all the threads in our hands before we act. If we'd rushed that place we would have got you out all right, but we'd have been too late to pinch Lord Gavin and, apart from that, we haven't yet succeeded in getting on to the London organisation.'

A sardonic smile twitched at Gregory's thin lips. 'So you took a chance. . . .'

The Superintendent laughed. 'Not a very big one. We knew they wouldn't shoot you unless you did something stupid. The lady made it quite clear about the way they'd bump you off. You didn't know, of course, but there were some of my chaps within a stone's throw of that cottage from three o'clock on, with orders to rush it if anything went wrong. Meantime Sir Pellinore and I went off into Ramsgate and fixed a boat all ready with life-lines; so as to get you out after they'd done their stuff.'

'But what the hell did you want to wait till the last minute for?' Gregory snapped. 'Apart from what we went through you were darned nearly too late to get us out at all.'

'It wasn't quite as bad as that, sir. We were in our boat by half-past four, lying concealed under the cliffs to the north of the bay with our night glasses out, all ready for the performance. Then their boat came down the channel and they chucked you overboard. We could have reached you within two minutes but we wanted to wait, if it were possible, until they'd gone back up the creek and couldn't spot us and guess we were on to their little game. Our scheme went like clock-work. They think you're dead and that they're safe as houses; so no alarm will have been given. You're out of it and we'll be able to pull them in just when we wish.'

Gregory nodded. 'Good staff work, I suppose, but devilish hard on the nerves, and you've made a pretty fine mess of my poor old carcase.'

'Maybe, but did you get anything? That's what I had to wake you up to know.'

'I did,' said Wells with new enthusiasm. 'I managed to spot the address on that case before they grabbed me. Mitbloom & Allison, 43, Barter Street, E.1.'

'Good boy,' the Superintendent chuckled into his double chin. 'I'm leaving for London now and we'll take a look over the place tonight. The doctor tells me there's no damage done to either of you; although you'll be a bit sore in the ribs for the next few days. You'd both better take it easy, I'm think-ing, while I get on with the job.'

Gerry Wells sat up, suppressed a groan, and said: 'Half a minute, sir. This is my pigeon. Surely you're not going to do me out of it; just because I took a chance on getting caught last night.'

'I don't want to do you out of anything if you're fit to carry on, but the doctors seem to think you ought to rest up for a day or two, at least.'

'I'll be all right, sir. I've no bones broken. It's only a bit painful where the ropes cut into the skin on my chest and back when you pulled me out. What time d'you mean to raid Mit-bloom & Allison?'

'I shan't raid it. That would give the game away. I shall have a search warrant made out, and pray to God I won't be called on to show it, then pay the place an unofficial visit sometime in the early hours tomorrow morning. I'll find out in the meantime if they keep a night watchman. If they do I'll think up some scheme to get him out of the way for a bit. Then we can go in and have a snoop round without anyone being any the wiser.'

'If I caught the last train up then I could be in on it—couldn't I, sir?' Gerry Wells pleaded.

The Superintendent nodded. 'Certainly if you're fit. Best stay here for a bit though and see how you feel this evening.'

Gregory eased himself over on to his tummy. 'We'll be with you. Old soldiers never die. Just order some dinner for us and a car to take us to the station; both items on Sir Pellinore's account. He owes us that for his day at the seaside.'

The doctor, who had been warned to attend again when the patients were woken, was summoned. He said that there was no danger in their getting up and only advised against it owing to the pain which must result from their bruised muscles. Where the ropes had cut into them he dressed the broken skin with soothing ointment and fresh bandages. When he had finished Superintendent Marrowfat and Sir Pellinore left them, to return to London, while the two patients turned over to doze and rest.

At eight o'clock the manager of the hotel called them in person, inquired most kindly after their health, and superintended the preparations for an excellent meal ordered by Sir Pellinore, to be served in their room.

They both felt terribly stiff, but apart from that, and the soreness under their arms, perfectly fit and well again after their thirteen hours in bed. Dressing proved a painful operation, but once it was accomplished and they had been heartened by a good dinner, washed down with a fine bottle of Burgundy, they felt as keen as ever. A car was waiting for them when they came downstairs and they caught the 9.8 to London; arriving at Charing Cross two minutes before midnight.

At the Yard all preparations for the secret raid had been completed. Mitbloom & Allison proved to be a firm of wholesale tobacco merchants. Their warehouse, so the Superintendent had ascertained, was fitted with electric burglar alarms but they did not employ a night watchman. Arrangements had been made for the electric current to be cut off at the main between the hours of one and three so that the police would be able to make an entry without the alarm going off and, unless they were very unfortunate, no one would suspect on the following day that the place had been searched in the early hours of the morning.

The Superintendent, Gregory, Gerry Wells, a lock expert from the special department, and another detective, squeezed themselves in one of the bigger Flying Squad cars at a quarter to one, and the driver turned its nose eastward.

They ran down the Strand which was still fairly busy with traffic passing to and from the great restaurants; Fleet Street, now given over to swift-moving newspaper vans lining up to collect and distribute the early copies of the great national dailies; then up Ludgate Hill and through Queen Victoria Street, strangely silent and deserted compared with the swarming thousands who throng those great business areas in the day time. Passing the Bank of England, they sped on to Liverpool Street, then turned right, into that maze of thoroughfares into which the wealthier population of London and the suburbs so rarely penetrate.

Barter Street proved to be a dark canyon between high brick buildings. It contained no residential houses and was given over entirely to tall warehouses; some of which had dusty-looking old-fashioned offices on the ground floor. Dustbins lined the pavements; a solitary cat minced its way forward in leisurely manner across the street upon its nightly prowl.

They parked the car at the end of the street leaving the driver with it. A city policeman touched his helmet to the Superintendent, having been warned of their visit, and remained on the corner to keep watch while the others made their way along the narrow pavement to number forty-three.

Grimy window panes stared at them blankly from the street level; above, the big hook and ball of a crane for hauling merchandise to the upper floors dangled over their heads. The Superintendent looked at his watch.

'Five past one. Go ahead, Jim,' he said.

The lock expert produced a bag of tools and, selecting one,

started work on the door. 'Lock's easy enough,' he murmured. 'Old-fashioned piece.' With a twist of his wrist it clicked back into its socket.

Pushing the door open the five men entered the building. The Superintendent switched on his torch. It showed a dusty hallway with a flight of stone steps leading to the upper floors and, on their left, two glass-panelled swing doors giving on to the offices. Thrusting them wide the fat Superintendent led the way in.

The beam of his torch, as he flashed it round, showed shelves with rows of faded letter files upon them; an old-fashioned clerk's desk, with high stools in front of it, and a rusty brass rail which carried a number of leather-bound ledgers. The place had the odour of dreary old-fashioned commercialism where men toiled half their lives in a perpetual twilight for a pittance. Another door with a frosted-glass panel, upon which was painted 'Private' in black letters, showed to the right. The Superintendent walked over and tried its handle. The lock expert set to work again and soon had it open.

The inner office was little better than the one they had just glanced over. It gave on to a deep well, and was lit in the day time only by glass reflectors swung on chains at an angle to the windows. A few faded photographs of elderly side-whiskered gentlemen, probably long-dead directors of the firm, were hung upon the whitewashed walls above a skirting of pitch pine. A rolltop desk occupied a corner near the window; a meagre square of turkey carpet failed to conceal all but a small portion of the worn oilcloth with which the floor was covered. An open bookcase contained piles of old trade journals, samples, and miscellaneous paraphernalia.

'We'll come back here later,' said the Superintendent. 'First I want to see the contents of the warehouse.'

They trooped out behind him and up the stone stairs to the first floor. It was an empty barn-like room; containing only several stacks of cases. The Superintendent pointed: Wells and the extra detective pulled one out from the middle of a stack and, by means of a jemmy which the lock man produced from his bag of tools, opened it up. It was a longish coffin-shaped case and contained tins of leaf tobacco.

They hammered back the nails carefully, so that it should not appear to have been opened, and replaced it in the centre of the stack.

The contents of four other cases were investigated from different portions of the room and the Superintendent noted down particulars of the goods they contained in his pocket book. Then they visited the upper floor and the same process was gone through with other consignments of merchandise which they found there. The top floor and the one below it were empty.

'We'll get down to the offices now,' the Superintendent said and, with an elephantine tread, led the way downstairs again.

They all had torches and began a rapid search through the clerks' desks and papers. It was impossible to examine them all in so short a time but the police officers made various notes of invoices, addresses, and dates of correspondence, without coming across a single item which tied up the place with its illegal source of supply.

Gregory wandered into the inner room. If there were any, it was there, he felt certain, that important papers would be kept.

The lock expert had already opened the roll-top desk and the Superintendent had gone carefully through it without finding any papers other than those connected with apparently legitimate business. Gregory stared round the place, scrutinising the photographs upon the grey-white walls and the miscellaneous collection of samples and trade papers, hoping for inspiration. Then his eye fell upon the lower shelf of the bookcase.

Half-buried under stacks of dusty documents there were a long row of books. He bent down and flashed his torch on them. It was a set of Shakespeare's works in forty volumes. As a book collector himself he knew it well. It had been published by an American company, just after the war, and remained at an exceptionally low price. The volumes were bound in grey boards with a strip of blue cloth down their spines on which were paper labels. Each contained one of Shakespeare's thirty-seven plays, except the last three, which were devoted to the sonnets and poems.

He stared at them for a moment; thinking how queer it was that the owner of this grim business office should be sufficiently interested in Shakespeare to keep a set in his depressing work room. Then he noticed that whereas the tops of thirty-nine volumes were grey with dust, the fortieth, number sixteen in the set, was comparatively clean and stood out a little from the others as though it had been recently used and hastily put back.

'When you are ready,' he said to the Superintendent who was standing in the doorway, 'we'll quit. I don't think you'll find much here but, if you'll provide me with a copy of *The Tempest*, when we get back to the Yard, I think I'll be able to decode that famous telegram for you.'

18

The Deciphering of the Code

At Scotland Yard Gregory settled down in the Superintendent's room with a thin paper edition of Shakespeare's plays, a pencil, and some blank sheets of foolscap. He knew that any ordinary combination of figures could have been deciphered by the decoding department at the Admiralty, to which Sir Pellinore had first sent the Corot telegram. The fact of its having defeated the experts showed quite clearly that the numerals referred to the lines of a certain book known only to the sender and recipient or their associates. His discovery of *The Tempest* as the only book in the set of Shakespeare, reposing so incongruously in the dusty warehouse of Mitbloom & Allison, which had recently been used, made him feel certain it held the key to the cipher.

He spread out the telegram before him and re-read it: COROT CAFE DE LA CLOCHE CALAIS SIXTH 41 44 11 15 THENCE 46 SEVENTH 43 47 EIGHTH AGAIN 47.

Turning to the play he looked up line 41, which read: '*. . . drown? Have you a mind to sink?*'

Then line 44: '*Work you then.*'

Next, line 11; which only had the single word: '*Enough!*'

Line 15 was, '*Where is the master, boatswain?*'

And line 46: '*. . . noise-maker. We are less afraid to be drowned than . . .*'

It simply did not make sense so he tried another method.

Treating the first numeral in each pair as indicating an act of the play, and the second numeral the line, which gave him:

41 '*If I have to*'
44 '*Amends; for I*'
11 '*Here, master: what*'
15 '*Ourselves aground: bestir, bestir.*'

This did not seem to make sense either so, for a quarter of an hour, he worked on all sorts of other possibilities; trying out the numbers against full speeches or as lines in various acts and scenes, but none of them gave any results until it occurred to him to try the songs of the Fairy Ariel.

There were four songs in the play and he wrote them down.

I. Act I. Scene II.

1. *Come unto these yellow sands,*
2. *And then take hands:*
3. *Curtsied when you have and kiss'd*
4. *The wild waves whist:*
5. *Foot it featly here and there;*
6. *'And, sweet sprites, the burthern bear.*
7. *Hark, hark!*

Bow-wow.
The watch-dogs bark:
Bow-wow.
Hark, hark! I hear
The strain of strutting chanticleer:
Cry, cock-a-diddle dow.

2. Act I. Scene II.

Full fathom five thy father lies;
Of his bones are coral made;
Those are pearls that were his eyes;
Nothing of him that doth fade,
But doth suffer a sea-change
Into something rich and strange
Sea-nymphs hourly ring his knell.
Ding-dong.
Hark! now I hear them—Ding-dong, bell.

3. Act II. Scene I.

While you here do snoring lie,
Open-eyed conspiracy
His time doth take.
If of life you keep a care,
Shake off slumber, and beware:
Awake, awake!

4. Act V. Scene I.

Where the bee sucks there suck I:
In a cowslip's bell I lie;
There do couch when owls do cry.
On a bat's back I do fly

5. *After summer, merrily.*
6. *Merrily, merrily shall I live now*
7. *Under the blossom that hangs on the bough.*

On taking out the lines, in accordance with the number in the telegram, he arrived at the following:

(Song 4, line 1). '*Where the bee sucks, there suck I.*'
(Song 4, line 4). '*On the bat's wing I do fly.*'
(Song 1, line 1). '*Come unto these yellow sands.*'
(Song 1, line 5). '*Foot it featly here and there.*'
(Song 4, line 6). '*Merrily, merrily shall I live now.*'
(Song 4, line 3). '*There do couch where owls do cry.*'
(Song 4, line 7). '*Under the blossom that hangs on the bough.*'
(Song 4, line 3). '*There do couch where owls do cry.*'
(Song 4, line 7). '*Under the blossom that hangs on the bough.*'

This little collection seemed by far the most hopeful h had achieved yet. There was a reference to '*yellow sands*' an another to '*owls*', which suggested the Brown Owl Inn. Th words '*foot it featly*', too, immediately conjured up in hi mind a vision of long dancing limbs clad in silk stockings.

Bearing in mind that the first four lines referred to th SIXTH of August, when he had witnessed the smugglers' operations at Calais, he went over them again. '*Where the be sucks, there suck I*', seemed to suggest the depot at Calais from which the smugglers drew their supplies. He did no know where they had landed on that occasion but, now that h was acutely conscious of the vast stretch of *yellow sands* a Pegwell Bay and their base a little way inland from it at As Level, it looked as though that was the spot where the smugglers had dropped their cargo on the night of the SIXTH.

Going on to the SEVENTH, the Brown Owl Inn on Romney Marshes was plainly indicated, as he knew that they ha landed there that night, and the repetition of it for th

EIGHTH, when they had landed there again, confirmed his guess.

He was puzzled for a moment about the line '*Under the blossom that hangs on the bough*', but, in view of the fact that they had discovered tobacco in Mitbloom and Allison's warehouse, he soon decided that the inference must be to leaves, and that both the cargoes he had seen landed at Romney on the two previous nights were shipments of tobacco. When he had finally re-drafted the telegram on these assumptions, it read:

COROT, CAFE DE LA CLOCHE, CALAIS. SIXTH. *I AM COLLECTING SUPPLIES FROM OUR BASE AT CALAIS. THEY WILL BE DESPATCHED BY PLANE TO PEGWELL BAY AND THE FREIGHT ON THIS OCCASION WILL BE A CONSIGNMENT OF SILKS. THENCE I SHALL PROCEED TO THE CARLTON AND ON THE* SEVENTH *A FURTHER CONSIGNMENT WILL BE LANDED AT THE BROWN OWL INN ON ROMNEY MARSHES CONSISTING OF TOBACCO. ON THE* EIGHTH *THE LAST OPERATION WILL BE REPEATED AND WE SHALL LAND AT THE BROWN OWL INN* AGAIN *WITH A FURTHER CARGO OF TOBACCO.*

'There you are'—he pushed it over to Wells and the Superintendent, 'that all fits in—doesn't it?'

The Superintendent nodded. 'Good work, sir. If you're ever out of a job I think we could find you a billet. Unfortunately, though, this telegram only carries us up to the night of the eighth and it's already the ninth, or rather the morning of the tenth I should say now, so we are stuck again. Otherwise, if I could only catch them red-handed landing a cargo, I'd bring them in now we've got on to Quex Park, Ash Level, Romney Marshes, Calais and at least one of their London depots.'

'Yes, we're at a bit of a dead end now,' Gregory confessed,

'and the new moon's due in two days' time. They'll stop operations then until the dark period in September unless I'm much mistaken. I've a hunch, though, they'll put another lot of stuff over tonight and on the eleventh so if you get your people to cover their three known landing grounds you ought to be able to catch them at it and capture their fleet tonight or tomorrow night.'

'Well, I'm for bed,' said the Superintendent. 'I was up all night last night chasing down into Kent, after Sir Pellinore got on to me to pull the two of you out of the mess you'd landed yourselves in, and you've both had a pretty sticky time, too. I think we'd best meet again here and talk things over later in the morning. How will eleven o'clock suit you?'

'Fine,' Gregory agreed. 'I got in a good sleep today at Ramsgate, but my chest's still devilish painful from the gruelling I had with that life-line, so a few hours in bed wouldn't do me any harm. I expect Wells feels much the same way.'

The Inspector drew himself up but winced as the bandages under his armpits pulled at the raw skin. 'I'm game to go on,' he said, 'but there doesn't seem anything to go on with at the moment, so I think you're right, sir. We'd best pack up for the night.'

A taxi carried Gregory swiftly through the deserted streets to Kensington. It was just four o'clock as he inserted the spare key he had telephoned Rudd to send up to the Yard in the side door of No. 272 Gloucester Road and let himself in. The terrifying experience through which he had been had taken a lot out of him and he wearily mounted the stairs covered by their worn carpet.

In his sitting-room Rudd had left, as usual, drinks and biscuits set out on a tray. He mixed himself a badly needed whisky-and-soda, threw off his coat, and drank it slowly.

His thoughts had turned to Sabine. The police net was closing upon Lord Gavin's organisation. She was still at Quex Park sleeping all unperturbed and unconscious, no doubt, of the approaching danger. By telephoning Sir Pellinore on the previous night she had undoubtedly saved the lives of

Wells and himself, but how much would the police let that weigh in her favour when they came to pull her in as one of the gang. And what was Wells's promise worth, when he had said that he would do his best for her, two nights previously, as Gregory had gone overboard from the aeroplane, trusting in the parachute to save his neck.

The police would have to charge her. They couldn't avoid doing that; and when she came before a court she would certainly be sentenced. The authorities could do no more than state that she had saved the lives of Wells and himself by giving timely information of their intended murder. It would reduce her sentence very considerably, no doubt, but she would be sentenced all the same, because she had refused to turn King's evidence when he had asked her to. She would be sent to prison and be faced with a hideous company of female gaol birds. Somehow or other he had got to save her from that.

For a moment he contemplated getting out his car and running straight down to Quex Park again, throwing the police overboard, telling her everything, and getting her out of the country by aeroplane if necessary, before they decided to arrest her. Yet if he did that, the whole of the police campaign would fall in ruins; all the work and risks taken by Wells and himself would go for nothing.

That did not matter so much, but the terrible thing was that Lord Gavin would escape and his secret organisation remain unbroken. He would create new bases farther north, perhaps upon the Essex coast, and start the game all over again. Soon, when the time was ripe, agitators and saboteurs would be landing there from his planes to pass unsuspected into the great industrial areas where they would ferment strikes and engineer every sort of trouble. He couldn't let that happen—just because he was in love. Sabine was at Quex Park and she must take her chance that he would be able to get her out when the police made their general clear up.

He opened the door of his bedroom. The light behind him was enough for him to see his bed. Upon it, stretched out on the eiderdown, her head buried in the pillows, and sleeping as soundly as a little child was Sabine.

19

Joy and Frustration

Gregory paused there in the doorway staring at her. Then, as though feeling his presence in her sleep, she stirred and, as he stepped forward, her eyes opened.

'So you are here—at last.' She raised herself on one elbow. 'I thought that you would never come and I was so tired I dropped off to sleep.'

He sat down quickly on the bed beside her and took her hands. 'My dear! How did you get here? Who let you in?'

'That nice man, Rudd. He said you were at Scotland Yard and that he had just sent up a spare key of the house for you. He offered to telephone to say I was here, but I would not let him and, not knowing how long you would be, I sent him back to bed again.'

A slow smile lit Gregory's lined face. 'You can have no possible conception how terribly glad I am to see you.'

She slid an arm round his shoulders and, pulling herself up, let her cheek rest against his. 'You are safe, *chérie*, safe. That is the only thing which matters.'

'Yes, thanks to you, but how did you know they managed to get us out of those devilish sands in time?'

'Sir Pellinore. All last night and all today I have been almost crazy with anxiety. I got out of the Park early this morning, before anybody was up, and telephoned to Carlton House Terrace from the village. Sir Pellinore was away and no one there could tell me where he had gone to. After that, I had no chance to phone again. I dared not do so from the house, in case Gavin cut in on the line, and all through the afternoon he kept me busy, typing out endless sheets of figures for him because, you see, I have acted as his secretary for all his most confidential business. After dinner he made me play backgammon with him and I thought I should go mad trying to conceal my desperate anxiety from those sharp eyes of his. At eleven o'clock we went up to bed and I had to give him a little time to settle down; but by midnight I had crept out of the house again and down to the village. Sir Pellinore was in when I called him up. He told me that you were safe back in London, so I knocked up a garage, hired a car and drove straight here to you.'

Gregory smiled again, a little bantering smile. 'Have you come to me for good?'

'Yes, if you want me.'

'Sabine, you know I do! But you mean to cut clear of this Gavin Fortescue business for good and all—don't you?'

'Yes. You were right about him. I did not know it, because he has always been so good to me, but that man is the devil in human form, I t'ink. Last night, when the Limper telephoned him that you had been caught, he sat there and told me quite calmly what he intended to do with you and the police inspector. I was horrified. Smuggling is one thing but murder another; and what a fiendish mind he must have to conceive such a terrible way of killing his enemies. I determined then that I must get away from him at whatever cost to my mother and myself; yet I had to pretend complete indifference at the time so that he should have no suspicion of my intentions. Immediately he left for Ash Level I telephoned to Sir Pellinore.'

Gregory nodded. 'It must have been grim for you, darling. It was grim for us, too; because they didn't get us out until the very last moment. I really thought our numbers were up.'

'But why? The tide was not low till half past six and I warned Sir Pellinore in ample time.'

'The police wanted Gavin and the Limper to remain under the impression they had done us in; so our rescue was not attempted until the Limper's boat had got back to land and we were buried up to our armpits in the quicksand. I take it Gavin doesn't know that we escaped, does he?'

'No, otherwise I am sure he would have spoken of it to me during the day. He seemed to have brushed the whole affair from his mind as though it had never happened; that was what made it so terrible for me. I felt quite certain that I should have heard of it if the police had raided his base at Ash Level. I waited hour after hour on tenterhooks, but no news came and I feared most terribly that something had happened to Sir Pellinore, so that he had been unable to pass my warning on to the police at all.'

'You poor darling; but never mind, we're safe enough now and it's the next move we've got to consider. Time's important, so I think, if you're not feeling too done up, you had best come up to Scotland Yard with me. We'll get Superintendent Marrowfat out of bed again and you must tell him all you know.'

She drew quickly away from him. 'But no! It is impossible for me to do that. To break away from Gavin myself is one thing, but to betray him quite another. How can you ask me to, when you know he saved my mother and me from starvation, and that he has been as generous as any father to me, giving me everything that I've ever had.'

'Now listen, Sabine,' he turned a little and faced her squarely, 'you've got to be sensible about this. I value loyalty myself above any other quality in a man or woman but Gavin Fortescue has placed himself outside the bounds of any decent code. Whatever he may have done for you in the past was done entirely for his own ends. When he saw you first, as a little girl, he had the sense to realise that one day you'd be a very beautiful woman and, even then, you probably showed signs that you'd be a very clever one, too. He realised that by an outlay, which meant nothing to him with his immense wealth, he could forge in you an instrument which would be of the very greatest use in furthering his scheme a few years later; and his foresight has been justified. You've already paid him back, more than paid him back, by taking criminal risks which he had no earthly right to expect of you, for every penny he spent on your education or allowed your mother.'

'That may be so, but nothing would induce me to *trompé* him.'

'But, my darling, you *must* think of yourself. You don't seem to realise that you've committed yourself to all sorts of criminal actions. The net is closing in on the whole of Gavin's organisation now. You'll be arrested with the Limper and the others and charged like any ordinary female crook. The Court will deal lightly with you compared with the others, because you gave information which saved myself and Wells from death, but they won't let you off entirely. You'll be sent to prison, Sabine. Don't you understand what that means. You can't, of course, or you'd never hesitate, but for a woman like you it will be a living hell and there's only one way you can save yourself from that: you've got to turn King's Evidence before the balloon goes up, so the court may use their full discretion in your case.'

'I can't, I tell you. I will not.'

'Please, Sabine, I beg you to.'

'No, Gregory, no. Whatever he has done, he has also been my friend. If I did as you wish—my self-respect—it would be gone for ever.'

'Then there's only one thing for it; I've got to get you out of England before the police decide to act.'

'That would mean your having to give up your job—no?'

'Oh, to hell with the job! I would have given a lot to be in at the death, when we corner Gavin and the Limper, but that's a bagatelle compared with your safety.'

'Are there not extradition laws so that they could bring me back?'

'There are, but I don't think they would apply them. You see, your having saved Wells and myself makes the police reluctant to prosecute you in any case now. It's only that they're bound to do so by the law—if they catch you.'

She nodded thoughtfully. 'Where could we go?'

Gregory stood up and, forgetting the abrasions on his chest and back, stretched himself. He grimaced suddenly and lowered his arms. 'The world's big enough and there are plenty of places where the two of us could lose ourselves very happily for a time.'

'When—when do we start?' she asked a little timidly.

'Mid-day will be time enough. Nobody knows you're here and zero hour for mopping up Gavin's crowd will certainly not be before tonight. They may even leave him on a string for some days yet; until they're satisfied they've gathered together all the threads of his organisation.'

'By mid-day he'll know that I've left him. Don't you t'ink that may make him uneasy. He knew I liked you. That, I think, was why he did not speak again of the business at Pegwell Bay all through today. He mentioned at lunch, too, that he had sent up to London for some sapphires that I might like to see; as though such things could possibly compensate me for your murder! It was horrible! But he is clever. When he finds I've left him he may think I cared about you far more than I said and have gone to the police to tell them how you died.'

'That's true; and if he does think that he'll hop over to France in his plane so as to be out of the way until he's certain you haven't split on him. Then the police will miss him, after all; which would be a tragedy. I wish to God you'd change your mind and come clean with the people at the Yard. We wouldn't have to make a moonlight flitting if you did and, with the information you could give them, the police would be able to fill in their gaps. Then they could raid Quex Park right away. If we acted now there would just be time for them to get Gavin in his bed before he finds out you've cut adrift from him.'

'It's no good, Gregory. I will not give evidence against Gavin.'

'All right, my dear, in that case we must get out at once. The police don't know you're here so we'll have a free run to Heston where we can pick up the plane. Before I leave I'll telephone the Yard that if they don't pinch Gavin within the next two hours they'll lose him. I need not say what makes me believe that; or where I got my information.'

'But you should rest. You're worn out—*mon pauvre petit*—and you've been through a time incredible. How can you possibly talk of just walking out of the house and flying the Channel when you must be so desperately tired.'

He shrugged and put a hand up to his bandages again. 'I'm all right. Slept all through the day at the Granville Hotel, Ramsgate. Bit sore where the ropes cut into me when they pulled us out of those blasted sands—that's all. It's been worse for you than for me, really. You had no sleep last night and a gruelling day worrying your lovely head whether I was alive or dead'o. But you can sleep in the plane once we're in it.'

'You are a very wonderful man, Gregory—the most wonderful man. I did not think that there was anybody in the world quite as wonderful as you. I love you.'

He bent above her. 'The gods are being kind to me in my old age. Most beautiful women are either good, stupid or vicious. And you are the marvellous exception. Lovely as a goddess, clever as an Athenian and a bad hat like myself, yet one who still has decent feelings. I'm going to kiss the lips off you once we land in France.'

The temptation to set about it now was strong within him, but time was precious: it was already after five o'clock. He had to get his car, take Sabine down to Heston in it, and see that his plane was fuelled for a cross-Channel flight. He did not intend to telephone Scotland Yard until the last minute before leaving. It was doubtful if Superintendent Marrowfat would be able to reach Birchington before Gavin Fortescue was up but he could telephone the local police with orders to prevent him leaving the Park until the Yard men arrived.

Gregory bent down and pulled a couple of suitcases from under his bed. 'Pack for me, will you?' he said. 'Anything you can lay your hands on that you think will prove most useful. Rudd sleeps down in the basement so it would only waste time for me to go and dig him out of bed.'

She stood up at once and began to collect things from his dressing-table.

'I'll go round and get the car,' he told her. 'It's garaged in Elvaston Mews, about ten minutes' walk away, but I'll be back in a quarter of an hour. Bless you.'

'Bless *you*,' she echoed, as he smiled over his shoulder, and his tall, slouching figure disappeared through the door. She heard him let himself out and his footsteps echo along the pavement of the deserted street in the silent hour that preceded dawn. A greyish light already filtered sluggishly through the chinks in the window curtains of the bedroom. She pressed the electric switch, flooding out those signs of approaching day; then she set to work rummaging through Gregory's drawers.

In less than five minutes she had the two cases crammed to capacity with the things she thought would prove of the greatest use to him and carried them out to the sitting-room where she put them all ready, just behind the door, with the little dressing-case which was all she had been able to bring with her.

As she set them down she suddenly grew tense. She had caught the sound of cautious footsteps on the stairs. Gregory could not have got back so soon she felt sure.

A second later a key clicked in the lock. The door swung open and she saw the Limper standing there with two other men behind him.

Before she had time to scream he stepped into the room and had her covered with his automatic.

'So we were right,' he said. 'The wife of the garage man in Birchington only overheard you say the word "Gloucester" when you knocked him up, but, as I had some of Sallust's letters from when we searched him on the marshes, I had a hunch you'd said Gloucester *Road*, and we'd find you here.'

Sabine stared at him with wide distended eyes; then backed slowly away before him. 'What d'you want?' she whispered, tonelessly.

'You,' the Limper smiled. 'The Big Chief's a light sleeper.

He heard the crunching of your feet on the gravel, looked out of his window, and saw you making your get-away from Quex a few hours ago. It wasn't difficult for him to find out from which garage in Birchington you got a car. He telephoned me at Ash Level to come up and get you.'

'Get me,' breathed Sabine, her face gone ashen.

'That's it,' said the Limper slowly. 'He was afraid that because we bumped off your boy friend you might have ratted on us and told tales to the police. We can't afford to have that sort of thing happening, you know, and it's lucky for you that you came here instead of going to Scotland Yard. Why did you come here, though—as Sallust is dead?'

'I—I thought I might get some of his papers, find out just how much he knew, which would have been useful to us,' lied Sabine.

'Who let you in? I got in with the keys we took off him the night before last—but you couldn't have. Who let you in here?'

'His servant Rudd. He doesn't know yet that his master's dead and he knows me because I've been here once before. I said Sallust had telephoned me to come but he might not be here for an hour or two. Then I sent Rudd off to bed.'

'I see; so that's the way of it, but if you had this bright idea of collecting Sallust's papers why didn't you tell the Chief what you meant to do?'

Sabine suddenly straightened herself. 'I am answerable to him and not to you.'

'Got the papers?'

'I'd just finished searching the place: there is nothing here that matters. He evidently keeps any notes he has somewhere else.'

'Right then. We'll be moving. I don't believe your story and I doubt if the Chief will either; but he's mighty anxious to see you again and put you through it. Come on; get downstairs to the car.'

Sabine hesitated only a second. Gregory would be returning soon now. How could he possibly overcome three armed men if he was taken by surprise by them on entering his sitting-room. They believed him dead, but if they found that their last attempt upon him had failed they were capable of shooting him out of hand, and they had silencers upon their automatics. The thought of trying to explain her movements under the steady gaze of Lord Gavin's cold soulless eyes, terrified her; but Gregory's life lay in the balance.

When he drew up before the house a few minutes later a large car was just disappearing round the corner of the street. Upstairs he found the bags packed and ready; but no sign of Sabine. He called aloud for her but there was no response. The flat was empty. With a bitter, hopeless feeling of distress he suddenly concluded that, for some incomprehensible reason, she had changed her mind and left him once again.

20

The Terrible Dilemma

For a moment Gregory tried to cheat himself by the thought that she might have slipped out of the house on some errand but even the dairies and fruitshops were not yet open. If she had wished to telephone the instrument stood there on a low table. He could think of no possible reason which might have caused her to leave the flat; except that she must be so frightened of Gavin Fortescue that her courage had failed her at the last moment and she had decided to go back to him.

He threw himself down on the sofa and dropped his head between his hands. While Sabine had been with him he had been buoyed up by the joy of her nearness and the need for new activities with the world opening wide before them both as they flew towards the rising sun—out of England. Now, the terrible strain of the last few days was beginning to tell on his iron constitution.

Except for the packed suitcases and the crumpled bed, where Sabine had been sleeping when he arrived, her presence there might have been a dream. He was faced again by exactly the same problem as that with which he had battled on his way back from Scotland Yard an hour and a half earlier. Should he risk wrecking the whole of the police campaign by going down to Quex Park and either cajoling or forcing Sabine to cross the Channel with him, before she was arrested, or must he take a chance upon being able to get her out of trouble later; so that the police might have a free hand to round up the whole of Gavin Fortescue's organisation in one swift move.

If smuggling only had been concerned he would not have hesitated for a second but have gone to his car and driven down into Kent right away. It was Sir Pellinore's insistence that Gavin Fortescue's fanatic hatred of Britain would lead him to use his fleet to import numbers of agitators and saboteurs, without the knowledge of the immigration authorities, which perturbed Gregory so seriously.

Of course, that might not occur until September but, on the other hand, the events of the last few days had probably rattled Gavin Fortescue badly. The affair with Wells in Deauville, just a week ago this coming night, had informed him that the police were on his track; the Limper's capture of two spies on Romney Marshes, that they were hot on his trail. It was doubtful if Sabine would be able to get back to Quex Park before he was up; so he might well suspect that her midnight absence had been caused by a journey to London to lay any information against him.

The thought of what would happen to her if that occurred made Gregory momentarily feel sick and giddy; but Sabine was clever. On the journey back her quick wits would surely devise some plausible explanation to meet Gavin's inquiries if her absence from the Park had been discovered.

In any case, it seemed that so shrewd a man as Gavin Fortescue would have seen the red light and would, therefore, bring his operations to a close, either that coming night or the next; before the new moon came in. On one or other of them the chances were he would land those men who might do such incalculable harm to the peace and prosperity of Britain.

Between the two necessities—for preventing that dire calamity and saving Sabine from prison—Gregory rocked mentally as he sat with his head buried in his hands. It was the most distressing problem he had ever had to face and he could reach no definite decision.

At last he got slowly to his feet and began to ease his clothes from his sore back and chest. The police net would not close until the following night at the earliest: that fact alone seemed reasonably certain. Therefore, he still had a good twelve hours in front of him before he need make the final plunge one way or the other.

Ordinarily he was a man of quick decisions, but in this case he felt the old adage 'sleep on it' was true wisdom. A few hours of blessed oblivion would recruit his strength for whatever desperate part he was called upon to play that coming night. He would keep his appointment with Marrowfat at the Yard at 11 o'clock that morning, and only then, when he was in the possession of any further information which the police might have obtained, decide definitely upon his future plans.

Five hours later he entered the Superintendent's room, punctual to the minute; spick and span again and ready to cope with any situation.

Wells was already there and Sir Pellinore arrived almost on Gregory's heels. Marrowfat nodded a cheerful good morning and, as they sat down, pushed a telegram across his table towards them.

'They'll be out again tonight,' he said. 'Though we're not quite certain where, yet. It looks as if they mean to use a base we haven't tumbled to.'

Gregory picked up the telegram. 'How did you get this?' he asked.

'Usual way,' the Superintendent grinned. 'We tipped off

the Post Office to let us have copies of any telegrams which came through for Mitbloom & Allison.'

Gregory read out the message: 'MITBLOOM 43 BARTER STREET LONDON E.1. TENTH 21 33 COROT.'

Wells held a slip of paper in his hand. 'According to the key you worked out last night from Ariel's songs, that means:

'Full fathom five thy father lies;
His time doth take.

Doesn't seem to make sense, does it?'

Gregory sat thoughtful for a moment then he said: ' "*Full fathom five thy father lies*" sounds like another base, as you suggest. Somewhere on the coast, I suppose, but where goodness knows!'

'I take it to mean some place where the water remains five fathoms deep even at low tide,' said the Superintendent. He spread out a large scale map of Kent and all four men bent over it.

'In that case it can be nowhere on the sea-coast,' Sir Pellinore remarked, 'but there are plenty of places round Sheppey or in the channel of the Medway, running up to Chatham, that are quite close inland and never less than five fathoms.'

'That's about it, sir,' Wells nodded. 'There's any number of quiet spots among all those islands; but which is it? That's the question.'

'Why should they mention the depth of the water?' Gregory spoke thoughtfully. 'I wonder if Gavin Fortescue is employing fast motor boats as well as planes to land his cargoes. It's a possibility you know; when the contraband is of a heavy nature.'

'That's a fact,' agreed the Superintendent, 'and the second number, 33, should give us the nature of the cargo, shouldn't it? It doesn't offer much to go on though; "his—time—doth—take". *Time*, is about the only word in it worth thinking about.'

'Bombs with time-fuses, my friend,' announced Sir Pellinore quietly. 'They would certainly constitute weighty cargo.'

'By jove, you're right, sir.' Wells backed him up. 'They're landing a cargo of bombs at some place in the Thames Estuary where the Channel is never less than five fathoms deep at low tide.'

For a moment they stood silent round the table, then the Superintendent said: 'If only we knew the place I'd pull them in tonight. Since Lord Gavin caught Mr. Sallust and Wells he must know we've been watching some of his people; although he's probably not aware yet that we have the Park under observation. He may decide to quit any moment now and, as the new moon's on the 12th, this may be the last cargo he'll chance running.'

The grip of Gregory's muscular hands tightened a little on the arms of his chair. The Superintendent was no fool and summed up the position precisely as he had himself a few hours before. That made it more imperative than ever that he must make up his mind what he intended to do about Sabine.

'You might raid the Park and get Gavin Fortescue tonight in any case,' suggested Sir Pellinore. 'After all he is the centre of the whole conspiracy.'

The Superintendent shook his big head. 'I'd rather work it the other way sir. If we nab him first it may prevent him giving some signal which is the O.K. for his men to run their stuff; then we'd lose the bulk of them. Far better let them land, take them redhanded, and bring in Lord Gavin immediately afterwards.'

'Have you had any news from the Park?' Gregory inquired.

'Nothing that's of any help to us.' Wells looked up quickly. 'My man Simmons rang up early this morning to say Mademoiselle Sabine had slipped off on her own round about midnight; telephoned from Birchington and then hired a car in which she drove away towards London. She turned up there again this morning though, just before eight, in a different car and three men were with her. The Limper was one of them.'

Gregory remained poker-faced at this piece of information. So she *had* gone back to Gavin Fortescue. But why had three of the others been with her? It flashed into his mind that perhaps she had not gone back to Quex Park of her own free will and that they had been sent to get her. But if that were so how had the Limper and his men discovered where she was. It was more probable, he considered, that Sabine, having no car of her own, had taken the early train to Canterbury and then telephoned for them to fetch her.

While the rest were poring over the map of the Thames Estuary and discussing the most likely spots where a landing might be effected at low tide Gregory began to wonder if Wells had passed on the whole of the information which had reached him in the early hours of that morning. It was possible the police had traced Sabine's car from Birchington to Gloucester Road and that Wells was concealing the fact. Knowing something of the efficiency of the police organisation Gregory thought it highly probable. If so, they were aware of her visit to his flat and assumed already that he intended to double-cross them. He would have to be extra careful now as the chances were that they were watching him; just as they had on the day he had spent with Sabine in London.

'I'll think it over,' said the Superintendent suddenly. 'Maybe we'll raid Quex Park tonight; maybe not. We'll phone you later in the day as to what we've decided.'

'Fine,' replied Gregory with a cheerful smile, concealing his inward perturbation that now, suspicious of him, the police did not intend to let him in on any further plans they might make.

'Let me know too will you?' Sir Pellinore said quietly. 'If there's going to be any fun I'd rather like to be in it. That is if you have no objection.'

'Certainly, sir. It will be a pleasure to have you with us,' Marrowfat assured him.

On that the conference broke up; Sir Pellinore and Gregory leaving the room together.

From Scotland Yard they crossed Whitehall, entered St. James's Park at Birdcage Walk and, turning left, crossed the Horse Guards Parade towards Carlton House Terrace.

The fine spell was over. London had had her week of summer and, although the weather continued warm, grey clouds hung low overhead. The Park looked dry and dusty; the flowers had wilted in the recent heat wave. Most of them were fading and, as the gardeners had not yet had time to clear the beds for fresh varieties, many of them presented only a tangle of overgrown greenery. A spattering of idlers lay sprawled upon the tired parched grass and here and there a handful of children played within sight of their knitting nursemaids. The atmosphere was heavy and depressing.

Gregory and Sir Pellinore did not exchange a word as they walked on side by side until they reached Waterloo steps and were ascending them towards the terrace.

'You'll lunch with me?' asked Sir Pellinore. 'That will pass a little of the time while we're waiting.'

'Thanks, I'd like to. D'you think they'll raid Quex Park tonight?'

'I haven't a doubt of it. Marrowfat is not a fool and Gavin Fortescue must realise by now that the tide is running swiftly against him. He's probably making his preparations for departure at this moment. If the police don't rope him in tonight they will have lost an opportunity which may not recur for months to come.'

'In that case I may not be with you.'

Sir Pellinore grunted. 'I had an idea that might be so. You're a clever feller, Gregory, and I doubt if they spotted anything at the Yard but I know you so well. You're worried about that young Hungarian baggage, aren't you?'

'I am,' Gregory agreed. 'Damnably worried. If they pull her in with the rest of the gang she'll be sent to prison.'

'Her sentence will be considerably reduced on account of

the fact that she enabled us to come to your assistance the other night.'

Gregory shrugged impatiently. 'That's no consolation. It might be for a down and out who's been used to sleeping in doss-houses and queueing up for charity grub. But think of a girl like Sabine in prison. Every month she gets will be like a year in hell. Have you ever visited a women's prison? I have. The smell of the place alone is enough to make you sick. Sour, sterile; cabbage soup, disinfectant, soap-suds—all mixed up. Think of the irritation to her skin from the coarse garments they'll make her wear; how her stomach will heave when she has to swallow the skilly to keep herself alive, and her hands with broken nails, red and raw from the wash tubs and floor scrubbing. Think of the ghastly creatures she'll have to mix with too. It's well known that women criminals are ten times as vicious as male crooks. They'll torture her every moment of the day from sheer loathing of anyone better than themselves. . . .'

'I know, I know,' Sir Pellinore broke in. 'I would do anything in my power to save her from that if I could; but even my influence is not sufficient to secure a free pardon for her unless she is prepared to turn King's Evidence.'

They did not speak again until they had entered the house and were seated in the big library overlooking the Mall; then Sir Pellinore rang the bell.

'Tell Garwood to send up a magnum of Röederer '20,' he said to the footman who answered his ring, then he turned back to Gregory.

'Nothing like champagne; only possible drink when you've been working overtime and are worried into the bargain. Gives you just the right fillip to carry on without doping you a hair's breadth. The twenties are getting on in age now, of course, but they're still grand wines if they've been well kept and, in my opinion, the Röederer was the best of 'em.'

Gregory nodded. 'It's been well kept all right if you've had it in your cellar for the last ten years.'

'Yes. Nothing like leaving good wine to rest quietly in the

same temperature till you want to drink it. I always buy 'em when they first come out and forget 'em till they're drinkable.'

Garwood arrived, portly, priestlike: preceding the footman who carried the double bottle in a bucket of ice and two large silver tankards on a big tray.

'Shall I open it, sir?' the butler asked. 'It hasn't had long on the ice but coming from the cellar it will be at quite a drinkable temperature.'

'Go ahead,' said Sir Pellinore, and the two tankards were filled till the bursting bubbles topped their brims.

'Good thought of yours to order a magnum,' Gregory remarked. 'Wine always keeps so much better in magnums than in bottles and in bottles than in pints. The only trouble with a magnum is, it's too much for one and not enough for two.'

Sir Pellinore brushed up his fine white moustache and smiled. 'Plenty more where it came from. We'll knock off another with our lunch if you feel like it.'

The servants had left the room; yet both men displayed curious reluctance to speak again of the topic which was really occupying their minds.

Gregory drank deep and sighed. 'How much better this stuff drinks out of a tankard,' he said slowly. 'The same thing in a footling little glass wouldn't be half as good.'

'You never said a truer word my boy. Think how horrid tea would taste in a port-wine glass, or burgundy in anything except a big round goblet, just half-full, so that one can get the aroma. Brandy too—although, curiously enough, all the other liqueurs lose their flavour in big glasses and are better in thimbles—provided one has the thimbles refilled often enough—but champagne's a tankard wine, not a doubt of it.'

They fell silent again until Sir Pellinore said, at last, with a swift look at his guest:

'Well, what're you going to do?'

'Go down and get her out before they raid the place tonight.'

'Risky—isn't it? Hundred to one they're watching you.

Some flatfoot in a bowler probably kicking his heels outside this house even now.'

'I know, that's the big difficulty. I can get rid of him all right. I've played tip and run before. Any tube station or big store with several entrances will provide the means for me to throw him off my track; but the devil of it is that these blokes know me. Another of them will pick me up on the station if I go by train or one of his pals will spot me if I motor down. I dare not move till after dark and we have no idea what time that clever old elephant Marrowfat will get to work.'

'You're taking a pretty nasty risk you know,' said Sir Pellinore quietly. 'Obstructing the police in the execution of their duty, aiding a known criminal to escape from the country, and all that sort of thing. You'll be a sitting pheasant for three months in prison yourself if you're not darned careful.'

'I know it. But what the hell! I've got to get her out of it somehow, haven't I?'

'Of course. I should feel just the same, but you've got your work cut out and I'll be devilled if I see how you're going to do it. Got any sort of plan?'

'No. I'm absolutely in the air at the moment and I'm not liking the situation one little bit. I'll tell you just how I stand.'

Gregory refilled his tankard, sat forward in the deep armchair, and told Sir Pellinore how things were between himself and Sabine; ending up with an account of her visit to his flat on the previous night.

When he had done Sir Pellinore looked unusually grave. 'From what you tell me the situation is worse than I imagined. You don't even know if the wench is willing to quit, so maybe you'll have to get her out of Gavin Fortescue's clutches against her will, as well as clear of the police.'

'I'll manage somehow,' said Gregory doggedly.

'You won't act too early and make the police campaign abortive, will you. It's frightfully important they should smash up Gavin Fortescue's organisation. Without any flag-wagging it means a hell of a lot to the country that they should.'

'Don't I know it,' Gregory agreed. 'If it weren't for that

I shouldn't be here but snooping round the Park at Birchington by this time.'

Garwood appeared to announce that lunch was served.

Sir Pellinore stood up. 'All right. I know I can leave the whole question of your private interests to your discretion.'

Over luncheon they talked of indifferent things but neither had any real interest in the conversation and long periods of silence intervened between each topic that was broached. The air was electric with their unspoken thoughts.

It was after lunch, when they were well into the second magnum, Sir Pellinore having decreed that no liqueurs should be served, that a call from Wells came through.

Milly had been on the telephone to him from a call box in Birchington. She reported that Sabine and Lord Gavin Fortescue had had high and bitter words that morning after breakfast; 'a proper scene' was the way she phrased it, and Mrs. Bird, who had butted in on their quarrel inadvertently, described his little lordship as having been 'positively white with rage'. Half an hour later Sabine had been taken up to her room and locked in. She was virtually a prisoner there but Mrs. Bird had been allowed to take her lunch up on a tray and reported her to be pale and silent.

Milly's real reason for ringing up, however, was that she had overheard a scrap of conversation which she thought might prove useful. She had been passing an open window of the downstairs room in which Lord Gavin and the Limper had been sitting after lunch. She had heard Lord Gavin say: 'Tonight at Eastchurch Marshes I wish you to . . .' That was all, and she had not dared to linger, but had slipped out of the Park to telephone Wells from the village right away.

In the library Sir Pellinore got out a big atlas, and soon discovered Eastchurch Marshes on the south coast of the Isle of Sheppey. The river Swale separated Sheppey from the mainland of the North Kent coast and a tributary of it marked Windmill Creek, just below Eastchurch Marshes, ran up into the island.

'That's it,' said Sir Pellinore, placing a well-manicured,

square-nailed finger on the spot. 'You'll see that apart from sandbanks, the Swale and Windmill Creek still carry five fathoms of water, even at low tide. That's the place they mean to make their landing and Wells said just now that the police will concentrate there after dark tonight.'

Gregory heaved a sigh of relief. 'Thank God they'll be busy then, and that the place is well over twenty miles from Quex Park, apart from being on the far side of the Swale. While they're on the job of rounding up the gang I'll have a free hand at the Park to get Sabine out of it before they come on there.'

'They'll probably surround the Park as well,' suggested Sir Pellinore.

'Perhaps, but it's a big place and well wooded. Marrowfat said himself this morning he wouldn't attempt to pull Gavin in until he mopped up the rest of the bunch. That should give me a chance to get clear of the house before they raid it.'

Sir Pellinore nodded. 'I told Wells you were here and he asked me to pass it on to you that the Flying Squad are leaving London for Queenborough at seven o'clock. Do you intend to come with us?'

Gregory shook his head. 'No. I've got a perfectly good excuse in the gruelling I received yesterday. I'd be grateful if you'd tell them I'm absolutely played out; so done up that I can't appear in the last act after all. If you'll give them that message, when you turn up at the Yard a little before seven, I can throw off any shadows they put on to my trail well before that and be down in Kent again. I think I'll leave now to get busy with my preparations.'

'All right, my boy.' Sir Pellinore laid a kindly hand on Gregory's shoulder. 'Please remember me kindly to your very lovely lady. It would break my old heart too, I think, to see such a gracious child sent to prison; and she will be unless you can prevent it. If I can do anything to help you know I will.'

His eyes were troubled as he watched Gregory go, a lean bent figure, from the front door to which he had escorted him a few moments later.

Sir Pellinore had geen right in his guess that the police were covering Gregory. He spotted two big men chatting together on the corner as he turned down past the Carlton Club into Pall Mall. Their boots were not unduly large and they both wore soft felts instead of bowler hats, but Gregory was quite certain that they were plain-clothes men. He did not bother to throw them off his trail since he assumed, with good reason, that another couple would be watching his rooms as well. Instead, he walked as far as the Piccadilly tube quite openly and when he reached his flat he was not at all surprised to see that the shorter of the two men was only a hundred yards behind him.

He had planned to repack his bags, collect his car and set off at about six o'clock, twisting through the streets of South East London to throw any following police cars off his track; then to drive by a circuitous route through Tonbridge, Cranbrook, Ashford, and so by by-roads, north-west to his destination. But Rudd was waiting for him in his sitting-room, hard at work polishing a brass ashtray cut from a 5.9 shell case: a souvenir of the old days of the war. He immediately produced a note which he said he had found half an hour before on the hall mat. It was unsigned, but Gregory realised at once that it had come from Gavin Fortescue, for it read:

Dear Mr. Sallust,

It seems that in spite of the almost foolproof precautions which I took to prevent your interfering any more in my affairs you are still active and impertinently curious.

This is to inform you that Sabine is once more in my care and to warn you, very seriously, that if you presume to lift one finger to interfere further in my business the matter will be reported to me by my people who have you under observation.

If you value Sabine's happiness, as I have reason to suppose you do, and by happiness please understand that I refer to her capacity for ever enjoying anything in this world again, you will not only refrain from troubling me further yourself;

you will also use your best endeavours to persuade your friends at Scotland Yard that, for any reason which you care to invent, it would be wiser for them to defer any visit which they may contemplate paying to myself, or my various bases, for the next few days.

If you fail in this, you may be quite sure that you will never see Sabine alive again.

21

The Trap is Sprung

When Sir Pellinore Gwaine-Cust arrived in Superintendent Marrowfat's room at Scotland Yard that evening at seven o'clock he was naturally a little taken aback to find Gregory there. He hid his surprise under an affable greeting to the Superintendent, Wells, and some other men who were present; assuming, quite rightly, that some new occurrence had caused Gregory to alter his plans completely.

Gregory sat silent in front of the Superintendent's desk puffing a little more rapidly than usual at a cigarette. Lord Gavin's letter had shaken him worse than any other incident that had occurred in his decidedly exciting career.

For an hour he had wrestled with himself once more; turning over in his mind again and again all the possibilities which might develop from the alternative sequence of actions he might take. Sabine was now a prisoner and he had not the faintest doubt that the soulless, deformed, little monstrosity, round whom the whole conspiracy centred, meant to kill her out of hand if he had the least suspicion that his warning had been disregarded.

In the face of that all Gregory's courage had temporarily ebbed away and, single-handed as he was, he had felt that he simply dare not risk raiding Quex Park. Lord Gavin would almost certainly be protected by his gunmen; Sabine was a prisoner in an upstairs room and in addition the situation was horribly complicated by the presence, outside the Park, of members of the police force who would have been told off to watch for him.

Later, he had been sorely tempted to throw discretion to the winds, go in bald-headed, and chance what might happen; but in his saner moments he realised that the odds were so terribly against him that it would be sheer madness to do so. If Sabine were taken by the police it meant that she would receive a prison sentence; but by making a premature move he would place her life itself in jeopardy.

Cursing the necessity of deferring personal action, he had decided that his only hope now lay in leading the police to suppose that he was completely loyal to them. Lord Gavin could know nothing of the projected raid on Eastchurch Marshes; by participating in it Gregory saw that he would at least learn of all new developments at first hand. Such information might prove invaluable and he just trust to his judgment, once the raid was made, as to the best moment to slip away from the police and act independently. He had brought Rudd with him to Scotland Yard knowing he could rely upon that loyalist's co-operation in any circumstances; now he sat listening intently, but saying nothing, as the big Superintendent outlined his plans.

Marrowfat's oration was brief. With a map spread before him he pointed with a stubby finger to various places on it. The Kent constabulary were co-operating with them; special levies drawn from Rochester, Chatham, Sittingbourne and Maidstone would take up their positions on Sheppey Island directly dusk had fallen. The Thames River Police had also been called in. With launches manned to capacity they would slip down the north coast of the island after dark, rendezvousing near the Ham Fishery buoy in the deeper water a couple of miles or more to the north of Shell Ness. Sound detectors would be on board some of the launches and they would lie in wait there until the motor barges of the smugglers passed south of them up the channel of the East Swale; upon which they would move in and close the mouth of the river. The Superintendent's own party, consisting of some Special Branch men, Sir Pellinore, Gregory and Wells would leave by car immediately and, crossing the West Swale to Sheppey, rendezvous at Queenborough. Small arms and ammunition were then to be served out.

A quarter of an hour after Sir Pellinore's arrival at the Yard the little crowd of muscular big-chinned men shouldered their way out along the passageway from the Superintendent's room, down the stairs, and into the waiting line of swift supercharged cars.

Gregory had brought his own car for his own perfectly good reasons. He got into the back with Sir Pellinore; leaving Rudd to drive it and a plain clothes man beside him to decide on the route they were to take.

As they ran out of the courtyard behind the others Gregory found his thoughts distracted from Sabine for a moment by admiration for the police organisation. There was no fuss or bother; no disturbance of the traffic. The fleet of cars did not form a procession, but separated immediately, all taking different pre-arranged routes down into the City and through Southwark, on the south side of the Thames, to the scene of their midnight activities.

They were at Queenborough before half past eight and, having already had his instructions, the plain-clothes man beside Rudd conducted them to the police station which served the docks. Wells and Marrowfat had just driven up but there was no sign of the squad of Special Branch men who had left the Yard with them.

Sir Pellinore and Gregory got out and followed the Superintendent into the station. In the private office there he introduced them to the Chief Constable of Kent and a number of local officers from Chatham, Rochester and Maidstone. Standing in front of a large scale map, which hung upon the wall of the plainly furnished room, the police chiefs spent half an hour discussing the positions which were soon to be taken up by their various bodies of men on both banks of Windmill Creek and along the southern coast of the Isle of Sheppey.

A local Inspector who had reconnoitred Eastchurch Marshes that afternoon gave them a brief description of the terrain where the landing was expected.

'We shall proceed to Eastchurch village,' he said, 'and leave our cars there; parked out of sight in garages for which I've already arranged. We shall then go on foot down the by-way leading south from the village. It's about a two-mile walk through low-lying unwooded country. There's a little cultivated land here and there; but it's mostly marsh which is waterlogged in winter. However, fortunately for us, it's dry enough to walk on without any danger of being bogged this time of the year.

'You'll see from the map the track I'm speaking of doesn't run right down to the water so, at the bend, just at point 13 which marks a slight rise in the ground, we shall turn right and cross the fields for about five hundred yards until we strike that second track which actually leads to the creek. That's probably the road they'll use. That, or the third track half a mile to the right again, which ends at the creek where it's marked "Hook Quay".

'The only buildings between the second and third tracks are a collection of empty tumble-down sheds near Hook Quay and a new cottage on the river bank about two hundred yards south of it which was only built a few months ago. The cottage is inhabited but, as the people who live there may be in with the crowd we're after, I didn't like to risk rousing their suspicions by going near the place when I was having a look round this afternoon.'

The whole party then left the station and, piling into four cars, drove off along the good road to the north of the island until they came to the little village of Eastchurch.

Having garaged the cars they began their walk, crossing the railway line at Eastchurch Station half a mile south of the village, and proceeding after that into the gathering dusk which had now descended upon the lonely stretch of country before them.

They left the lane at point 13 and struck across the low-lying ground with its coarse tufts of high marsh grass, found the road to the east and turned south along it, until they arrived on the banks of the creek; a sluggish stream set between sloping muddy levels.

The opposite bank was about a hundred and fifty yards away and, although scores of police were now lurking in the neighbourhood, not a soul was visible in the failing light. The only life apparent in that desolate waste was an oyster catcher pecking in the mud and a few screaming seagulls which wheeled overhead.

The Chief Constable's party turned inland along the bank towards Hook Quay, making a detour to avoid passing within sight of the new brick cottage which the local inspector had described, and arriving just before ten o'clock at the cluster of empty sheds.

It was dark now and producing their torches, once they were inside the ramshackle buildings, the police made a thorough investigation of them.

They were quite empty but showed signs of recent use. Their windows had been boarded over so that no lights could show and gaps in the wooden walls had been pasted over with brown paper. The earthen floors showed marks where heavy cases had been thrown down upon them and in two of the larger sheds cartwheel tracks were visible.

'It looks as if they work things differently here and store the stuff instead of getting it away immediately,' Wells remarked. 'Although, of course, a fleet of lorries may come rumbling down the lane outside to meet them when they turn up.'

'I doubt it,' replied the Superintendent. 'A dozen lorries rumbling along the Ashford road or anywhere behind all those coast towns in Thanet wouldn't call for special comment. But here in Sheppey it's different. The roads don't lead anywhere so convoys passing in the middle of the night, even once or twice a month, would be certain to arouse some inquisitive person's suspicions. They wouldn't dare risk that. In my opinion they store the stuff here and local farm carts come along later to collect it. The carts probably deliver the goods to some other depot on the west end of the island, south of Queenborough, where it would be easy to transfer them to the railway with so much goods traffic passing from the docks there up to London.'

Gregory drew Rudd outside and into a smaller shed near by where they were quite alone together. Kneeling down on the floor he spread out his map and shone his torch upon it.

'See where we are now—Hook Quay?' he said in a low voice.

'Yes sir,' muttered Rudd.

'Right. Think you can find your way back to the village?'

'Easy. Straight up the track that leads from here. 'Crorst the railway at the level crossin'. Turn right along that second-class road south of the one we come to Eastchurch by for half a mile and there we are. Simple as kiss me 'and.'

'Good lad.' Gregory patted his arm affectionately. 'Now I want you to fade out when no one's looking. Go back to Eastchurch, collect the car, and drive it to the farm marked "Old Hook" on the map. That's just half-way up the track between these sheds and the railway. I daren't let you bring it nearer in case the people here catch the sound of the engine, send a man to investigate, and finding it's my car tumble to what I'm up to. When you reach Old Hook turn the car round and park it at the roadside, facing north, ready for an instant getaway. If one of the local coppers who're playing hide-and-seek all over the countryside tonight ask what you're up to just say you're acting on Superintendent Marrowfat's orders. We must risk their disbelieving you and coming over to report. When you're through, leave the car and join me here again to let me know everything's all right. That clear?'

'You bet it is. I'll be back under the hour sir.'

Rudd slipped out of the hut and vanished in the darkness. Gregory folded up his map and rejoined the others. Just outside the largest shed Wells was standing; peering down at the small wharf which jutted out from the bank into the sluggish stream.

'What about having a quiet look at that cottage the local man mentioned,' Gregory suggested, coming up behind him.

Wells nodded. 'Righto. It's very unlikely anything will happen for an hour or more, so we've plenty of time.'

The two left the shed together and made their way cautiously along the bank of the creek. Six hundred yards from the shacks they came round a sharp bend and saw a light directly ahead a little way in front of them.

'That'll be it,' muttered Gregory. 'I'll bet the earth whoever lives there is in this thing.'

Picking their way carefully they approached nearer to the small two-storied house. It had no garden, only a back yard filled with rubble that the builders had left, and no road or lane led to it. The light came from a downstairs window; covered by a thin cretonne curtain.

'I'd lay any money that Gavin built this place,' Gregory went on, 'and I'm pretty sure I can tell you why he picked this site, well away from either of the lanes, too.'

'All right, let's hear your theory,' Wells whispered.

'The sheds at Hook Quay are round the bend of the creek so no light shown there could be seen for more than five hundred yards down stream. That's probably why Gavin chose it as the actual landing-place, but it has one drawback, they can't signal from it. Now this place is right on the bend of the river. A light in the upstairs room of the house, on its far side, could be seen for five miles at least, right down at the entrance of the Swale. That's how they signal to the incoming fleet of luggers that the coast is clear, or if there are any suspicious-looking people about, and the smuggler boats had best hang off for a bit.'

'That's sound enough. I see they're on the telephone too,' Wells remarked, jerking his head towards a stout pole only a yard away from them. 'That in itself is suspicious; seeing it's only a jerry-built place miles from anywhere. It must have cost them quite a bit to get a line brought down from Eastchurch Station; far more than ordinary people who lived in a little place like this could afford.'

They were crouching behind a pile of debris, left by the builders, about thirty yards from the cottage. 'I wish we could get near enough to look in at that window,' Gregory said thoughtfully; but Wells shook his head.

'Too risky. If they spotted us they'd be on the telephone to warn their pals the game was up before we could get inside. Now we've seen all there is to see I think we'd best get back to the others.'

In one of the sheds Sir Pellinore, the Chief Constable, Marrowfat and the rest, were gathered, seated on the dry earth floor busily engaged in eating a picnic supper. Producing their own packets of sandwiches Gregory and Wells joined them.

When they had finished Sir Pellinore, who had refused offers of various drinks, produced a large medicine bottle from his pocket, removed the cork, and took a long pull at it.

'Not allowed to drink with my meals,' he lied cheerfully, winking at Gregory, 'gives me such awful indigestion. That's why I have to take this medicine.'

Gregory kept a perfectly straight face as he listened to this barefaced lie. He had often seen that interesting medicine bottle before. Whenever Sir Pellinore was compelled to accept an invitation for dinner at a house where he distrusted his host's choice of wines the medicine bottle always travelled with him. He left it outside in the hall and sent for it after dinner; having first pronounced his glib tarradiddle about suffering from indigestion. The medicine it contained was in actual fact an ample ration of his own impeccable Napoleon Brandy.

At eleven o'clock they switched off the shuttered electric lamps they had brought with them. The Chief Constable and his party remained seated in the darkness of the shack, except Marrowfat, who went out to check the final dispositions of the Special Squad men he had brought with him from the

Yard. One of these sat in the doorway with a box-like apparatus before him and a pair of telephone receivers clamped over his ears. It was a small portable wireless set.

Soon after Marrowfat had left them Gregory got up and strolled outside. He waited for a little on the edge of the wharf keeping a watchful eye upon the end of the track to landward. He was desperately impatient now for something to happen, so that he could submerge his gnawing anxiety for Sabine in the necessity for action, but he scarcely moved a muscle when a familiar figure sidled up to him out of the darkness.

'All present and correct sir,' came Rudd's husky mutter.

'Fine. Keep close by me from now on and be ready to bolt for the car the second I do.' Gregory turned and walked slowly back to the shed with Rudd beside him.

As reports came through that the various forces on the north Kent coast and in the island of Sheppey had taken up their positions, the man at the wireless spoke in a low voice to a stenographer who sat beside him, his pad held under a boxed-in light. Before eleven most of the land contingents had already reached their stations and the river police now reported themselves ready at their rendezvous by the Ham Fishery Buoy.

After that they spoke little. To Gregory the period of waiting seemed interminable. He tried to keep his mind clear and alert, but he could not free it from the thought of Sabine, and fruitless speculations as to where she was, and what might happen to her in the next few hours.

At length a message came through from the river police. Their sound detectors had picked up the motor engines of a numerous convoy moving in the direction of Clite Hole Bank north-east of Herne Bay. A little later another report gave the convoy as directly south of them, off Pollard Spit at the mouth of the East Swale, and the river police stated that they were now moving in.

At a quarter to twelve the little group who waited in the darkness of the shack estimated that the smugglers must be entering Windmill Creek itself; then a message came through from the river police that they had closed the mouth of the Swale and were running up it.

Five minutes later a report came by wireless from another police post, a mile away at the entrance of the creek, that a fleet of six motor barges were proceeding past them at that moment without lights. The Superintendent's party stirred into activity.

'They may land here,' Gregory said in a low voice to Wells, 'but the centre of the trouble's going to be at that cottage. Let's get down there.'

'We've got it covered by a dozen men,' Wells answered, 'but I think you're right and I'd like to be in at the finish.'

They put out their cigarettes and hurried along the bank. The light in the window of the cottage had disappeared, but they turned inland, skirting it at some distance and, on reaching its farther side, saw that Gregory's surmise was proved correct. The upper window made an oblong of bright light; naked and uncurtained. The only thing that marred its symmetry was the outline of a black cat seated, apparently, upon the sill inside.

For a few moments Gregory watched the cat. It remained absolutely motionless and, as he was standing only about twenty yards from the window, he suddenly realised that it was not a cat at all; but a black silhouette in the form of a cat, either painted or stuck on the lower section of the window. It was a sign which would arouse no suspicion in a casual passer-by but, with good glasses, it could probably be seen miles away down the river as a black outline against the rectangle of light. Obviously it was the signal to the smuggler fleet that all was well.

As he crouched there peering at it the soft chug-chug-chug of motor engines came to him out of the darkness from the river. He crouched lower, pulling Wells down beside him, so that their forms should not be visible against the skyline. Rudd, just behind them, was already on his knees.

Six large motor barges chugged swiftly by and rounded the corner of the stream.

'Will Marrowfat pounce on them the moment they land?' Gregory whispered.

'No,' Wells whispered back. 'He'll give them a chance to unload some of their cargo and wait until the river police close in behind them.'

The noise of the motors grew less; then ceased. Silence settled again over the low, apparently deserted, stretch of country. It was broken only at intervals by the faint sound of men's voices, drifting on the night air, as the first barge was moored against Hook Quay and the others came up alongside it.

Wells and Gregory waited with what patience they could muster. The Inspector knew that one of his men was squatting ten yards away to their right, another down on the river bank to their left, and that a dozen more were hidden in the marsh grass close at hand all round. Touching Gregory on the elbow he began to make his way stealthily towards the creek where he took up a fresh position from which he could see the front door of the cottage.

They had hardly reached their new post when two men came along the little-used footway leading to the group of shacks. From the lower ground Gregory could see them in the faint dusky light sufficiently to recognise the taller of the two, who dragged his leg a little, as the Limper.

A new sound came from down the creek, the rapid throb of other, more powerful, motor boat engines. The Limper caught it at the same second as Gregory, and paused, silhouetted for a moment in the lighted doorway of the cottage, listening intently.

Suddenly the shrill blast of a whistle pierced the muted roar of the engines. Marrowfat, lying in wait behind the shacks, had heard the approaching police boats, as well, and sent his men into action.

22

Desperate Methods at Windmill Creek

The Limper dived into the cottage. The Superintendent's piping blast was still shrilling through the night when Wells's whistle took up the note, and springing to his feet, he leapt up the bank.

Instantly a dozen forms, hidden before, came into view; racing across the coarse grass and broken rubble towards the cottage. The Inspector reached the door first; his men were close behind him. Gregory had charged in at a different angle, making for one of the downstairs windows. The glass shattered and fell as he bashed at it with the butt end of his borrowed police pistol.

The door was bolted; the police were throwing their shoulders against it to break it down. Gregory and Rudd had stripped the lower window frame of its jagged glass, parted the curtain, and were peering into the room.

The Limper, two other men, and a thin pinch-faced grey-haired woman, were inside. The Limper was bawling down the telephone.

'Drop that!' yelled Gregory, pushing his head and shoulders through the shattered window. 'Drop that or I'll drop you!' He thrust his pistol forward aiming for the Limper's body.

The crook spun round, still clutching the instrument, and stared at Gregory; but the police had broken in the door and were crashing into the room.

The scuffle was short. By the time Gregory had left the window and walked in through the door the Limper and his companions had been overpowered.

When a brief silence fell again they could hear shots and shouting coming from the direction of Hook Quay. Marrowfat and the rest were already on the barges. The police were there now in such overwhelming numbers that the smugglers had no possible chance of escape.

Immediately order was restored inside the cottage Wells said abruptly to his men: 'Take these other two and the woman into the next room.' Then he faced the Limper.

'Now then, we've got you. You'd best come clean. Where were you telephoning to just now?'

The Limper's sullen face displayed only anger and contempt.

'You go to hell,' he snarled. 'You've got me, and I know it, but you won't get the Chief.' He turned his sneering eyes on Gregory.

'As for you! you've asked for all that's coming to you. That is if you care about the girl. It's she who's doublecrossed us: given away somehow the place where we meant to do this job tonight. But, blast your soul, I had time to phone; so she'll be for the high jump. I'll go to prison but you can go and buy a wreath for her.'

Gregory's brown face had gone a shade paler. He did not reply. Instead, he snatched up the telephone and, a moment later, got the operator.

'This is police business,' he said, 'urgent! The last call that was made from here—only a couple of minutes ago—what was it?'

There was a short pause then he turned to Wells.

'Thank God! There's an intelligent man on the end of this line. This brute called the Quex Park number and said: "21. 35. 19". He repeated it twice before we got him.'

In a second Wells had out his note-book. '21, "*Full fathoms five thy father lies*"—that's here, 35, "*Shake off slumber and beware*"—19, "*The watchdogs bark*:"—two lines of warning; that's evidently their code signal for an extreme emergency.'

Gregory dug his nails into his palms. The warning had been given. Quex Park was over twenty miles away as the crow flies. If Gavin Fortescue believed, as the Limper obviously did, that Sabine had given the information about the night landing which had enabled the police to lay their trap her last hope of any clemency from him would be gone. He might be giving orders now for her murder before he got away safely to France.

Little beads of sweat stood out on Gregory's forehead as he realised what a colossal blunder he had made. He should have gone straight to the Park and chanced everything instead of coming here with the police in the hope of obtaining knowledge which would improve his situation later. By waiting for the police launches to come up Marrowfat had unwittingly bungled the affair, and allowed the Limper time to telephone, wrecking all Gregory's hopes of a successful raid on Quex Park.

While he stood there, sick with anger and apprehension, one of Wells's men had been running over the Limper and emptying the contents of his pockets on to a kitchen dresser. Among them was a buff form.

Wells snatched it up. It was a telegram, despatched from Birchington that afternoon to Creed, Poste Restante, Rochester. He read out the numbers on it: '44. 32. 27'.

The Inspector glanced swiftly down the lines in his notebook and said: '44, "*On the bats wing I do fly*"—32, "*Open-eyed conspiracy*"—27, "*Sea-nymphs hourly ring his knell*".'

Gregory stepped forward. 'That means the fleet of planes are out again as well as the barges and "*open-eyed conspiracy*"—good God! Gavin guessed the game was up this afternoon so he's risking everything on a last throw to land his bunch of communist agitators tonight.'

'That's it,' exclaimed Wells, 'but where? "*Sea-nymphs hourly ring his knell*" gives the place all right but it's one we haven't had yet.'

A new light of hope lit Gregory's eyes. If the planes were coming in at that moment with the most important cargo of all it was almost certain that Gavin Fortescue would be there to meet them. He would have left Sabine at Quex Park, so although a warning had been sent there it could only be telephoned on to him, and he might be many miles away on some desolate stretch of coastline to the south or east. Perhaps, when the warning reached him, he would leave the country at once with the returning planes without risking a return to the Park to deal with Sabine. On the other hand he might have taken Sabine with him; in which case her situation would be every bit as desperate as it had been before. In a sudden spate of words he voiced his thoughts to Wells.

The Limper laughed. 'That's right. You're clever enough and a hell of a lot of good may it do you. The Chief'll get out all right while you're batting your head about *sea-nymphs*. And you bet he's got Sabine with him.'

Rudd, who was lurking now in a corner of the room, said quickly: 'Sea-nymphs. That sounds like mermaids ter me. I reckon the old man's at some bit of a pub called the Mermaid, or the Mermaid Tavern, or the Mermaid Arms. Must be a local of that name somewhere round abart this coast.'

'Good for you,' nodded Gerry Wells. 'Run along to the shacks will you. Tell the Superintendent we've got our man and ask him if he can come along with the local inspectors if he's mopped up the crowd on the barges.'

Rudd departed at the double.

The Superintendent had already dealt with the main body of the smugglers. Rudd met him with Sir Pellinore and the Chief Constable already on his way to the cottage; so that no more than three minutes elapsed before they all crowded into the little room.

In a few brief sentences Wells told his superior of the call they had traced, the telegram, and its interpretation. Marrowfat spread out his map upon the bare deal table, but he shook his head angrily.

'Mermaid Tavern! Mermaid Arms! must be dozens of pubs with names like that scattered round the Cinque Ports and the North Kent coast.'

'That's right,' sneered the Limper. 'I'll bet you fifty quid you don't pick on the right one.'

The Chief Constable consulted with his principal officers

from various districts who had pushed their way in behind him. Marrowfat proved right: each of them added to the list by some little house or tea-garden hotel called the 'Mermaid', in towns and villages as far apart as Hythe, Broadstairs and Whitstable.

Marrowfat and his colleagues acted with amazing promptitude. In less than five minutes the Yard Squad had been disbanded and told off to accompany local officers to twenty different places on the Kent Coast; where a 'Mermaid' tavern might prove the key to Lord Gavin's secret rendezvous.

Wells was left in charge of the Limper while the Superintendent's party hurried off to Canterbury; which he had selected as the most central place for their new headquarters.

Five minutes after their arrival the little kitchen-living-room of the cottage was empty again, except for Gregory, Rudd, Wells, the Limper and the two officers who held him.

Gregory stood there staring at the floor. He was faced once more with an appalling choice of courses and if he selected the wrong one Sabine's life would prove the forfeit.

With the whole of the Kent constabulary in a ferment of activity there was little doubt that they would discover the new base within the next half hour. A fleet of aeroplanes might land at a quiet spot unobserved upon a normal night but they could not do so with hundreds of police out on the watch for them all over the county. Should he wait until news came in, over the humming telephone wires, which 'Mermaid' Tavern or hotel was the focus for the aeroplane landing; or should he make direct for Quex Park on the assumption that the Limper was lying and Lord Gavin had left Sabine there.

The more he thought of it the more certain it seemed that if Gavin Fortescue had made his last throw that night he would surely have already arranged to leave the country by one of the returning aeroplanes himself; therefore he would have taken Sabine to the 'Mermaid', wherever that might be, with him.

How long would the police take to find it? Half an hour, an hour perhaps. By that time it might be too late, or, if they were lucky enough to arrive before Sabine was murdered and Lord Gavin gone, she would be arrested with the others. Gregory saw clearly now that, somehow, he must find out where the 'Mermaid' was and not only get there, but get there before the police.

He glanced at Wells. 'Can you spare me a moment outside?'

The Inspector nodded and followed him from the cottage into the dark, now silent, night.

'Listen,' said Gregory. 'I want you to do something for me.'

'What?' asked Wells cautiously.

'I want you to call your chaps out here and remain with them while I have a word alone with the Limper.'

'Why?'

'Never mind why. Rudd can remain there with me. The Limper won't get away from both of us and you'll be outside with your men to pinch him again if he did manage to knock the two of us out.'

Wells shook his head. 'Sorry, I can't do that. He's under arrest.'

'You can—and you're darned well going to,' Gregory said with a friendly grin. 'You'll be a made man when this case is over, and, in a few years' time, the youngest Superintendent in the force. You've done a lot to deserve that yourself but you owe it even more to the help I've given you. You remember too the night I jumped out of your aeroplane; risking my neck with that blasted parachute. You promised then you'd give me a break later if I needed it and a few minutes' conversation with the Limper isn't much to ask.'

'You win,' smiled Wells. 'I'll call the boys out and post them by the windows. In you go.'

A moment later Gregory was facing the Limper across the kitchen table. Rudd stood, a silent spectator, in the corner.

'Now,' said Gregory grimly, 'you're going to tell me the place indicated by that phrase "*sea-nymphs hourly ring his knell*". I've got no time to waste—so be quick about it.'

'The hell I am!' the Limper sneered.

Gregory pulled the table to one side. 'Rudd, you'll stay where you are,' he said quietly, 'and see fair play.' Next second his left fist shot out and caught the Limper in the stomach.

The Limper had already raised his arms to guard his face. He doubled up under the unexpected blow. Gregory's right fist jerked like a piston and catching him on the ear sent him sprawling to the floor.

'Now, are you going to talk?' rasped Gregory, standing over him.

For a moment the Limper lay gasping for breath upon the ground. Suddenly he dived for Gregory's legs, clutched him below the knees, and sent him hurtling backwards. But Gregory kicked out as he fell. The Limper lost his hold and the two men rolled in different directions.

Both staggered to their feet and stood panting angrily as they faced each other. The Limper was much the bigger of the two, but Gregory was far more agile. He feinted, then hit out again, and his fist crunched on the Limper's nose.

The Limper staggered as water gushed up into his eyes, blinding him momentarily; but he shook his head and charged in like a bull, raining a hail of blows upon his smaller opponent.

Gregory grabbed at the edge of the table and fell. The Limper came down on top of him and kneed him in the stomach.

For a second Gregory squirmed under him, white with agony, then he buried both his thumbs in the flesh of the Limper's neck, gave his head a sudden violent twist and rolled from under him.

Clear of each other, they stumbled up again, bleeding and breathless. The Limper charged but, quick as a cat, Gregory leapt to one side and dealt him a terrific blow on the side of the chin as his head shot forward.

The floor shook under the weight of the Limper's body

as he fell sideways on it. He muttered something then lay there, face downwards, on the boards.

'Now will you talk,' gasped Gregory. 'If you don't, I'll beat you till you're dead. *I've got to know* and the life of such scum as you isn't going to stop me.'

The Limper pulled himself up on to his hands and knees. 'You devil,' he croaked, 'I won't. You can do your damnedest.'

'You will. I'm going to make you.' As the Limper came rocking to his feet Gregory caught him another frightful blow full in the mouth, sending him crashing backwards into a corner.

He lay there moaning; blood trickling from his broken nose and the corner of his mouth.

'Talk, damn you,' shouted Gregory, his eyes blazing. 'If you don't I'll murder you.'

Groaning, the Limper feebly shook his head.

Gregory seized him by the collar of his jacket and threw him over on his face. 'All right,' he muttered. 'Rudd, get me that clothes line.'

Rudd jumped to obey. In spite of the Limper's renewed struggles they soon had his wrists tied tightly together behind his back with one end of the stout cord. Then, between them, they hauled his heavy body across the floor.

'Take the other end of the line and put it over that big hook on the door,' Gregory ordered Rudd. 'This bird is going to squeal if I have to break both his arms to make him do it.'

Rudd ran the cord over the hook, which was about five feet from the floor, keeping the loose end of the line in his hands.

'Right, heave away,' Gregory said tonelessly.

Rudd obeyed with a will. As he drew the line taut the Limper's pinioned wrists were drawn up behind his back until his arms were stretched to their limit and began to bear the weight of his prostrate body.

'Go on, heave I said,' shot out Gregory mercilessly.

As Rudd threw his whole weight on the cord the Limper's shoulders came off the ground with a jerk and his head hung down towards the floor between them. He let out a sudden gasp of agony.

'Are you talking?' asked Gregory, with a sudden quietness.

'Let me down—let me down,' moaned the tortured man.

'Not till you talk,' said Gregory pitilessly, 'and I haven't finished yet by half.'

As the Limper remained silent he strode over to the gas stove; picked up a wax taper and lit it.

In two strides he was back beside the hanging man. He pushed the lighted taper a few inches below the Limper's face for a second then withdrew it quickly.

'See that?' he asked. 'You'll tell me the truth about that message or I'll burn your eyes out.'

'Good God, sir, you can't!' exclaimed Rudd, suddenly paling. 'It—it's fiendish.'

Gregory swung on him. 'You fool! My woman's life depends upon my loosening this brute's tongue and I mean to do it.'

Rudd shuddered. 'Sorry, sir. Looked at like that o' course you're right.'

Gregory thrust the taper under the Limper's face again, nearer this time, but only for an instant.

Suddenly he let out a wail and cried: 'All right, I'll tell you.'

'Go on,' ordered Gregory, holding the taper ready, so that he could push it under the man's face again if he regained his courage; but the Limper was broken now and he sobbed out in gasping breaths: 'You—you got the message wrong—it wasn't sea-nymphs—or mermaids. "*Knell's*" the key word in the sentence. That means the Bell tower—Quex Park. The planes are landing in the Park itself tonight, but—but they'll be gone before you get there—blast you!'

'Let him go,' snapped Gregory.

Rudd loosed the straining cord letting the Limper's body fall to the floor with a bang. They pulled it from the doorway and rushed outside. Wells was standing about fifteen yards away from the cottage.

'What've you been up to?' he asked dubiously.

'Never mind. Your man's inside, or what's left of him,' Gregory panted. '*Bell* was the word, not *Mermaid*. I give you that in return for what you've done for me. Think it out.' With Rudd hard at his heels he dashed away into the darkness.

23

Where 'Sea-Nymphs Hourly Ring His Knell'

Side by side Gregory and Rudd dashed along the half-obscured footway to the shacks at Hook Quay. The police were still moving there and taking notes of the contents of the barges. A group of some thirty prisoners, heavily guarded, stood by the wharf ready to be marched away to the main road where a fleet of police vans would now be waiting. A car was parked at the end of the track which led inland and Gregory recognised it as the long low sports model in which he had previously seen the Limper; evidently it had brought him and his companion, half an hour earlier, to meet the barges.

They hastened past it at a quick jog trot and away from the creek towards Old Hook. Another four minutes and they were in the car Rudd had parked there ready for their get-away; hurtling over the uneven track towards the level crossing and the road.

'We'll never make it, sir,' gasped Rudd when he had partially regained his breath. 'By road, Quex Park's near on forty miles from here. Can't do that much under the hour; even if we take a chance on being pinched by speed cops.'

'God knows if we'll be in time,' Gregory groaned, 'but

we'll be in Quex Park under a quarter of an hour—bar accidents.'

'Go on, sir, that just ain't possible.'

'It is, you big sap. You don't think I was ass enough to rely upon the car alone—do you? Before we left London I telephoned Heston and had a hired pilot fly my plane down here in readiness for us.'

'S'truth! Mr. Gregory, you're a wonder, but where is it?'

'Parked on the racecourse half-way between Queenborough and Sheerness. That's the only decent landing ground I could think of for the hired man to fly it to. We'll be there in less than a couple of minutes.'

They had already crossed, and re-crossed, the railway and were roaring down the straight of the second-class road to the south of it. A moment later they swung north on to a better road.'

As Gregory pulled up he glanced at the clock on the dashboard. To his satisfaction, but momentary amazement, he found that it was only ten minutes past twelve. The smugglers had attempted their landing at a quarter to and all the excitemen which had ensued, together with their brief journey, had occupied no more than twenty-five minutes.

They flung themselves out of the car at the entrance of the racecourse and dashed in through a gate beside a tall deserted stand. Some bright flares were burning in the open space before it which picked out the silver wings of the waiting plane.

The racecourse keeper and a couple of his men met them near the plane and began quick expostulations but Gregory brushed them aside with the terse explanation: 'Police business. No time to talk.'

A rapid handshake with the hired pilot; then Gregory and Rudd scrambled on board. The engine stuttered and burst into a roar. Another moment and the plane taxied forward sailing into the air. It banked steeply and swung away east by south, over Sheppey Island, then across the entrance of the

Swale. They picked up the land again near the Reculvers and headed dead for Quex Park.

The twenty miles of air were eaten up in less than seven minutes and, as they zoomed towards the tree-surrounded enclosures that were now so familiar, Gregory was sorely tempted to land upon one of the grassy stretches which he knew lay between the coppices. Next second he caught sight of lights right in the centre of the Park; Gavin Fortescue and his people were still there. To bring the plane down anywhere near them would give the alarm prematurely.

He banked again, cursing the heavy clouds that obscured the stars, as he sailed low over the black belt of trees fringing the eastern end of the Park. Then he switched on his landing light and planed down towards his old landing ground outside the gates.

They came down with a horrible bump which made their teeth rattle in their heads, bounced up, sailed on and hit the ground again. There was the sound of rending fabric as the plane crashed to a standstill. One of its wing-tips had caught a pylon bearing the electric cables of the grid system.

'Gawd!' exclaimed Rudd, grabbing the zip fastener of the emergency exit at the top of the cabin.

'To hell with the plane,' Gregory shot back flinging open the door, which fortunately had not jammed, and tumbling out.

Rudd was after him in a second, and they were running again, towards the lane. They had landed within a hundred yards of the east gate of the Park. Gregory seized the ironwork and pushed it violently. The gate swung open. They slipped through, jumped a fence that divided the drive from the fields, and ran on over the ground which Gregory had covered in his first visit.

Panting for breath they reached the coppice where Gregory had lain hidden, thrust their way through it, and came out upon the other side into the open space before the house.

Gregory gasped with relief as he saw no sign of imminent departure about the fleet of planes. A few men stood near them but many more were gathered in little groups, talking quietly, in front of the house. They were waiting for something; Gavin perhaps, but orders might be given for the pilots to fly their machines back to France at any moment. There was not a second to be lost.

Gregory shouldered his way back into the undergrowth and, with Rudd following him, crossed the drive; then slipped round to the back of the house. The front windows had been lit but here all was dark and silent.

At the far end of the building they turned again, stole swiftly between the outhouses, and came to the servants' quarters. Gregory drew his gun and approached the door. It was unlocked; so he entered it and tiptoed down the passage to the housekeeper's room. That was in darkness too but, as he thrust open the door, a faint whimpering came from one corner.

Pulling out his torch he switched it on and flashed it in the direction of the sound. Milly was crouching there wide eyed and shivering. She did not recognise him behind the glare of the torch which blinded her and thrust out her hands as he approached seeking to fend him off.

'Don't be frightened,' he whispered. 'It's Gregory Sallust and Rudd.'

With a little sobbing cry she sprang up and flung herself towards him grabbing at his coat with her hands.

'Oh thank God it's you,' she wailed. 'Terrible things have been happening here—terrible. They're killing people and if they find me they'll kill me too.'

The muscles in Gregory's cheeks twitched in a spasm of fear. Killing people: that meant Sabine. He was too late after all. But he must keep his head and quiet this hysterical girl. Perhaps she was mistaken.

'Steady Milly,' he said gripping her firmly as she clung to him; shivering with terror. 'Pull yourself together my dear and tell us about it. Please! It's frightfully important we should know everything without the least delay. Where's Mrs. Bird?'

'They—they locked her in her room,' Milly sobbed, 'about twenty minutes ago and I—I daren't go up and let her out in case I meet some of them on the stairs.'

'Who have they been killing then?' His voice trembled a little.

'Gerry's men. Poor Mr. Simmons and—and his two friends. I crept out to—to let them know what was happening and I found them in a heap beside the drive. Oh it was horrible!' Milly burst into a sudden hysterical wailing and, fearful that her cries would draw some of Gavin's men to that wing of the house, Gregory muffled her face against his chest.

'Steady now! steady, for God's sake,' he pleaded. 'Finding them like that must have been a frightful shock. But try and tell me what started the trouble.'

For a moment the girl's slender shoulders shook with uncontrollable sobbing, then she choked back her fear and stuttered: 'We—we've been worried all day: ever since that awful row Lord Gavin had with Mademoiselle Szenty this—this morning. I telephoned to Gerry . . .'

'Yes, I know that. Gavin locked her up in her room and you were able to tip us off about hearing him speak to the Limper of Eastchurch Marshes. That was fine work, but go on. What happened this afternoon?'

'Nothing; nothing much. We sat about wondering what was going to happen. Half a dozen strange men turned up about tea time and one of them asked Aunty the quickest way down to the post office because he had to send a telegram. After dark they all set out in different directions from the house to—to patrol the grounds, I suppose. It must have been then they caught Simmons and his friends at their different posts. Aunty wanted me to go up to bed at half past ten but I wouldn't because I thought I might be useful to take a message. You see, I didn't know—I didn't know then that poor Simmons was dead.'

'It was brave of you to want to do that,' Gregory said quickly as the girl showed signs of collapsing into another fit of hysterics. 'You're going to be brave again now, aren't you, and hang on to yourself until you've told me all you can?'

She gave herself a little shake and stared up at him with tear-dimmed eyes. 'Two of the men came back to the house. The others stayed in the grounds I suppose. It was half past eleven when Aunty left me here to go and have a look round outside. When she came back she said that three bright lights were shining from the top of the steel mast above the Bell tower. There have never been any lights there before as far as we know. She—she said she thought we ought to let Simmons, or one of the others know—in case they hadn't seen them—so that they could telephone Gerry at Scotland Yard.

'I slipped upstairs to get a coat, because it's turned so chilly, and it was from my bedroom window that I saw the men in the grounds were walking about with torches. They seemed to be laying out lines or something.'

'What time was this?' Gregory asked.

'Just on twelve.'

'They were setting up them flares for their planes to land by,' murmured Rudd.

'Go on,' Gregory urged the girl, ignoring the interruption.

'I was just coming down the stairs again when I heard the telephone ring. It stopped and, almost immediately afterwards, one of Lord Gavin's men came running out of the room below. He leapt up the stairs three at a time. I've always been terrified of these people; before he saw me I'd slipped back on to the landing and behind a heavy curtain. He rushed past me and I was just coming out from behind the curtain when I caught a glimpse of the other fellow. He was standing in the hall staring up the stairs—so I stayed where I was.'

'I reckon it's well you did,' Rudd muttered. 'That telephone call must have been the one the Limper made; warning them the game was up.'

'After a moment,' Milly went on breathlessly, 'the first man came back to the landing with Lord Gavin. They all seemed terribly angry and excited. The man at the bottom of the stairs called up to them "that—that slut of yours has squealed on us". The two men started swearing then in the most frightful way. But Lord Gavin banged his stick on the parquet floor and silenced them. Then he said—he said something like this:

' "You stupid fools. Why do you waste time blaspheming. Nothing is lost yet. We only have to keep our heads. The police spies who were set to watch us here have been dealt with. Sallust, Wells, and the Flying Squad, if they have called it out, are miles away on Sheppey Island. We're safe here for a good half-hour. The planes are due at 12.15, so they will be in any moment now. Once they've landed their human freight will separate. Arrangements have already been made for that. We shall leave again by them immediately for France. Go and get Mrs. Bird now. She knows nothing of what's been going on but she might prove troublesome. She's still up because I saw a light in her room only ten minutes ago. Take her up to her bedroom, truss her up, and lock her in there. Then, on your way downstairs, you can deal with the Szenty woman. Tie her up too and take her out to my plane. Get a large stone and lash it to her feet. We'll drop her overboard when we're half-way across the Channel," ' Milly moaned. 'His voice was icy—terrible but that's what he said as well as I can remember.'

'And then?' snapped Gregory. 'Go on, quick.'

'I remained there till they had dragged Aunty, struggling up the stairs, past me. Directly they'd gone I rushed down and out of the house by the back way. I hadn't understood then what Lord Gavin meant when he spoke of the police spies having been dealt with. Then I found them all in a—all in an awful heap—there in the driveway only fifty yards from the house. I heard aeroplanes coming in as I stood there, feeling sick and faint, and saw through the trees that a lot of bright flares had been lighted on the lawn. I—I was so horrified at the sight of those dead men I don't know what I did next. I think my brain must have gone blank but I suppose I ran back here. The next thing I knew was that I was crouching in the corner shivering with terror when you came in and flashed your light on me.'

'I wonder why they didn't lock you up too,' Gregory said suddenly.

She shook her head. 'I don't think they even know I live here. Aunty got Lord Gavin's consent to my boarding with her when she took the place but he's so queer about her never having visitors we were afraid he might change his mind afterwards. That's why I've always kept out of his sight. They've been here very little until the last few days and I've never met any of them face to face.'

Gregory's sharp questions and Milly's stuttering replies had occupied no more than a couple of minutes, but time had slipped by while Gregory and Rudd were running from the plane, and later creeping round the back of the house. In spite of their well-organised getaway from Hook Quay over half an hour had elapsed since they left Wells staring after them as they raced off into the darkness.

It was now twenty minutes to one and, from Milly's report of what Lord Gavin had said when the Limper's message came through just about midnight, the planes had been due to arrive at a quarter past twelve. They must have been there then for over twenty minutes and would be leaving any moment now.

From Gregory's glimpse of the lawn through the trees, before he had entered the house, he knew that fifty or sixty men at least were gathered there. He might find Gavin's plane and get Sabine out of it but someone was almost certain to spot him and the odds were hopelessly against his being able to get her away safely.

He almost wished that he had surrendered to the certainty of Sabine's arrest, given the police the information which he had beaten out of the Limper, and enabled Wells to concentrate the forces of the law here; but it was too late to think of that now. Standing there, grim-faced and silent, he racked his brain for some refuge to which he might take Sabine if only he could deal with the pilot of Gavin's plane; but every second was precious and he dared not wait to formulate any complicated plan. Suddenly he turned to Milly.

'Do you know if there's a spare key to the Bell tower?'

She nodded towards the sideboard. 'I think there's one in the drawer on the left. Aunty keeps all the keys in there.'

Rudd wrenched the drawer open. Gregory shone his torch down into it and Milly snatched up a heavy old-fashioned key from among the rest.

'This is it.'

'Right,' said Gregory. 'Rudd must come with me; I need him. We don't want you mixed up in the fighting but are you prepared to act like a little heroine?'

'I—I'll try,' she stammered.

'Bless you! That's the spirit! Now this is what I want you to do. As they've been signalling from the Bell tower the door of it is probably open already. You know the Park and the path round the back from here, across the drive, up to the tower through the wood. That's well away from the lawn so it's unlikely you'll run into anyone. If you hear any of these people you can hide in the woods till they've gone past. I want you to get to the tower, see the door's open, and put this key into the lock on the inside—on the inside remember. That's what's so important. Think you can do it? Gerry'll be mighty proud of you if you will.'

That reference to Gerry Wells was just the psychological touch needed to give Milly renewed courage.

'All right,' she said, throwing up her head.

'Well done!' Gregory squeezed her arm. 'Directly you've got that key in the door go in among the trees and hide there until the trouble's over; get as far from the lawn as you can. Blessings on you my dear.'

The three of them left the house together. Milly to skirt its back and make her way through the dark shrubberies; Gregory and Rudd together, past the museum buildings and the conservatories, into the coppice which lay to its right front; at the far end of which, they knew, lay the hangar that housed Lord Gavin's plane.

For tense moments they stumbled through the undergrowth, not daring to show a light, then they emerged cautiously from behind the hangar into the open. Two hundred yards away, on the far side of the lawn, they could see the dark bulk of the other coppice with the Bell tower rising from it. No lights showed at its steel mast now. Its purpose of guiding the planes in had already been served.

Gregory peered out beyond the angle of the hangar. Bright flares still lit the lawn. The planes reposed before them in an irregular row. One or two men, the pilots probably, stood near each but the majority were gathered in a solid crowd on the gravel sweep before the house. At the open front door Lord Gavin's small hunched figure, supported by two sticks, was silhouetted against the bright light of the hall. He was evidently giving the foreign agitators, whom he had imported, his last instructions before they dispersed to spread anarchy in the great industrial areas.

His plane was already outside the hangar; its nearest wing-tip no more than a dozen yards from the spot where Gregory crouched. For a second the wild thought entered his head of attempting to make off in it; but the men by the other planes were within such easy range it seemed certain he would be shot down before he could scramble on board and get the machine into the air. Besides, he was not sure yet that Sabine was in the plane. If she were not he would have bungled things for good and all.

He turned to Rudd. 'Got your pocket knife handy?' he asked in a quick whisper.

'Yes sir.'

'Good. We'll need it to cut her free if she's there. Don't wait to be shot at but shoot first if they try to stop us. Ready now? Come on!'

Going down upon his hands and knees he came out into the open and crept swiftly towards the waiting plane. Now, he blessed the friendly darkness and the clouds that hung, low and threatening, obscuring the stars. The nearest men visible in the flickering light from the flares were a good fifty yards away.

With a last crouching sprint Gregory reached the body of

the plane and wrenched open the door. The light on the far side of it came through the windows sufficiently for him to see the interior of the cabin. A long bundle lay in the after part of it behind the two rear seats. It was Sabine, a cloth wound round her face, her arms and ankles lashed with rough cords and a couple of weighty iron bars fastened to her feet; trussed ready for Gavin's men to heave into the sea once they were well away over the Channel.

Swiftly but cautiously Gregory and Rudd drew her limp body out and laid it on the grass. Rudd's knife bit into the cords. Gregory unmuffled her face, pressing his hand lightly over her mouth to prevent her screaming before she realised that it was he who was manhandling her.

Another moment and they had her on her feet, limp and half-dazed, supported between them.

'Think you can run, my sweet?' Gregory said softly.

She flung one arm round his neck. '*Mon dieu!* those cords, they almost stop my circulation,' she whispered, 'wait, I will be better in a minute.'

'Hang on to her,' Gregory breathed, removing her arm from his neck and gently passing her to Rudd. Then he went down on his knees again and, creeping forward a little, peered under the nose of the plane. Its pilot, who had been hidden by the bulk of the machine before, was standing within seven yards, his back turned, looking towards the house. A murmur came from the gravel drive and then the sound of crunching feet. Lord Gavin had finished his address to the red servants of evil and the crowd in front of the doorway was breaking up.

There was not an instant to lose. Gregory dived back behind the plane and spoke to Rudd. 'They're coming; you'll have to carry her. Fireman's lift and gun in your right hand. Too late to make a detour, we'll have to chance a dash across the open.'

Rudd stooped and threw Sabine across his strong shoulders as though she had been an infant. Without a word he plunged forward straight for the Bell tower. Gregory followed, walking swiftly backwards, ready to fire instantly they were spotted and covering Rudd's retreat.

Rudd had traversed sixty yards before they were seen; then a cry went up from one of the men by the flares. In a second Gavin's pilot swung round with a drawn pistol in his hand. He fired from his hip and the bullet sang past Gregory's head; but Gregory had had him marked already. His pistol cracked, the man's knees gave under him, and he crashed forward on his face.

Gregory ducked to escape the bullets of the men by the flares. As he did so a series of sharp coughs told him that they were firing at him with pistols which had Mauser silencers attached. Suddenly he sprinted forward, covered fifty yards before he stopped, swung round, and fired again. One of the men by the flares staggered sideways with a scream.

The lawn was full of racing figures now. The scattered group by the house was surging forward in a long irregular wave. Lord Gavin still stood on the doorstep, waving one of his sticks and shouting something which Gregory could not catch. Rudd had already covered two thirds of the way to the Bell tower when Sabine cried: 'Put me down! I can manage now.'

He slipped her from his shoulders. She stood rocking for a moment then began to stagger forward while he turned and fired at the nearest of the running men. The man ran on, Rudd fired again. The fellow spun round and fell.

Rudd's intervention gave Gregory another chance. He bounded forward. Both of them fired twice into the mass of shouting figures that were thundering across the grass, then they turned and ran on together.

A bullet ploughed up the ground at Gregory's feet, another whistled past his ear, a third hit the gun in Rudd's hand, knocking it out of his grasp.

Gregory halted and emptied the remaining contents of his automatic into the oncoming mob. Rudd lurched forward, grabbed up his pistol, and dashed on again. Next instant he came up with Sabine. She was now no more than twenty yards from the Bell tower.

Jamming his now useless automatic into his pocket Gregory pounded up beside them. Each caught Sabine by an arm and half-carried, half-dragged her towards their goal.

'Come on! Come on!' shrilled a treble voice and Milly's form loomed up by the tower. She was holding the door wide open for them.

'Good God!' gasped Gregory as they dashed through the entrance. 'Why didn't you hide as I told you to?'

She shook her head. 'I had to stay and help if I could.' Then she flung her frail weight against the heavy door and banged it to. Rudd grabbed the key and turned it in the lock.

For a moment they remained there panting in the close musty darkness. Sabine was lying on the ground; Gregory leaning against the wall as he sought to ease the strain of his bursting lungs. He pulled his torch out of his pocket and flashed it on. Rudd and Milly were standing just behind the door.

'Get back, you fools!' he shouted. 'They'll be shooting through that door!' Rudd grabbed Milly and thrust her away from it into a safe corner.

Sabine was on her feet again. She snatched Gregory's torch and turned in on the door; then she sprang forward and shot the bolts at its top and bottom.

'That's better!' her voice came huskily. 'They could have blown in that lock.' As she spoke a bullet crashed through the door splintering its woodwork. She swung round towards Gregory.

'Why—why did you bring me here? It would have been safer to have hidden in the coppice near the hangar. You could have carried me there without bringing this hornets' nest about our ears.'

'I thought of that,' he replied swiftly, 'but there are dozens of them. When they found you missing from the plane it wouldn't have taken them five minutes to beat the coppice for us. We'd have been caught with no protection.'

A thunderous beating came upon the door. Shots thudded into its stout oak panelling; one clanged upon the metal lock. Gregory remained leaning against the wall. He only shrugged now at this fresh clamour and smiled in the darkness.

'Don't get scared any of you. That door's old and solid. It'd take them an hour to break it in and they can't spare the time. They know every policeman in Kent is on the look-out for them and that they'll be caught if they don't get away from here before one o'clock. It's five to now.'

Sabine stretched out a hand and grasped his quickly. '*Mais non*,' she cried. 'Gavin believes all the police are concentrated miles away on Sheppey Island. He's killed the men who were set to keep a look out here. There is no one to give a warning of what they do and the village is too far for anyone there to hear the shooting. Gavin will send for saws and cut the bolts out of their sockets; or get a battering ram for all that mob to break down the door. He thinks he is safe here for an hour—two hours yet. If help doesn't arrive soon—*nous sommes tous morte*.'

While the battering outside continued Rudd was flashing his torch round the lofty chamber. From holes in its wooden ceiling ten ropes dangled; the last few feet of each covered with a thick wool grip. They looked like a group of inverted bulrushes.

'All right,' said Gregory with sudden decision. 'If we've got to summon help after all we'll use the bells.' He sprang forward and caught at one of the ropes bearing down his full weight upon it. A loud clang sounded high up in the tower.

Rudd seized another rope and Milly a third. The noise outside the door was drowned in a horrible cacophony of vibrating sound. Without rhythm or music the great bells above their heads pealed out in horrid irregular clamour—clash—boom—dong—bing—which seemed to shake the very ground on which the bellringers stood.

Sabine ran to Gregory and shouted in his ear: 'The lights on the steel mast! The controls are in the next room. I will make signals with them.' She dashed away and a moment later was tapping at the instrument—S O S—S O S—S O S.

Rudd now had a bell rope in each hand and was swaying from side to side as he pulled them alternately with all his vigour. Gregory tugged at first one, then another until the whole peal of ten bells was in motion; thundering out a vast and hideous discord which could be heard over half Thanet.

After a couple of minutes Gregory left Rudd and Milly to keep the din going, rushed up the narrow winding stairs in a corner of the chamber until he reached a long slit window cut in the thick stone wall, and peered out.

From it he saw that the attempt to force the door had been abandoned. Gavin Fortescue was standing near the flares; waving his sticks and evidently ordering the pilots to their various planes. As Gregory watched, a new commotion started. A car roared up the driveway and halted in front of the house. Dark figures sprang out of it. Another car and then another came in sight.

The bells were so deafening that he could not hear the coughing of the silenced automatics, but stabs of flame, piercing the darkness near the museum building, told him that a battle was in progress between the reds and the constantly arriving squads of police.

He glanced at his wrist watch and saw that it was one o'clock. The bells could not have been pealing for more than five minutes. How could the police have got here so quickly, he wondered, but he did not pause to think of possible explanations. Instead, he leapt down the narrow stairs, yelling for Sabine, and waving his arms to stop Rudd and Milly tugging at the bell-ropes.

As they ceased their pulling he shouted: 'The police are here! Quick! Open that door, Rudd. I've got to get Sabine away. We'll use Lord Gavin's plane while they're fighting it out together.'

Rudd wrenched back the bolts. Milly unlocked the door and tugged it open. All four of them ran out into the half-light which came from the flares.

The bells were still clanging faintly behind them, but now they could hear the sound of shots as the waves of police, descending from fresh cars and lorries which were arriving by both drives every moment, dashed into the fray a hundred yards away. Lord Gavin had disappeared. The backs of his men were now towards the tower.

As Gregory and the rest burst out of its entrance there was a crashing in the undergrowth behind them. A body of police who had been sent to take the conspirators in the rear were just emerging from the coppice.

Someone called upon Gregory's party to halt, but he took no notice, urging Sabine on beside him. They raced across the open lawn towards the hangar, but, as they reached it, another phalanx of police emerged from the opposite coppice and Marrowfat's voice boomed out into the semi-darkness. 'Halt there you, or I fire.'

They were caught between two forces; as the police who had emerged from the Bell tower coppice were hurrying up in their rear. Another moment and they were surrounded.

With a sinking heart Gregory realised that the game was up.

Beside Marrowfat loomed the tall figure of Sir Pellinore, the bulky form of the Chief Constable, and the tall but slighter Gerry Wells.

As Gregory halted he gulped in a quick breath, and then stared at the Inspector. 'How did you manage to turn up here so quickly?'

Gerry Wells grinned. 'When you tipped me off about Bell being the word instead of Mermaid I tumbled to it at once that meant the Bell tower at Quex Park. It took me five minutes to phone Canterbury, so the Superintendent could concentrate the others when he go there, and you'd obviously sneaked your car round near Hook Quay. You had the heels of me but I didn't lose much time, once I got started, and the others seemed to have arrived here altogether.'

Milly stepped forward and touched his arm. 'It's been terrible,' she murmured. 'But I feel safe, now at last—because you're here.'

Most unprofessionally he put his arm round her slim waist. Marrowfat stepped quickly up to Sabine.

'Mademoiselle Szenty,' he said gruffly, 'this is an unpleasant duty but I have no option. I arrest you as a confederate of Lord Gavin Fortescue upon the charge of having been an accessory to an attempted murder.'

'But you can't,' cried Gregory. 'It was she who saved our lives by warning Sir Pellinore that our murder was to be attempted.'

'I'm sorry,' Marrowfat shrugged his vast shoulders. 'Of that charge, of course, the lady will doubtless be able to clear herself; but there are others. Three of our men were done to death here in the Park tonight. Whether she had any hand in that I don't know but, in any case, she is heavily implicated in the importation of contraband. Suitable charges will be presented in due course. I proposed to hold her on this one for the moment.'

The scene was quieter now. Three hundred police had rounded up Lord Gavin's agitators and saboteurs. Not a single plane had got away. The wounded were being carried to ambulances that had arrived on the heels of the police from Birchington, Westgate, Margate and Herne Bay. A score of Inspectors were questioning the captives and taking down material for charges in their note-books. Sir Pellinore, the Superintendent, Wells, the Chief Constable, Gregory, Rudd and the two girls stood apart, a hundred yards from the shifting crowd on the far side of Lord Gavin's plane.

Suddenly there was a movement in the undergrowth near by. A flash of light streaked past Rudd's face. Milly screamed as a knife caught her in the shoulder.

Gregory guessed the thrower instantly. It was Corot, whose fanatical blood lust had tempted him into this last bid for vengeance; the knife had probably been intended for Wells. Milly collapsed against the Inspector, sobbing, as he swiftly drew out the knife and dabbed at the wound. His eyes blazed with a murderous desire to get to grips with the apache but, supporting Milly as he was, he could do nothing.

It was the Chief Constable who, nearer to the coppice than any of the others, dashed into the undergrowth swinging his heavy stick high above his head. He had caught sight of Corot's white face, gleaming there, within a second of the knife being thrown. His stick descended; catching the murderous Frenchman a terrible blow right across the eyes. Corot went down moaning among the bushes. Sir Pellinore and Marrowfat had already started forward to the Chief Constable's assistance.

Gregory's distress that poor little Milly should have been wounded was almost instantly displaced by the wild thought that the ensuing commotion had given him one more chance.

Sabine was standing close beside him. 'Get into the plane,' he muttered swiftly.

Without a second's hesitation she turned, tore over to it, and threw herself in. Hard on her heels he scrambled up beside her. Rudd sprang to the door of the cabin and slammed it after them as Gregory pressed the self-starter.

Wells was facing in their direction but he was supporting Milly. He was quick enough to see that he had the one perfect excuse for not attempting to interfere.

The Superintendent realised what had happened only a moment later and swerved out of his heavy trot, towards the bushes, in the direction of the plane; but Sir Pellinore grasped the situation at the same instant.

He seized the Superintendent by the lapel of his coat. 'A great day sir,' he said swiftly. 'I must congratulate you.'

'Dammit, let me go,' boomed Marrowfat, but his voice was drowned in the roar of the aeroplane engine.

'You must lunch with me,' shouted Sir Pellinore above the din. 'I'll have the Home Secretary to meet you.'

Marrowfat thrust his great hands forward and tried to push Sir Pellinore off, but the older man showed unexpected toughness.

'Must tell the Monarch,' he bawled, his mouth glued almost

to the Superintendent's ear, 'His Majesty will probably honour you with some decoration.'

'Let me go, sir,' burst out Marrowfat his face gone purple. 'Let me go or I'll arrest you for interfering with the police in the execution of their duties.'

'What's that! I didn't hear,' Sir Pellinore yelled back. The plane ran forward; a hundred faces turned towards it but no one was foolhardy enough to try and stop its progress. It turned into the wind, rose, bounced once, then sailed close over the heads of the police and their prisoners.

'Next week,' Sir Pellinore shouted a little less loudly; as he clung still to the frantic Superintendent. 'I'll let you know what day the Home Secretary can lunch with us. You must bring Wells; splendid feller, Wells. Sallust shall join us too —*if* he's in England.'

Rudd was grinning from ear to ear as he waved after the departing plane. It lifted above the house-top missing its chimneys by no more than a dozen feet. A mile of land spread below it and then the sea. Gregory placed his hand on Sabine's.

'Where do we go from here?' he asked. 'You can bet the plane's fuelled to capacity.'

'I don't mind,' she whispered, letting her head fall on his shoulder. 'This last week we've been drawn into a strange and terrible adventure, but now, thank God, it's over.'

'That's where you're wrong,' he laughed, as the plane zoomed away over the water. 'Our real adventure has only just begun.'

Below are details of the most recent Dennis Wheatley title to appear in paperback:

EVIL IN A MASK

This latest of the Roger Brook stories continues his saga through the years 1807–1809. Napoleon is at the height of his powers. By now the complete autocrat, lusting for more power, he had warred against Prussia, Austria and Hanover, struck through Poland, towards the Baltic and into Russia. The needless wars were bleeding France white.

Roger Brook, still the most valuable and resourceful of secret agents, moves amongst the centres of power of Europe and beyond, and owing to mischance and intrigue is carried to Turkey, Persia, Portugal and Brazil.

But, interwoven with the historical pattern, runs the thread of Roger's passionate involvement with the lovely Lisala de Pombal—a woman as licentious as she is beautiful—who plays her part in leading him from one desperate situation to another.